I Got You, Love

Desiree DuBois

Author's Note

Hello lovely reader!

Thank you so much for taking a chance on my spicy Why Choose Romance. I hope you love these three as much as I do. A few content warnings: there are on-page sexual assaults that occur but are cut short, a video taken and shared of a half-naked minor without her consent, and a lot of alcohol use. Other than that, I hope you enjoy reading a lot of sex, because once these three figure out that their feelings are returned, things go from zero to sixty fast!

One last thing: I'm Canadian! I chose to use American spellings for the most part, but I kept the Canadian spelling of pyjama. I hope you don't mind my eccentricities.

Love you all! Mwah!

Desiree DuBois

Part One:

First Day
Home from
College

Amanda Beyer woke up the morning of her first day home drenched with sweat. She lay in bed, heart pounding, and clit throbbing with need, trying to get her breathing under control. *As if I were a randy teenager again. Shit, I did* not *need this today!* she wailed internally. At twenty-two, with her undergrad degree freshly under her belt, she'd come home for the summer before moving to Boston with her best friends in the world. She glanced at the clock. It read 6:55 in the morning. *At least I've got time to do something about it.*

She reached over to her bedside table, slid open the top drawer, and dug under a couple pashmina scarves for her small finger vibrator. Flicking it on, she rolled onto her back and lifted her shirt.

It was one of James's old soccer shirts, his last name printed across the back. It was a little small for her now, only reaching her waistband and pulled almost obscenely tight across her boobs, but it was still her favorite nightshirt. She hummed along with the vibrations as she circled her nipples, drawing them into tight nubs that she pinched with her free hand. The mild pain was like lightning streaking down her body to her clit, and her hips jumped, eager for her touch.

Sticking her thumbs in the waistband of her underwear, she scooted them over her hips and down her legs before kicking them off under the covers. She spread her knees wide, her finger strapped with the vibrator finding her clit with the ease of familiarity. She gasped and arched her back against the onslaught of pleasure.

Amanda's free hand moved down between her legs and two fingers slipped inside. She pumped them a few times before a third joined in.

"Oh my God!" she moaned, her breath catching in her throat. Unbidden, the faces of her two best friends, James and Tony, flashed behind her closed eyelids. Her hips jumped again. "Yes yes yes," she murmured, chasing her climax.

Her cell phone rang on her bedside table with the ringtone she'd assigned to James.

"You'll just have to wait," she muttered. Quickening her pace, she rubbed the vibrator against her clit. Her phone stopped ringing. "So close!"

Amanda groaned when her phone started ringing again, this time Tony's ringtone. She crooked her fingers inside herself and came with a cry.

Panting heavily, she slapped the top of the table, reaching for her phone without looking. Grabbing it off the wireless charger, she put it on speaker. "Morning!" She tried to sound like her normal chipper self.

"Good morning, darlin'." Tony's Texan accent rarely slipped out, but when it did, it gave her the best kind of shivers. "You sleep through our first attempt to wake you?"

"What's that buzzing sound?" James asked.

Embarrassed, Amanda flicked the off switch on her vibrator. "I was... massaging."

There was silence on the other end of the line.

Finally, Tony blew out a long breath. "'Kay." His voice squeaked.

"Moving on," James said bracingly. "First day back, what are we planning? A run, jump in Amanda's pool, play some games?"

"Sounds good to me," said Tony, voice normal again.

"Are we planning on going to Glenn's party this evening?" Amanda asked.

"I think I'd like to go," James said.

"I haven't seen most of our graduating class since, well, since we graduated high school four years ago," Tony added.

"You okay with that? Carolina will probably be there," James asked.

"I'll be fine." Amanda was a little anxious about seeing her nemesis again. "I have to get used to seeing her at some point, especially since she's going to be working at the front desk of the sports complex this summer."

"Ugh, I forgot about that," Tony groaned. "I hope she leaves me alone."

She hummed sympathetically. "She was pretty clingy with you all through high school, wasn't she?"

"Even after I made it incredibly clear that I wanted nothing to do with her after she exposed you in junior year," Tony snarled.

Amanda winced. "Let's not go over old dramas. We're all adults now, hopefully more mature. Now, this party." She cleared her throat. "Even if people we don't necessarily want to see are there, it won't matter because we'll be together."

"We'll stick to you," Tony said.

"Like glue," James finished the sentiment.

All three of them burst into laughter.

"Breakfast?" James asked, getting their plans back on track.

"Energy bars now, breakfast before we jump in the pool," Amanda said, chuckling.

"You're a harsh task-master," Tony groaned.

"Hey, Glenn's parent's place isn't too far from here, right, Tony?" James asked.

"Yeah, a couple blocks. He's hired a DJ and there'll be more than a few kegs. Should be a fun time." They heard rustling through the line on Tony's end. "He's a decent guy."

"Sleepover on the hammock tonight?" Amanda suggested.

Amanda's parents had a hammock the size and shape of a king bed on their back porch. It was a great place to cuddle up on colder nights, or to sleep on warm ones.

"Perfect."

"See you guys in five minutes," Amanda said and hung up.

Amanda stretched and rolled out of bed, tossing her vibrator back in the drawer after a quick wipe down with a wet wipe. She stripped off her shirt and dug through her dresser for workout clothes. She forewent underwear and slipped on black short shorts before yanking on a bright green zip-front sports bra. It hooked in the middle before zipping; her favorite kind.

A hot, sticky breeze was already blowing through her yard as she brought socks and running shoes out to the front steps. She smiled as she sat down. Days like this reminded her of the day that Tony's family had moved to Northampton, Massachusetts in early July almost eleven years ago.

Chapter Two

Flashback: First Meeting

"I spy the enemy, Captain," whispered Amanda, twelve years old. She pushed her bangs off her forehead, sticky with sweat. "Shall we ambush him or wait to see what he does?"

Captain James, also twelve, thought for a moment. "I think it would be more profitable to know where he's going, First Mate. Steady on."

The Captain and his First Mate held their breath as the enemy crept closer to their hiding place. He kept pausing, looking around as if he felt their eyes on his back. Finally, he reached his destination, climbing swiftly up the wire fence around the garden and heading directly towards the iceberg lettuce.

"We've got him now!" cried the First Mate. "Charge!"

Sliding down the pole out of their treehouse, Amanda and James charged at the squirrel, who stopped digging at the base of the lettuce head and scurried away as fast as he could.

"After him!" shouted James. "Let him never forget who protects these lands!"

"And my lettuce!" Amanda roared as her battle cry. They chased the squirrel towards the fence separating the backyard from the front. He squirmed underneath. They had to waste precious seconds opening the gate, and then continued on their way.

The squirrel darted up the tree near the street, tail whipping behind him. He scampered along a branch and leapt for the tree in the next yard. In two heartbeats, he was several houses down. James and Amanda stopped, breathless, and shook their fists after the squirrel.

"And don't come back!" shouted Amanda. They collapsed in the shade of the big maple. "Now what?"

"Now we make that garden squirrel-proof," replied James.

"How? I thought we had! We got Daddy to buy chicken wire and posts to make a fence. What will keep the squirrels away from my garden?" Amanda pouted.

James made a face. "I really thought that would be enough. Maybe my parents will have an idea. I'll ask them tonight when they get home from work."

Just then, a moving truck drove past them and started to back into the next-door neighbor's driveway. Amanda and James watched eagerly, waiting to see the family moving into their neighborhood. They had helped the previous owners sort through and pack up their belongings over the past few weeks, but their parents had met the new owners while they were still in school. The tweens had been waiting for the moving van since lunch, and Amanda's mom had told them that they had their parents' permission to help unpack. The Carlsons were driving across the country from Texas, and they'd texted the night before to let them know that they'd made it to Harrisburg, so they'd be getting in around mid-afternoon today, depending on the traffic.

"I'm going to miss Mrs. Giambaldo's cookies," said Amanda sadly.

"Mr. Giambaldo probably would have known what to do about the squirrels," added James. "Pity we didn't ask him before they left."

The truck shuddered to a stop and went silent. The door opened and a blonde man climbed out stiffly. He stretched slowly before closing the door to the cab. "Hey, you two!" He called out to them. "Did you see a car drive up before I got here? A woman and a boy your age?" The passenger side door opened and a blonde teenage boy climbed down from the cab.

"No," replied James, before Amanda cut him off excitedly.

"Our parents said we could help you unpack!" she called over.

Before James could add any more, a car drove up. A dark-haired boy and a blonde woman got out; she hurried to the man and gave him a hug.

"You okay, honey? We lost you on the highway at that accident, and then we got lost after taking the wrong exit." She rubbed her hands over his shoulders and down his back, as if checking for herself that he had sustained no injuries from driving a fully packed truck.

Amanda and James exchanged small smiles. They were used to their own parents showing affection in front of them, and seeing it in their new neighbors was a good sign.

The older boy had opened the back of the truck and was examining its contents. "Nothing seems out of place," he announced. "But we won't know if there's any damage until it's all out."

"Well, come on then," said the man as he waved the kids over. "You must be Amanda and James. Your parents were very welcoming when we flew over to sign the paperwork two months ago. I'm Mr. Carlson; this is my wife and my sons. Adam is behind me, grumpy because we moved him across the country from his friends before his last year of high school, and this is Anthony, who is going to be in seventh grade this fall, same as you."

"Tony." The boy scowled.

"Sorry, Tony." Mr. Carlson beamed at everyone. "Shall we get started?"

Tony examined his new neighbors. Amanda was petite, almost a full head shorter than himself, and had blonde hair with reddish hints up in a ponytail. She had a tiny, upturned nose that was covered with freckles and blue eyes that sparkled with excitement. James was as dark as she was pale. His hair curled around his head in an afro, and his skin and eyes were dark brown. James flashed his white teeth in a wide smile, and Tony couldn't resist smiling back.

As he was looking them over, they were doing the same to him. Tony was slightly shorter than James, with inky black hair that fell forward over his forehead. His eyes were a light hazel that contrasted with his naturally tanned skin. He had angular cheekbones and a thin nose. They immediately decided that they liked him.

The rest of the afternoon was spent unloading the truck. The Giambaldos had left the beds for the two spare rooms and most of the basement furniture behind for the new owners, but the Carlson family still had a lot of boxes and suitcases, as well as the principal bedroom furniture, a sofa, dining room table and chairs, and several bookcases. James's dad joined them when he got home from work and was greeted by tired cheers, as they had left the heaviest pieces until they had more adults to help.

During the course of the move, Amanda and James helped out where they could, carrying boxes to this room or that, teaming up to carry an immense Monstera plant, and then helping to unpack the kitchen with Tony and his mother. James unwrapped the dishes, Tony washed, Amanda dried, and Mrs. Carlson decided where things should go.

"Although newspaper is a great choice for wrapping dishes, it is unpleasant having to wash everything before putting it away," said Mrs. Carlson. "I'm happy to have such great helpers!"

A dish that James was handing to Tony fell to the floor with a crash. All four of them jumped with surprise.

"It's not my—" started Tony.

"I'm sorry, Mrs. Carlson," said James. "I didn't make sure that Tony had a good grip on that before I let go."

"Don't worry about it, Tony, James," said Mrs. Carlson. "Nobody move until I get all the shards cleaned up." She quickly left the room.

"But it was part of a set!" said James, still clearly upset with himself. "Is there any way to replace it?"

"Why were you so quick to assume blame?" asked Tony, a curious tone to his voice.

"Because it was my fault," said James.

"Seriously, boys, don't worry about it!" Mrs. Carlson had come back with a broom and dust pan. "I'm glad I knew where these were!" She brandished her tools.

"But..." started James.

"Let me tell you a little bit about this set of dishes. They belonged to my grandparents—" She was interrupted by James.

"An antique! You can't replace—" James closed his mouth when Mrs. Carlson raised her eyes from the floor to look at him.

"May I finish?" There was a twinkle in her eye. After James nodded, she continued. "They belonged to my grandparents, yes, but they were not antiques. They bought them for their cottage from a flea market. It contained two versions of the same set, so they could have all the children and grandchildren visit at once. The whole thing cost about ten dollars. Okay?"

James nodded again, weakly.

"Besides, although there are many memories attached to this set, I dislike the pattern!" She chuckled and got to her feet with the pieces. "It just seems like a waste to get rid of it when there's nothing wrong with it."

Amanda, Tony, and finally James, all laughed with her.

"We'll just finish this box, and then I think we all deserve a break. I'm glad no one got hurt." She dumped the broken dish into the garbage can, and then left the room again.

"I like your mom," said Amanda, hip bumping Tony.

"Yeah, me too," he replied quietly.

Later, while they were all sitting on the back porch and licking popsicles, James asked his dad about the squirrel problem that was plaguing Amanda.

Tony, overhearing, muttered, "Dog hair."

Amanda, who was sitting beside him, looked confused. "What about dog hair?" she asked.

Tony flushed. "Put dog hair in the garden. Squirrels will smell it, think there's a dog nearby, and won't come near it."

"Really? That's awesome!" Amanda bounced in her seat on the floor. "I can ask our old babysitter if I can brush her dog tomorrow morning! He's always shedding," she confided to Tony.

"What kind of dog?" asked Mr. Carlson, curious. He casually ruffled Tony's hair. Tony shook his hand off, but he couldn't stop the tiny smile that appeared.

"A Saint Bernard!" said James, grinning from ear to ear. "He's also always slobbering!"

Everyone laughed.

Chapter Three

Tony

Tony Carlson hung up the phone with his best friends and groaned, pressing his knuckles into his eyes. "Massaging?" he rasped, trying to ignore the raging erection that had appeared the minute Amanda had hesitated. She was a terrible liar.

It was one thing to watch your best friends grow up. It was another to realize you were incredibly attracted to *both* of them.

And then to have Amanda essentially tell them that she was pleasuring herself with a toy...?

Was it a vibrator or a vibrating dildo? How many times did she come this morning? And more dangerously, he let his thoughts go *there*: *Does she ever think of me when she touches herself?*

Feeling like the greatest perv of all time, Tony scrambled out of his boxer briefs and hissed as he gripped his cock. He was already close. Saliva pooled in his mouth and he licked his palm, easily finding the rhythm that had him on edge in seconds. All it took to topple over was a glance at his bedside table, where there was a picture of himself cuddled up with his two best friends. He came in white ropes that splattered up his tattooed torso, decorating his bronze skin like pearls. He let his head fall back against his pillow with a quiet groan.

Fuck.

He grabbed a couple tissues from the box beside his bed and wiped himself off. Rolling out of bed, he yanked a drawer open and rifled through. He pulled out a pair of plain black shorts and stepped into them, doing up the ties at the waistband with fumbling fingers.

In the bathroom, Tony glanced in the mirror, running his fingers through his hair before giving himself a shake. *It doesn't have to be perfect. We're going for a run. Stop being vain!* He tried to keep his steps light on the stairs to avoid waking his parents and left through the back door, running shoes and socks in his hands.

It was a short walk from his backyard through the gate into the Beyer's front yard. Amanda was already stretching, wearing nothing but a sports bra and the tiniest shorts in the world. Tony bit his lip firmly to distract himself and joined her on the lawn.

"I'm almost done with my stretches," she said, tossing him an energy bar.

Tony caught it one-handed. "Then I guess you'll have to wait for us."

The front door across the street opened and they both looked up eagerly, spotting the third best friend. James closed the door carefully behind him and jogged across the quiet street to join them on the grass. "I feel like I'm always late," he complained.

"He just got here, so don't fall for his act of innocence," Amanda teased Tony. She tossed the last energy bar to James.

"I see," James replied, a twinkle in his eye. "He also doesn't have his shoes on yet. I put mine on before leaving, that held me up."

Tony eyed his best friends' bodies appreciatively as they stretched. James was dressed similarly to himself, shirtless in simple jogging shorts. The muscles of his torso were well-developed and showed that he'd spent quite a bit of time in the pool during his four years at college. His dark skin tone was a little lighter than usual, but a summer outdoors was sure to change that. He still wore his hair loose, but he'd pulled it back with a bandana that revealed the shaved sides for this morning's jog. He looked like he'd stepped out of a magazine.

Amanda's shoulders were already starting to turn pink from the sun, despite how low it was in the sky. "Go get your sunscreen," Tony prodded her. "You can put it on while we're stretching."

She rolled her eyes. "Yes, mother hen." She got to her feet with a bounce that made her breasts jiggle. "Give me your wrappers and I'll toss them while I'm inside."

Tony let his gaze rest on her ass when she turned to go inside. *Those shorts aren't hiding anything,* he thought, watching them hug every curve of her body.

James poked him. "Hot today, isn't it?"

Humming noncommittally, Tony didn't look away until the door closed behind Amanda.

"Not subtle," James said.

"Wasn't trying to be." Tony stretched one leg out and leaned over it. "Nobody at college came close to turning my head."

"I thought you dated Wendy for almost a full year last year," James said, amused.

Tony pushed on James's shoulder. "You know what I mean." He switched legs. "Wendy was great, really. Just not for me. What about you and Nick?"

James flushed. "Nick was pretty special. Our goals just didn't match up. He wanted to travel the world. I want to get my Master's in Education and teach."

"You couldn't compromise for love?" Tony asked.

"I don't think it was love. Or at least, not the kind our parents have." James stretched his arms, the muscles in his abdomen rippling. "Not the kind you and Amanda and I share."

"Aww, you love me!" Tony launched himself at James, wetly licking the side of his face as they fell over.

"Dude," James chortled. "You need to learn how to kiss."

"My goodness, I didn't think I was gone for that long," Amanda teased. "What did I miss?"

"James declared his love for us," Tony said.

Amanda brought a hand to her chest. "Aww, babykins!" she cooed sappily. "I thought you'd never say it!"

"You two are the worst," James replied, his cheeks darkening in a blush. He succeeded in pushing Tony off and sat up. "Do you need any help getting your back?" he asked Amanda.

"Always. Thanks." Amanda squeezed a huge dollop onto her hand before passing the bottle to James. "You know the drill."

"I'm quite familiar."

Tony watched enviously as his friends worked together to cover every inch of skin that wasn't covered with the tiny sports bra and shorts. His fingers ached to touch her soft skin, to spread the lotion over it, but at the same time, he knew his body would betray him. It was better to watch from a distance.

"Want some?" Amanda asked him once she was done.

"Sure, why not."

Her small hands moving in firm strokes across his back nearly did him in. He rolled his eyes at James, who smirked at him.

But James wore a similar expression when she moved on to his back, so Tony didn't feel quite as bad.

After Amanda was satisfied with the amount of sunscreen they wore, she put it just inside the door and headed for the end of her driveway. "Are we racing or running together?"

"Race to the park and run together along the trails behind it?" James suggested.

"I'm game," Tony replied, bouncing on the balls of his feet as he got into position beside Amanda.

"On three," she said. "One—" She took off without warning, sprinting as fast as she could.

"She cheated!" Tony exclaimed.

"We'll catch up and pass her." James held up one fist and Tony bumped it. "Let's go."

Tony reveled in the whoosh of air, his legs pumping. He and James were both fast sprinters, and they stayed side-by-side for quite a while. They passed Amanda, one on each side of her, and she shouted after them, something about it not being fair that they had longer legs than she did. A burst of speed when he saw the brightly colored playground, and Tony reached it first, tapping the side of the swing set nearest the road with the palm of his hand.

"Good one," James panted, resting with his hands on his knees. "You've gotten faster."

"I've been training on the hills of San Francisco while wearing weighted vests. This is a breeze compared to that torture," Tony pointed out.

"Impressive," James drawled.

Tony frowned. "Not trying to be."

"Still is."

Amanda joined them, having slowed to a jog once she knew she wasn't going to win. "Run together now?"

"I'm all for that."

They started out slowly on the bike trail beside the park. There were a few kids playing in the park with their parents, the adults glancing up from their phones every once in a while and sipping from reusable cups.

"Do you remember that one time we went for a run and that cop car pulled up?" James asked suddenly.

"How could I forget?" Tony shuddered.

"Of course." Amanda shot him a glance. "Why do you ask?"

"I don't know. I was just thinking about it all of a sudden. Coming back here after being away at college... it brings back old memories, I guess."

"I'm glad it had a happy ending." Amanda reached out and squeezed his hand.

"Me too," the men echoed each other.

Chapter Four

Flashback: A Scare

James, Amanda, and Tony had been hired by their parents to wash all the family cars one day in August. It was the perfect amount of responsibility for the trio of twelve-year-olds. They finished up the Carlson's and Lavallee's, and were working on the Beyer's by mid-afternoon. The three of them were almost as wet as the cars they were washing, thanks to "accidents" from whoever was holding the hose at the time.

"Amanda, honey, you should probably put more sunscreen on. You're looking a little red on your shoulders," Mrs. Beyer greeted them, bringing out a towel and sunscreen.

"Ouch, yeah, you are." Tony took the sunscreen while Amanda toweled off. "Sorry about that. We'll pay more attention."

"Sunscreen train!" Amanda chirped happily, sitting on the grass and patting the spot in front of her for James. "Just because you don't turn red doesn't mean you can't get skin cancer!" James rolled his eyes but submitted, sitting in front of her. Amanda held out her hand for a squirt of sunscreen and started rubbing it over James's back and shoulders while Tony did the same for her.

"Right underneath the edge of her suit, Tony, or else there will be red burn lines," Amanda's mom commented, watching them.

"And then even wearing a bathing suit would be painful, let alone a shirt!" Amanda shuddered. "Once was enough. Never again."

"Hello!" A car had stopped in front of their house and Mrs. Beyer moved closer to talk to them. James watched as she gestured down the street, obviously giving directions.

Finishing each other's backs, they painted each other's faces and then did their own fronts, arms, and legs.

"You kids are doing a great job on the cars," Mrs. Beyer said as she returned to them.

"Thanks, mom!"

"What did they want?" James asked, curious about the car that had stopped.

"They were looking for the open house nearby. They took a wrong turn."

"Why didn't they use GPS?" James muttered. He gave himself a shake. He was being paranoid.

They returned to the car, this time actively trying *not* to get each other wet, at least until the sunscreen had a chance to soak into their pores.

"Want to go for a run after this?" Amanda asked, rubbing a soapy sponge over the headlights. "We can run to the hill and use it to practice."

Tony groaned. "Aren't you exhausted?"

"Not at all! This is fun!"

James laughed at Tony. "You'll get used to her endless energy someday."

"You're just glad that you're not trying to keep up with her by yourself anymore," Tony retorted, swiping a cloth over the front window.

"I'm game for training on the hill. You're the one who's complaining," James teased.

"I think we're done here," Amanda said, wiping the back of one hand over her brow, leaving a trail of soapy bubbles behind. "Get the hose, James?"

"On it." He sprayed the car down. "We did good work today."

They admired the car for a minute before Amanda pushed on their shoulders. "Go get your shoes and meet back here for stretching!" She ran up the steps to the front door of her house two at a time.

"She's exhausting," Tony said to James the instant she disappeared into the house.

James shrugged. "You don't have to come."

"Of course I'm coming!"

The boys separated to go to their own houses. James was the first one out and sat on Amanda's front lawn to stretch, reaching for his right foot.

A car rolled to a stop in front of the house. "Hey, you!"

James looked up. It looked like the same car that had stopped earlier. "Hi. Did you find the open house alright?"

The man scowled. "Do you live around here? Why are you loitering in front of this house?"

Heart rate spiking and palms sweating, James swallowed hard. "Yes, I do. I'm waiting for my friends so we can go for a run."

The man's frown deepened and he made a motion inside the car that looked like he put the car in park.

Amanda bounced out of the house and threw herself down on the grass next to James. "You were quick!"

"I didn't have to change out of my bathing suit." James kept one eye on the car.

"Neither did I." Amanda tossed her ponytail over her shoulder with a flick of her head and started doing the same stretch as James. "Easier to jump in the pool after our run if I just have to strip off my shorts and shirt."

"Good call." James noticed that the man in the car had moved on and hoped that they wouldn't be putting an offer in on the house around the corner. "I didn't change my shorts either for the same reason. What's taking Tony so long?"

"I'm here!" Tony panted, collapsing beside them, sneakers in his hands. "Couldn't find my shoes."

They finished stretching and headed for the hill. "This hill is the best place for sledding in the winter," James told Tony as they jogged down the street.

"Sounds good." Tony pretended to shiver. "I'm not looking forward to winter, but snow sounds like it could be fun."

"Winter's great!" Amanda enthused. "Race you to the hill!" She took off without waiting for their agreement.

"That's not how cross country training works!" shouted James after her.

"So we're not racing?" Tony asked, one eyebrow raised.

"Of course we are. Come on!" James lengthened his stride and picked up the pace, his feet pounding the pavement on the side of the road. He soon outpaced Tony and was quickly catching up to Amanda when a siren sounded. His heart thumped in his chest, not just because of the running, and he slowed to a stop.

"Hands over your head where I can see them!" said the police officer, getting out of the car. He immediately un-holstered his gun.

James slowly obeyed, his brain panicking. He said nothing.

"James!" shrieked Amanda, running back to him.

He didn't turn to look at her and hoped she wouldn't do anything to startle the officer. He saw Tony slow to a stop behind the man, looking as panicked as he felt.

Amanda moved to stand beside James, breathing hard. "Is there a problem, officer? My friends and I were training for cross country for school this fall."

"We got a report of a young man matching his description loitering in the area."

Amanda kept her arms loose at her sides while she talked calmly and clearly. "I'd like to call my father, please. The neighbors all know us. Can I ask to use one of their phones? We live here, across the street from each other, and have since he was one." Quietly, out of the corner of her mouth to James, she added, "Who the heck called this in?"

"That car," murmured James. "The one that asked for directions."

Amanda sighed and waited for the officer to say something.

"You live here?" the cop repeated slowly, lowering his weapon.

"We do." She looked at the houses around them and gestured at the red brick one. "The Smiths live there. They have a cat." The graystone. "The Fieldings live there. They have a new baby, so I wouldn't recommend knocking during naptime." The cream siding. "The Bakers live there. They have a yappy dog whose bite is *actually* worse than his bark." She let her arms fall to her sides and waited again.

The cop looked a little sheepish. "I guess it was a case of a newcomer in the neighborhood. Take care, kids." He reholstered his gun and got back into his car, driving away with a nod at them.

Amanda repeated the license plate under her breath a few times. She threw her arms around James's waist, pressing her face into his chest. "He's going to pay for that."

"No," James said into her hair. "No, that'll only make things worse. Forget it." He shuddered. "You were incredible."

"That was pretty wild," Tony said, walking up to them. "You alright?"

"Not really. It's kinda upsetting to have a gun pointed at you," James said wryly.

"At least the police are pretty responsive. That's good, right?" Tony said.

Amanda frowned at him. "They responded quickly because this is a rich neighborhood and there was a call about a 'potentially dangerous' Black boy hanging around where he shouldn't be. There was absolutely no reason to pull a fucking *gun* on James!"

Tony looked surprised. "He was protecting himself."

James's heart sank. "Were you scared of me the first time you saw me, too? Just because of the color of my skin?"

"No," Tony replied, a little too quickly.

"I want to go home," James said, shrugging out of Amanda's hug. He took off down the street at a sprint, leaving his friends behind before they could see his tears.

Not much later, Tony knocked on his bedroom door. "Can we talk?" he asked quietly.

"I'm not sure I want to listen," James growled, turning away from the door.

"Can I come in?"

"No." James knew he was being rude, but he wasn't feeling all that charitable at the moment.

Tony sighed and sat in the doorway. "Yes, I was scared the first time I saw you. I was scared of both of you. Because I don't exactly have a good track record of getting along with kids my age. It had nothing to do with the color of your skin and everything to do with my own issues."

"Is this a 'it's not you, it's me' speech?" James sneered, turning to face the door.

"Yeah, actually. I was homeschooled for sixth grade in Austin, did you know that? Because I didn't fit in with the kids at my school." Tony hung his hands between his knees and stared at them. "I really wanted you two to like me and I was terrified you wouldn't. I'm sorry I made you feel bad."

James looked at his dejected friend in the doorway. "It's hard to make friends. Amanda and I didn't have to *make* friends with each other, we just...*were*. I guess it helps to have moms who got along and put us together daily as we grew up. But we don't really have any other friends. It's been just the two of us for so long. But you fit. It was so easy to make friends with you, and even though it's only been a month, I'm finding it hard to remember what it was like without you." He sniffed and wiped his nose with the back of a hand. "One thing you'll learn about being friends with me is that cops are *not* always there to protect those that need it. There is a major bias amongst the force against anyone with Black skin."

"That's ridiculous!" Tony exploded. "Why?"

James shrugged. "Because most of *them* are white, and we don't look like them, I guess."

"That's a terrible reason." Tony punched a fist into his hand. "Can't they go to school to learn how to treat everyone the same?"

James shrugged again. "I wish I knew how to change it."

"How often has this happened to you?" Tony asked softly, all anger draining from his body.

"First time with a gun, so that's great," James said sardonically. "But I've been stopped five other times. It never gets any less embarrassing."

"Embarrassing? Why would you be embarrassed?"

"The feeling of powerlessness," James replied. "There's rarely anything I can do or say to stop the situation from happening. Amanda has stepped up every time to talk for me." He smiled softly. "She's gotten very good at it."

"Is that why she knows everyone in the neighborhood?" Tony asked, playing with the edge of the carpet.

"Yeah, once we were old enough to walk to the park without adult supervision, she had her father go with us and we introduced ourselves to every single house on the way to the park." James shook his head with a smile. "The hill is just behind the park, and the trails lead to it, so we didn't have to do it again in the winter. It was nice to get to know the neighbors. Even if not all of them understood *why* we were doing it, they were all very courteous."

"When was that?"

"Two summers ago."

"And she still remembers all their names?" Tony whistled, impressed.

James chuckled. "No. Not everyone. Just the ones that were memorable."

"Still."

"Yeah." James smiled. "So how long did she yell at you before you agreed to come apologize?"

"There was no yelling, only a really disappointed expression with tears in her eyes."

"Ouch."

"Yeah." Tony got to his feet. "Did you want to try the run again?"

"Maybe skip it and head straight for the pool?" James suggested. "I'm still feeling a little jumpy."

Tony nodded. "You sure you don't want Amanda to complain to that bastard's boss?"

"I'm sure. It would only make things worse."

"Alright. Last one to the pool is a rotten egg!" Tony took off down the stairs, James hot on his heels.

"Be back later, mom!" James called as he ran out the door.

"Have a good time!" Mrs. Lavallee shouted back as James closed the front door behind him.

Chapter Five

James

By the time they got back to their houses, each of them was glistening with sweat. James was torn between letting his gaze rake over his friends' bodies and grant them the respect they deserved.

His efforts produced mixed results that left him even more sexually frustrated than he had been earlier this morning.

A drop of sweat glided between Amanda's breasts, behind the enclosure that he wanted to unzip with his teeth.

He glanced away, only to find himself staring at Tony's heaving chest, tattooed muscles gleaming in the early morning sunlight. James wanted to trace the Monstera leaves that decorated his skin with his tongue. His and Amanda's names were hidden within the black ink on Tony's arm, a claim that James wished desperately could come true.

Eyes back on Amanda, he focused on her face this time, but the wisps of hair that had escaped her blonde ponytail were damp with perspiration and curling, and he couldn't help but wonder if her sex face was even hotter than how she looked just then.

"Meet at the pool in five minutes?" Tony asked them.

"I'm going to need help in the kitchen," Amanda reminded him.

"Meet in the kitchen in five minutes," James amended.

"Great."

They headed to their own houses to get dressed in their swimsuits. James toed off his shoes at the door and took the stairs two at a time, knowing his parents were both at the hospital by now. Both were very successful in their own fields; his mom in obstetrics, his dad in palliative care. They liked to joke that their jobs were polar opposites, life and death.

Shaking thoughts of his parents out of his head, James unpeeled his running shorts from his body and tossed them into his laundry basket. He'd already found a pair of swim trunks earlier that morning, but didn't relish the idea of yanking them over his sticky body. He decided to jump into his shower. The cold water made him yelp, but it felt good on his overheated skin. After a quick rinse, he pulled on trunks with blue flames licking up from the knees, and ran back down the stairs. He slipped on his sandals and was across the street in less than the proposed five minutes, entering Amanda's house through the kitchen door.

The first thing he saw was Amanda bent over in front of the fridge. She was wearing a very tiny royal blue bikini that barely covered anything at all, and he had to bite the inside of his cheek to stop all the blood from rushing to one organ in particular as if he were a teenager again.

"That was quick," Amanda said, not looking up from what she was reaching for. "Take this, please?"

James wasn't sure how he managed to follow her directions, his eyes not leaving the thin strip of bikini as if he could penetrate it with wishful thinking. He took the pitcher of orange juice and several bowls of fruits from her, putting them on the island in the middle of the kitchen.

"I was hoping I could find whipped cream," Amanda said, standing up straight with a pout. She smoothed the wisps of hair back from her forehead with one delicate hand. "Waffles with fruit are just crying out for whipped cream, you know?"

James nodded in agreement, not trusting his voice not to crack. The triangles that covered her breasts were also small, revealing soft swells on either side of the material.

Just then, Tony arrived. "I swiped this from my parents' fridge, just in case you didn't have any," he said, tossing a can at James, who managed to catch it instinctively.

"Whipped cream!" Amanda cheered, bouncing in place. She crossed the kitchen to kiss Tony's cheek, rising on her tiptoes and pressing her body along his front to reach.

James smirked at Tony's expression, one of barely contained self-control.

"Can't have waffles without whipped cream," Tony said, a little shakily.

"I was just telling James that!" Amanda replied with a grin. "Eat here or outside?"

"Outside," James suggested. "As much as I appreciate the A/C, I'd rather stay hot before jumping in the pool."

"Patio it is." Amanda picked up two bowls and headed outside.

Together the three of them moved their breakfast onto the back deck, to the large table next to the door.

The three families had been close ever since Tony's family moved in next door, and they rotated who hosted the weekend dinners. The backyard and dining room furniture each family owned was suited to hosting the six adults and four children. Now that they'd grown up, it was a tight squeeze to fit everyone, but nobody seemed to mind.

James wondered if the parents had kept up the tradition while they'd been away in college. He hoped so. It wasn't just them who'd benefited from their close friendship.

They clustered around the end of the table, even though they could have spread out, and were silent as they prepared their breakfasts. James tracked Amanda's fingers as they plucked a strawberry out of the bowl and dragged it through the mountain of whipped cream on top of her waffles before popping it into her mouth.

She half-hummed, half-moaned, and he felt the blood in his body rushing south again. He immediately shifted his gaze over to Tony, who seemed to be having a similar issue. That was enough of a distraction, and James made himself focus on his food.

"Are you excited to be coaching at that sports camp again?" Amanda asked Tony, breaking the silence that comes with eating good food.

"Yeah." His face softened into a smile. "I missed it last year, helping the kids gain new appreciation for sports." This would be his seventh summer working with the Northampton Sports Complex. They ran day camps for kids and younger teens featuring a different sport each week. All of them had attended for several weeks when they were young enough to be campers, but Tony had been hired on as a junior coach when he'd been only fifteen. They'd liked him so much that he'd worked for them every summer since, with the exception of last summer when he'd stayed in San Francisco on placement.

"You probably won't be back next year either, right?" James asked. "Now that you've gotten into that specialized social worker program, you'll be hired right out of school next spring."

Tony crossed his fingers. "That's the hope. It's only a one-year program, but it requires a four-year college degree just to get in." He rolled his eyes. "I'll probably be as busy as the two of you, working on your Masters."

"That's why I plan on making the most of this summer," Amanda said, wiggling in her seat. "Relaxing, not having a care in the world, and hanging out with my best friends."

"And teaching lifeguarding courses," James teased.

"Psh, that's relaxing," Amanda said, waving a hand. "Besides, you'll be there with me, and we'll see Tony on breaks because we're working in the same complex." She gathered leftover whipped cream from her plate with a finger and popped it into her mouth. "Yummy."

James unclenched his hand from the edge of the bench he was sitting on, trying to avoid thinking about her little pink tongue lapping up the white cream. *Is everything going to look like an innuendo today?* he asked himself desperately. The image of her cleavage as she'd bent over was ingrained in his memory. "Who do you think they'll promote to senior coach once you're gone?" James asked Tony.

Tony shrugged. "There are plenty of coaches with the camp. One of the younger ones will get promoted just like I was. I'm not concerned. What about the pool where you two are working this summer? How will they fill *your* positions?"

"There are always new kids going through the lifeguarding program." Amanda continued to clean her plate with her finger. "They'll bump everyone up."

"Sounds like we're going to have busy summers." Tony smiled wryly. "Will we have time to see each other at all?"

"I already said we will!" Amanda looked shocked. "On breaks, at lunch. Plus we'll have evenings and weekends! We're senior guards; we get our pick of shifts. We'll have to take a couple random ones here and there when others get sick, but for the most part, we'll have lots of time together."

"*And* we'll be moving into an apartment in Boston together for the school year. That'll give us more than enough time to get sick of each other," James teased, imitating her tone.

"Bah, who's to say I'm not sick of you already?" Tony grumbled half-heartedly.

Amanda laughed at him. "You know that I know that you love me," she said in a singsong tone.

"Yeah," Tony muttered, blushing.

"All of us together in the same city for school," James mused. "It's been four long years of video calls."

"I can get hugs whenever I want!" Amanda cheered. She leaned over James and squeezed him tightly. "I used to get so sad when I needed a hug."

"Your partners not good enough?" Tony said with a chuckle, putting his fork down on his plate.

"It wasn't the same." Amanda shook her head solemnly. She got to her feet and collected empty plates and bowls. "Help me with the leftovers?"

James and Tony combined the fruit into one bowl and covered it with plastic wrap while Amanda headed for the front door to collect the sunscreen she'd left there before their run.

"I'm going to need more of *this* on more of *this*," Amanda said, shaking the bottle and pointing at her body when she returned to the kitchen. "I'd like to tan out the pallor before we're at one of the outdoor pool shifts. I always burn if I don't have a base tan first."

James winced. He remembered vividly how her burns had blistered their first summer guarding the outdoor pool. "Don't worry; I got you, love."

It didn't take long for him to cover her newly exposed skin with the sunscreen. Amanda took the bottle from him as they headed out to the pool.

"Just in case I want to sunbathe topless," she said with a wink.

James controlled his expression just in time. "You'll definitely want to put on an extra layer," he said calmly. In his mind, the video from their senior year of high school where she'd been pranked and shown topless replayed in his mind. She'd been stunning then, but her more mature body now was mouth-watering. *Note to self, if she does go topless, do laps. Anything to distract yourself from creeping her out.*

He exchanged desperate glances with Tony as they reached the crystalline blue pool. When they'd all hit puberty, Tony and James had confided in each other about their crushes on Amanda. It had been a relief to have someone to share that with. Amanda didn't know, as far as they knew. While they had all dated other people in college, they were all single now that they were home for the summer.

Single and flirtatious, if he was judging Amanda correctly. *Is she doing this on purpose, or is she just comfortable with us?*

There was no way of knowing without asking, and there was no way he could ask. Not without giving himself away. They were living together in Boston in the fall, and he didn't want that to be awkward. Hitting on Amanda when she wasn't interested would *definitely* make things awkward.

Amanda had already put the bottle down next to a lounge chair and was entering the pool by the stairs, her hands swishing through the water playfully. "It's wonderfully warm. Why are you still up there?" she asked them.

"Coming!" Tony said, cannonballing into the pool and making her giggle at the splash.

James stretched his arms over his head. "I was just thinking of our Bronze Cross class. Do you remember getting your first period?"

Amanda groaned. "That was *the worst*. Why are you bringing that up?"

"You've been taking a lot of trips down memory lane," Tony commented, making James shrug.

"I think I just missed you two." James headed for the storage bin. "Water polo?"

"Yes!" Amanda eagerly agreed.

Chapter Six

Flashback: Unexpected Visitor

Amanda scissored her legs under water, pulling a limp James to the edge of the pool. Quickly, she placed both of his arms on the side, tilted his head back, held his wrists with one hand, and hefted herself out.

"You're going to be just fine," she said calmly, trying to control her breathing.

She turned him around by his arms and struggled to get the hold right to lift him out of the water.

"One, two, three," she muttered to herself. Muscles in her legs straining, she dragged him up onto the wall, and then away from the edge of the pool. She laid him gently on his back.

"Check for breathing," she continued, tilting his head back to clear his airway.

"He is breathing," said the instructor's voice.

"Turn onto the side," Amanda said to no one in particular as she arranged James's body in the required position. "Can I get a blanket over here, please? How soon until the ambulance gets here?"

"Great job, Amanda," said Kelly, one of the three instructors for the fourteen year olds' pre-lifeguarding class. "You need a little more practice on the hold for the lift, to be a little quicker, but you reached him before anyone else got to their victims."

Amanda beamed. James hugged her around the shoulders.

"Switch up!"

Amanda stood up and went to the edge of the pool to dive in.

"Amanda, wait," said James. "You're... bleeding."

"What? Where?" Amanda tried to see over her shoulder. "I don't remember scraping myself on anything."

"Down the inside of your leg," replied James. "I think..." He stopped, chewing on his lip, hesitating in case she was uncomfortable discussing this with him.

Amanda bent to inspect her legs. "There's no cut," she said, confused.

"I think you got your period," James finished quietly.

"Ohh." Amanda turned scarlet. "What do I do?"

"What do you normally do?" he asked.

"I don't have a normal! This hasn't happened before!" cried Amanda, tears gathering in her eyes.

"Okay, it's okay," said James, reaching out to pull her into a hug. Amanda buried her face in his chest.

Kelly came back over to them. "Everything good over here?" she asked.

"Do you want to talk to Kelly?" James asked Amanda. "She would have experience with this sort of thing."

Amanda shook her head.

James sighed. "Can she be excused for the rest of the class? She needs to take care of something."

Kelly looked confused until she saw the trickle of blood trailing down Amanda's leg. "Do you have any tampons?" she asked Amanda.

She shook her head again.

"I can get you one," Kelly continued.

"I don't know how to use it," Amanda whispered, horrified.

"I don't have anything else," said Kelly sadly.

"I do."

Both girls looked at James, surprised.

"I always carry pads and tampons just in case they're needed," he said shyly.

"Okay, you need to go and get your clothes and go to the bathroom," said Kelly to Amanda. "And you go and get me a pad. I'll bring it to her."

They completed the exchange quickly.

"You're going to have to figure something out for class on Monday," she told Amanda through the bathroom stall door.

"My mom bought me a Diva Cup for when I got my period," said Amanda. "But I didn't expect to get it in the pool. I usually have the cup in my backpack, but I only bring my beach bag to class."

"You'll have the weekend to get used to it. It can be tricky to use," said Kelly.

"It's got to be better than this horrid thing," replied Amanda, opening the stall door. "I feel as though I'm wearing a diaper!"

"Welcome to being a woman," said Kelly sarcastically. "Why don't you watch the rest of the class? There's only fifteen minutes left."

Later that day, in Amanda's backyard, James and Tony were sprawled out on the giant king-sized hammock. Amanda came out of the house and sat gingerly on the edge.

"Thank you for the pad today, James," she said, blushing slightly. "I'm sorry I don't have a replacement to give you. Mom doesn't buy one-use products."

"Don't worry about it," said James. "Are you okay?"

"Other than some mild cramping, I feel fine. I can't even tell that I have the cup in." Her face flamed. "It will get easier to talk about this, right?"

"If you don't want to talk about it, you don't have to," said Tony, his face almost as red as hers.

"But we are definitely here for you if you *do* want to talk about it," added James emphatically, elbowing Tony.

Tony nodded.

"It doesn't gross you out?" asked Amanda. "I'm talking about blood coming out of my..." She gestured in the vicinity of her crotch. "My uterus."

"My parents are both doctors, remember. And my mom is graphic about her delivery descriptions. I'm used to talking about menstruation," said James. "It happens to about half the people on the planet. Once a month, give or take."

"We should be able to talk about this," Tony finished. "And it will get easier to talk about it the more that we do."

"I love you guys," said Amanda, her eyes filling with tears.

"No crying!" said Tony. "I love you, too."

"You've never said that to me before," gulped Amanda.

"Sure he has," said James. "Just not with words. Love you both, too."

"Hugs," demanded Amanda, holding out her arms to both of them, shrieking when they each caught one hand and pulled her towards them.

Chapter Seven

Playing water polo with the guys was extremely physical.

Usually.

Today, they seemed to be holding back from grabbing her and forcefully moving her out of their way. It was extremely frustrating. Her nerves felt like they were humming with anticipation. She wanted her best friends to touch her body, and they seemed to be doing their utmost to avoid it.

After she smashed down Tony's flutter boards yet again, Amanda lifted herself out of the pool to chase after the ball. Water sluiced down her body, leaving a trail of wet footprints on the hot patio stones before she stepped off them onto the grass. Bending over to pick up the ball, she made sure to give the pool the best view of her ass.

But when she turned around, the guys didn't seem to be paying her any attention at all, setting up the boards to mark Tony's net once more.

Okay, okay. So they see me as their sister. Amanda tried her best not to pout. *I can live with that, I guess.* "My fingers are getting wrinkled. Let's play some frisbee until we're less water-logged."

"I'm game," Tony said cheerfully.

"I'll get the frisbee."

Amanda bit her lip as the muscles in James's back flexed as he pushed himself out of the pool. His suit rode low, just barely covering the swell of his ass, and clung to his legs.

Her attention was diverted by Tony climbing the ladder. His muscles were similarly impressive. She let her gaze linger on both men as they squeezed the excess water from their trunks.

"Coming?" James said.

"Not yet," she muttered under her breath as she balanced the ball in the finger notch of the skimmer beside the pool. "I'm right here," she said, jogging out of the pool area and joining the other two in a triangle on the grass.

The frisbee flew gracefully from James to Tony, to Amanda, and back to James.

"Tackle frisbee?" Amanda suggested. "This is fun and all, but a little tame."

The men exchanged glances. "Yeah, sure," Tony said.

James nodded, and threw the frisbee towards her. Tony launched himself into its path and snatched it in midair.

"Oh, It is on!" Amanda shouted. She threw herself at Tony's back. One foot caught on the material of his trunks on his thigh, and she pushed up with it and her hands on his shoulders, trying to reach the frisbee over his head.

Tony threw the disc as if he weren't encumbered by her in the slightest, and she huffed, dropping off him since he wasn't holding it any longer.

Amanda glared at one and then the other. She knew that the second she ran to James, he'd throw it back to Tony and vice versa. Her only chance was to try to catch it midair the way Tony had. Unless they made a mistake. She briefly toyed with the idea of flashing them before discarding it. Without knowing how they felt about her, it felt icky, not getting their consent. *Okay, let's try this.* She walked slowly towards James. He smirked at her and tossed the frisbee high over her head.

It came down precisely where Tony was standing, thunking neatly into his hand. The game continued in this way for a couple passes, way over her head, and Amanda let them think that they had her giving up. But then James made a pass that went a little wider than usual, and she saw her chance.

Instead of running for the frisbee, Amanda sprinted for the spot where Tony would have to catch it. She arrived just after the disc, tucked her head down, and plowed into her friend's midsection with her shoulder.

They toppled onto the grass, Amanda on top of a gasping Tony. She crawled up and plucked the frisbee out of his fingers. "Gotcha!" she said, smirking down at him.

He raised his eyes up to her face. "You sure did," he wheezed. "Not sure I can feel my spleen!"

"Don't be a baby. I didn't hit you that hard." She moved back down again. Lifting his hand off his abdomen, she pressed a gentle kiss just under his rib cage on top of one of the black ink flowers. "There. All better."

Amanda sprang to her feet and threw the frisbee to James, who caught it just in time.

"Impressive tackle," James complimented her.

"Thanks." Amanda bounced a little as she returned to where Tony had been standing.

"Remind me not to underestimate you again," Tony said, exaggerating a limp as he walked between them.

"You underestimated me?" Amanda asked, bringing a hand to her chest. "Me?"

"I'm out of practice," Tony said ruefully, his gaze tracking the frisbee as she caught it.

Amanda tossed the frisbee back and forth between her hands, taunting him. "It's only been two years, and you forgot how competitive I am?"

"Guess so."

Amanda noticed his feet shuffling closer to James, moving slowly. She thought he might jump for the frisbee again, and then she paused. "Hey! Tony caught the pass that *you* made, James. You should have gone in the middle, not me!"

"Yup." James grinned at her. "But I'm not complaining. Can't go back now."

Amanda rolled her eyes. "Fine. Hope you get tackled." She threw the frisbee in a curve that Tony missed wildly, but James caught it easily.

"Nice one," James said. He tossed it back, but Tony jumped and grabbed it.

"Not so injured then, are you?" Amanda teased him.

Tony stuck his tongue out at her as he exchanged places with James. He flipped her the frisbee before she was expecting it, but James must have seen it coming, because he ran for it.

Amanda grabbed it at the last second and then shrieked when James collided with her, throwing them both to the ground.

"Are you okay?" James asked, his brow furrowed in concern.

He was so close his breath caressed her cheek. One large hand was behind her head, cushioning it from the ground. Mentally, she checked her body.

He was pressed against her from knee to chest, distracting her. "A little out of breath from the fall, but nothing broken," she whispered.

"Good."

She felt a tug on the frisbee in her hand and she grabbed it tighter. "Nice try. It's mine."

James grinned down at her. "Had to try."

"You did."

He still didn't get up.

"Uh, are we breaking for cuddles?" Tony's voice broke into their little bubble.

"He's trying to wrestle the frisbee away from me!" Amanda called back.

"Wrestling isn't the way to go about it," Tony said.

Amanda's eyes widened. She knew where he was going with that.

So did James, going by his smirk.

"Please," she murmured, surprised by how breathless she sounded.

James's dark eyes dilated, and the edge of sensuality crept into his smile. "Please what, Amanda?" His free hand ghosted over her belly, barely touching her skin.

She felt goosebumps erupt wherever he hovered, and she bit her lip, mentally willing his hand to go lower. Her breathing quickened and she felt herself get wet from anticipation.

James moved his hand close to her bellybutton, eyes scanning her face attentively. "Please *what*, Amanda?" he repeated.

Amanda whined quietly and his pupils dilated further.

"You're killing me with anticipation," Tony said. "Tickle her already!"

As if in a trance, James brushed his hand over to her ribs and danced his fingertips along them.

Amanda flailed with a shriek of uncontrollable laughter. Her ribs were the most ticklish spot on her body. Barely any touch was needed to send jolts of sensation to her brain, and James knew exactly how to make her lose control.

So did Tony, for that matter.

She forgot about the frisbee as James continued his assault on her ribs, until she gasped for breath. "Mercy!" she begged. "Or I'll pee right here!"

James chuckled and stopped, picking up the frisbee she'd dropped from nerveless fingers. He got to his feet and held out a hand for her. Once she was up, he tapped her ass with the plastic disc. "Off you go, then."

Amanda pushed his shoulder and adjusted her bikini. "It's not that dire now that I'm not being tortured!"

James raised an eyebrow silently.

She bit her lip, debating with herself. "Oh, alright. We should have lunch anyway."

"We've got bagels and tomatoes at my house," Tony suggested.

"Lettuce too?" James asked.

"Of course."

"What are we waiting for?" Amanda grabbed both their hands and swung them. "That sounds like a delicious lunch!"

"That was a good game," James said, letting go of her hand. Her heart dropped until he pulled her close with his arm around her shoulders.

"It reminded me of when we'd play soccer together in freshman year," Tony mused. "Do you remember that competition we went to in Philly?"

"Now who's reminiscing?" James chuckled. "How could I forget? We bunked with Damien and Ben, right?"

"Ugh. Don't remind me." Tony wrinkled his nose. "Those assholes."

"Weren't they on, like, all the sports teams with you?" Amanda asked.

"And then some. They played football too." James shuddered. "They got better as they aged, for the most part. They weren't very nice on that trip."

Tony rolled his eyes. "Understatement," he muttered under his breath.

The junior boys' soccer team exploded from the school bus and swarmed into the hotel, followed tiredly by their coach. He went straight to the desk to check in and get the keys. The young teenagers climbed on the furniture and jumped on the couches, screaming at one another in exhilaration. All but two. Tony and James followed their coach to the desk and waited quietly beside him, grinning.

"Did you win a game?" The receptionist questioned the two well-behaved teens.

"We won the tournament!" replied Tony, his grin practically splitting his face in two.

She smiled at them. They were vibrating with suppressed energy. "Congratulations!"

"Thanks!" said James. He threw an arm around Tony's shoulders. "It was mostly due to this guy!"

Tony flushed with pleasure. "You stopped more goals than I took shots. I think our win was due to you."

Beaming, James squeezed him tighter. "I'm just a defenseman. Our goalie stopped more goals than I did. You tore up the field as a midfielder!"

"It sounds like you work well as a team." Handing over the keys to the coach, she laughed. "Have a nice stay!"

The coach handed one key to the two boys. "Get your roommates and your bags from the bus." He sighed. "I wish more of the team was as calm as you two."

"I'm only calm on the outside." Tony smirked. "I feel like I could fly!"

Coach grinned. "Okay, I wish the team had your control. Off with you."

They found Damien and Ben trying to do handstands against the wall.

"Come on, we got our key," said James. "Let's get our shit and go."

The driver was removing the last of the bags from the bus when they exited the hotel. They found their bags easily and hauled them to the elevators.

"I need a shower," said Tony, wrinkling his nose as he stepped into the elevator.

James leaned over and took a sniff. "Yup, definitely. I'm not sharing a bed with you when you smell like that!" He grinned.

"You don't smell so fresh yourself," snorted Tony. "I call first dibs and then you can have it."

Damien smirked. "Why don't you just share? You share everything else." They got off the elevator at their floor.

Blinking in surprise, James looked over at Damien. "That's an odd thing to say," he said mildly. "What do you mean by it?"

"Oh, you know," Ben joined in. "You're sharing a bed, you share Amanda, why not share a shower?"

Tony looked confused. "Share Amanda?"

"Yeah, you're always all over each other. It's obvious to anyone with half a brain that you're both fucking her." Damien made an obscene hand gesture. "Damn, I wish I had grown up with her. Maybe she'd have let me fuck her, too. She's a tight piece of ass!"

Turning red with rage, Tony choked, spluttering, and turned to James. "He... I..." He gestured wildly, before attempting to launch himself across the hallway at Damien.

James grabbed his arm. "Not worth it," he muttered quietly into Tony's ear. To Damien and Ben's smirking faces, he said calmly, "We respect Amanda and are not having sex with her. She is our friend, and if you ever say anything like that about her again where we can hear it, I swear you'll live to regret it." The fierce look on his face told the boys he meant what he said. "As for sharing a bed," he shrugged, "so what? We do that all the time. Sharing a shower could get a little awkward, though."

Tony smirked at him. "You know you want a piece of this," he said, gesturing to himself. "Come on, Jamie, give in to your sexual urges!" He leaned in to kiss James.

Looking at his friend, James chuckled and turned his cheek to the proffered lips. Tony gave a wet sounding smack as he touched skin and then pulled away, grinning. "I think I'll be able to resist, thanks. There's nothing sexy about stinky hotel showers," James said, wrinkling his nose.

They continued down the hallway to their room, ignoring the other two boys trailing behind.

The next morning, James was woken by a clicking sound. He groaned and shifted on the bed slightly. Tony's sleep-heavy weight was pinning him to the mattress. He yawned and rubbed his free hand across his eyes, blinking as he opened them.

Damien and Ben were smirking at him from beside the bed. They were holding their phones.

"You are so gay for each other!" shouted Damien gleefully, not bothering to lower his voice.

Tony mumbled something into James's bare chest and tightened his grip on his waist, his eyes squeezing tightly closed.

James yawned again. "It is *way* too early for this conversation." He shook Tony's bare shoulder. "Wake up, sleepyhead."

"I'm awake," groaned Tony. "I don't want to deal with boneheads who think that being gay is an insult."

"You're gay!" Ben sneered at them. He waved his phone at them. "We've even got picture proof of it!"

"Yesterday, you were accusing us of sleeping with the same girl and now you say we're gay." James rubbed his hand over his face again, his fingers catching slightly on the satin scarf and tugging it askew. "You know what? I don't give a fuck what you say about us."

"Me neither." Tony yawned. "Can we go back to sleep now?"

James looked at the clock on the bedside table. "We have fifteen minutes before we have to be up." He glared at the boys staring down at them. "If you don't mind?" he asked pointedly.

"I don't want to sleep in the same room as a couple of fags," said Damien in disgust.

"Why? Afraid we'd take advantage of you in your sleep?" asked Tony, his eyes still closed. "Or are you more afraid that we wouldn't? Because I hate to break it to you, but you aren't my type."

James snickered. "Yeah, I'm really not into narrow-minded homophobes. Go on, get out of here."

After Damien and Ben had fled the room, James rubbed Tony's bare arm. "Think we handled that okay?"

Tony snorted. "If they'd gotten a picture of your morning wood, they would have had even more 'proof.' I'm fine with them thinking we're gay. Who cares? Amanda will get a laugh out of it."

"My wood?" James laughed. "What about yours? I can feel it digging into my hip through both of our pyjama pants."

"I can't help it. You're fucking hot."

They snickered.

Chapter Nine

Tony

"Is it just coincidence that Glenn is having his party on the first night we're home, or did he plan it so that we could be there?" Amanda asked, balancing on the curb as they walked the few blocks over to Glenn's parents' place.

"He got back earlier this week," Tony replied. "He told me that he considered having the party on Tuesday, but that nobody would come and get drunk in the middle of the week."

"Probably true," James agreed. "Cheaper for Glenn, then."

Tony chuckled. "Yeah, but his parents would've been home too. Not exactly a 'rager.'" He used air quotes.

"Where are they?" Amanda asked. "I was wondering if they'd be there."

"Some sort of spa retreat thing." Tony shrugged. "Probably need it after Glenn being home a whole week."

"I thought Glenn was one of your nicer sports friends?" Amanda asked, wobbling a little.

"I mean, he isn't a bad guy. Just..." Tony hesitated, drawing a breath in through his teeth. He held his hand out for her to grab if she needed it. "He's exuberant. Enthusiastic. All the time. You know what I mean?"

"Like me?" Amanda said, laughing a little.

"It's not the same," Tony argued. *I'm not in love with him,* his brain added silently.

"I didn't really hang around with him much in school, but he did seem like a nice guy," Amanda said.

"We wouldn't be going to his party if he wasn't," James pointed out.

"He's friends with all sorts of people, so we might bump into some not-so-friendly people as well," Tony cautioned. "Do we have a game plan?"

"Stick together," Amanda said promptly.

"Watch Amanda's drink," James added.

"Watch everyone's drinks," Amanda corrected. "You two can be drugged too."

"Stay with one kind of alcohol," Tony added. "And have water after each one."

They skirted around a line of parked cars leading up to a large house with a perfectly manicured lawn. They paused at the bottom of the driveway.

"This house is so pretentious," Amanda said. "It feels like it should belong in a movie about the social elites."

Tony snorted. "His parents would love that. Come on."

The music washed over them when they opened the front door, lights changing color to the beat. To the left was a large room, obviously normally a living room of sorts, with a DJ station tucked against the window seat. On their right was another large room with an abundance of chairs and sofas, obviously moved over from the room on the left.

"Kitchen's at the back," Tony shouted over the music.

"Yeah, I remember," James shouted back.

They made their way through the throngs of people to the kitchen. The music was a little quieter here. They spotted their host mixing a drink.

"So glad you could make it!" Glenn said loudly. "What can I make for ya?"

"Ooh, you have blue curacao. May I have a Blue Lagoon, please?" Amanda asked, bouncing a little on her toes. "It matches my shirt."

Tony glanced at her low-cut blue tank top before gritting his teeth and looking back at Glenn. The shirt fit her like a glove and it was obvious to everyone that she wasn't wearing a bra.

"Matches your shirt and your eyes," Glenn said smoothly, flipping bottles around and pouring them into a shaker. He shook it and then poured it into a tall glass with a straw, garnishing it with a maraschino cherry and a little folding umbrella. He offered it to her with a bow. "If you don't mind waiting while I serve your friends, can I steal a dance?"

Amanda smiled and blushed a little. "That would be great." She took a sip and her eyes widened. "Wow. This is *really* good!"

"I worked part-time as a bartender during college to make some extra cash," Glenn said. "And you get to benefit from it." He said that to the men, but he winked at Amanda, who blushed.

Tony swallowed back a growl. Amanda was allowed to flirt with whoever she chose. Just because he wanted to scoop her up in his arms and carry her off didn't mean that *she* wanted him to do that. "Long Island Iced Tea, please," he said instead.

"Classic. Nice." Glenn made it swiftly, with as many flourishes as he put into making Amanda's, and handed it over. "And for you?" he asked James.

"Mudslide, please."

Glenn nodded, whipped it up, and handed it over. "I'll be making a set of Screaming Orgasms in about half an hour, if anyone is interested," he informed them. He took Amanda's arm and led her to the door out of the kitchen.

"That's vodka, right?" Amanda asked.

"It is, sweetheart," Glenn replied.

"Then I will *definitely* have a Screaming Orgasm," Amanda said with a giggle as they exited the kitchen.

Tony turned to James, unsure what to do now. "Do we...follow her?"

"I think she can handle dancing with Glenn," James said wryly.

"How do you not feel as possessive as I do over her?" Tony demanded.

James clenched the hand that wasn't holding his drink into a fist. "Trust me, 'possessive' is not the only emotion I'm feeling right now. The way she looks tonight in that tight shirt and short skirt..." He closed his eyes and pinched the bridge of his nose. He let his breath out slowly before opening his eyes again, letting the full weight of his gaze fall onto Tony. "The alcohol will help."

"Alcohol will only make me worse," Tony muttered, taking a sip of his drink. "Oh damn, this *is* good."

James chuckled. "You going to have a Screaming Orgasm too?"

"I just might," Tony replied with a smirk. "You?"

"Why not? If a White Russian mixes kahlua and vodka, I'm sure I can handle a little mixing in my system."

"I kinda want to see Amanda dance," Tony admitted suddenly. "It's been a while."

"Prom," James said quietly. "That was a time and a half."

Tony winced. "Some good and some bad." He glanced at the door Amanda had disappeared through. "Fuck it, I'm going to watch."

James wasn't far behind him as he wandered through the doorway. He remembered this room having been a dining room when he'd visited during high school, and briefly wondered where the table had been stashed.

His musings were cut short, though, when he spotted Amanda dancing with Glenn. He was holding her close with one hand low on her back. It would almost look innocent, if her hips weren't swaying back and forth to the beat.

Tony turned around, bumping into James. "I can't watch her dance with another guy," he said, putting his lips near James's ear so he could hear. "I'm heading back to the kitchen."

"To sulk?" James teased.

"Shut up. You coming?"

"I think I'll stay here a little longer."

Tony nodded shortly and returned to the door. He glanced back before entering the kitchen and saw that a girl he recognized from Amanda's cheerleading days had approached James. *Kimberly, I think her name was,* he thought to himself, watching his friend react to the pretty girl in a short yellow sundress. *She was one of the nice ones.*

Kimberly seemed to be a little drunk, and she swayed into James as they danced, pressing herself against his body.

Tony leaned against the doorframe and took a sip of his drink as he watched, amused when James didn't seem sure about where to place his hands.

"Kimmy's always been into James," said a voice too close to his ear.

Tony stiffened, and not in a good way, upon hearing that voice. Sticky lips pressed a kiss to his bicep and long, sharp fingernails dug into his skin. "Carolina," he said, purposefully without any intonation.

Carolina giggled, the high-pitched tone assaulting his eardrums. "I knew you'd remember me!" she said breathily. She slid around to his front, squishing her breasts against his chest.

A quick glance down at her revealed that she was wearing a tank top similar to Amanda's, and he could see down her cleavage. Her red lipstick matched her shirt, and he made a mental note to check his arm for a stain.

"You're hard to forget," Tony replied truthfully.

"Aren't you the sweetest!" Carolina cooed. She trailed her hands up Tony's arms to his neck. "You've been working out. I *love* your tattoos. You look incredible."

"Thanks." The word almost got caught in Tony's throat, but he forced it out.

"When did you get home? You've been gone so long!"

"Yesterday," Tony gritted out.

Carolina's voice grated on his nerves, and he was grateful when the song ended, Glenn's voice resounding in the room. "Screaming Orgasms in the kitchen. Come on back if you want one!"

Cheers went up at this, and guests started moving towards the door. Tony backed out of the way, Carolina following him.

"You know, I've always had a thing for you," Carolina said, playing with the hair at the nape of his neck. "It's a pity we never got together in high school. Are you sticking around for the summer?"

"I'll be here before I move to Boston with James and Amanda in the fall," Tony replied tightly.

"You're still friends with them? That's so sweet!" She leaned closer and Tony realized she'd backed him against a wall. "I always thought that once they got together, they'd drop you. I mean, who would want a third wheel in a relationship?" She let loose a fluttery little giggle that set his teeth on edge.

"Well, I guess I have a little more time with them then. They're not together yet."

Carolina patted his cheek. "It's cute that you still think you have a chance with her. You'll see what she's really like."

Between the two of them, he knew Amanda better than Carolina did. He hummed noncommittally.

"We'll have lots of fun this summer, working together," Carolina continued blithely on. She pressed her breasts against his chest provocatively, doing absolutely nothing to his libido. "When the chips fall, I'll be here for you."

"I'll remember that." Tony tried not to let her words get under his skin. Unfortunately, Carolina was very good at pushing his buttons.

"Tony! There you are!" Amanda beamed at him as she bounced up to him. "Oh, hi Carolina," she said as if an afterthought. "Come on, Glenn's making shots." She grabbed Tony's hand and gave him a tug.

"You finished your drink already?" Tony asked, letting her lead him into the kitchen.

"Yes, and I've had a glass of water *and* went pee." Amanda stuck her tongue out at him. "You gonna chug that or finish after?"

"I'll finish now."

"Great. I'll go nab a shot for you."

She disappeared into the crowd surrounding the counter.

Tony finished his drink in two large gulps and then Amanda was back with two shot glasses.

"Wanna have a Screaming Orgasm with me?" she asked, a twinkle in her eye.

The alcohol in his belly was making him feel looser and less inhibited. "I'd never turn down an orgasm with you." He made a mental note to think before speaking.

Amanda beamed at him and clinked their glasses together before tipping it up to her lips.

The drink went down smoothly and they both gasped at the end. "He's good," Tony rasped.

"Too good." Amanda took Tony's glass. "I'm going to have to hold off on getting another drink for a bit. I'm already feeling these. Be right back with water for us."

"Can't wait."

Tony leaned against the cabinets, his gaze lingering on the swish of her hips as she headed for the sink. Her skirt just barely covered her ass. He wanted to put his hand on her thigh, sliding it up and up and... He closed his eyes, taking a deep breath.

"You fall asleep?" Amanda chuckled, pressing a glass into his hand.

"Not at all. I'm still on West Coast time," Tony teased. "Despite being woken up at seven this morning."

"Whoo, long day for you, poor baby." She pouted. "Mind you, I'm still on Texas time. I'm not far off from you."

Tony tucked a strand of hair behind her ear. "You've always been better on less sleep than me. I get to be a grump when I'm tired."

Amanda's eyes fluttered closed as he touched her hair. "You're not a grump."

"Not with you."

She hummed happily.

"Hey you two." James appeared, three shot glasses balanced in his hands. "Have you had a Screaming Orgasm yet?"

"Not from you," Amanda said playfully. She plucked out the middle glass. "This is my third. Seriously, no more for an hour after this, okay?"

"We've got you, love," Tony promised, taking the second glass.

The three of them clinked their shots together and tipped them back.

"Oooh that's good," Amanda moaned. She wobbled a bit and fell into James, who caught her. "Sorry." She giggled. "Lost my balance for a second."

"Drink your water," James advised. "Why don't we head outside for some fresh air after this?"

"Party games in the backyard!" Glenn announced over the excited chatter. "Be prepared to get a little physical!"

"That sounds like fun!" Amanda exclaimed happily, bouncing a bit. "Let's go!"

They played Human Knot, which Tony found a lot funnier with a bunch of drunk people than he thought he would. He made a mental note to add the game to the set of icebreakers at the start of camp this summer.

Then they played human twister. They were each given three colored cloth dots with safety pins, and were told to pin them somewhere on their bodies, the sexier the better.

"It's hands only," Glenn told them as he passed out the dots. "Don't want people falling over, trying to get their foot on someone else's shoulder!"

"This is so fun!" Amanda giggled. She pinned a red cloth to the left strap of her tank top. It flipped down off her shoulder to cover the top of her chest. "Where are you going to put yours? One should go on your ass. It's very grabbable."

Tony's eyebrows shot up. "You've never grabbed my ass."

"But I want to." She pouted. "Please?"

She's drunk and has no filter, Tony thought repeatedly. "If you'll help me pin it on."

"Yay!" She bounced a bit. "Turn around." She slid her hand in his pocket to protect him and pinned the circle on. "Put one on me, too, please?" She passed him a blue patch and turned around. "Don't prick me!"

"I'm going to have to go up your skirt," Tony said, exchanging glances with James.

"Not a problem." Amanda shrugged as she pinned a yellow dot over her belly. "James, you need one on your ass, too. Can I put it there?"

"Amanda," Tony said in a strangled voice, the back of his fingers grazing soft skin. "You're not wearing underwear!"

"Of course I am! I'm wearing a thong. It matches my shirt," she said chipperly. "James, I'm done. Where are you going to put your third?"

"Where do you think I should put it?" James asked.

Amanda studied him seriously for a moment. "You've got one on your pecs, one on your ass... The other place I'd want to grab on you is your cock. Do you think that's too much?"

Tony choked on nothing. The words coming out of Amanda's mouth tonight!

"I'm not sure I'm tipsy enough to have random people grabbing my crotch," James said dryly. "How about my lower abdomen? Is that close enough for you?"

"I suppose so," Amanda said with a sigh. "Maybe later."

"Sure, love." While Amanda was helping him pin the third patch on, James met Tony's eyes, widening his own with incredulity.

It was nice to see that James was as thrown by her lack of filter as he was.

"Okay, rules!" Glenn rubbed his hands together and the small group of people gathered around him. He looked around them approvingly. "Nice job everyone."

Most of the people that Tony could see had done what they had, but some had also included their breasts and crotches. Most of the latter were men, but some of the women had as well. He found himself wishing that Amanda had followed suit, but shook his head. There was no guarantee that the hand on her breast or crotch would have been his.

"You must not have both hands on the same person. Only one hand per patch. Since there's unlikely to be a person who gives up, we'll only play for ten minutes. Please return the patches to me afterwards, as they'll be used again later in the evening. That's it! Have fun!" He spun a dial. "Right hand, red."

Before Tony thought about it, he turned to Amanda and put his right hand on her left shoulder.

She grinned at him and put hers on James's lower belly.

Tony felt someone else's hand on his ass, but didn't care who it was, even when the hand gave a tiny squeeze. "Someone else thinks my ass is grabbable too," he whispered to Amanda, making her laugh.

"Right hand, blue," Glenn said gleefully.

James put his hand on Amanda's ass and turned himself so that Tony could see the blue cloth on his pants. "You know you want it," James said with a smirk.

"You bet I do," Tony replied without thinking, grabbing his best friend's left butt cheek.

Amanda's small hand felt up his pectoral where he'd pinned his blue patch. She moaned a little. "Your hand is so warm, James," she gasped. Her fingers tightened against Tony's muscles as she swayed into James's touch. "Feels good."

"Left hand, yellow," Glenn said.

"Amanda," Tony said teasingly. "Are you a horny drunk?"

Her glare was softened by her expression of bliss. "Shut up."

Tony huffed a laugh, meeting James's amused gaze with a matching one of his own.

"Right hand, red."

By the time Glenn called the end to the game, Tony was half-hard and ready to leave.

"I'm going to make some more shots, if anyone's interested. There's dancing inside, and you can play 'Find the Grape' out here."

"What's that?" Amanda asked.

"It's when someone hides a grape somewhere on their person and someone else puts on a blindfold. They can only use their mouths to find it," Kimberly explained.

"That's hot," Tony admitted.

"I'm going to grab another shot," James said. "Anything for either of you?"

"I'll take another, thanks," Tony replied.

Amanda tilted her head, her eyes half-closed as she thought. "I wouldn't mind feeling a bit more of a buzz. Yes, please!" She wrapped her arms around James and stood on tiptoe to kiss his cheek. "Mmm, you smell good," she hummed, brushing her nose against his cheek.

"Glad you think so." James passed her to Tony. "Keep an eye on each other," he said, giving Tony a meaningful look.

"I'm going first!" Carolina exclaimed, holding a grape between her fingers. "Who wants to search my body with their lips?"

Tony shuddered as he watched Damien, Ben, and Oliver leap for the pile of blindfolds on the table at the side of the patio. They had been on every sports team in high school and been the stereotypical jocks.

"You don't want to try?" Amanda whispered with a soft chuckle.

"I think 'fuck, no' is not strong enough," Tony replied, dipping his nose behind her ear. "I don't even want to know where her body's been."

Amanda continued to shake with laughter in his arms. "She slept around quite a bit during high school, and I can only imagine how much more she did after graduating."

"Not appealing."

"Are you saying that any woman who enjoys sex with multiple partners is unappealing?" Amanda asked, pulling back slightly.

"No." Tony shook his head so hard their bodies swayed in place. "That would be a huge double-standard."

"Good." Amanda melted into his embrace, her back to his front. "Because I know how many people you've slept with."

"Only a handful or so," Tony commented.

"Maybe their boob size," Amanda teased.

Tony tickled her ribs, making her squirm with laughter. They watched Carolina place the grape into her cleavage after the men had tied on their blindfolds. The men started mouthing along her arms and body.

"I'm not sure I can watch this," Amanda murmured.

Carolina moaned theatrically.

"Yeah, I'm done. Let's find James."

The kitchen was crowded with loud people waiting for their drinks. They spotted James in a corner. He waved them over.

"Why don't we skip this round and dance?" Amanda suggested. "I bet there's barely anyone there."

"What, there isn't enough room to dance in here?" Tony teased, spinning her under his arm until she bumped into somebody.

"Sorry," Amanda said with a giggle. "Come on you two." She took a hand from each of them and pulled them after her down the hall to the dance floor.

She'd been right; the dance floor had a few people on it, but there was plenty of room for the three of them.

Tony pulled her close and Amanda draped her arms over his shoulders, swaying her hips to the beat of the music. James stepped up behind her and put his hands just under Tony's on her hips. "Think we remember how to dance together as the three of us?" he murmured, just loud enough for Tony to hear.

"We'll figure it out." Tony shrugged. "This is so much better than Carolina pushing herself on me."

Amanda wrinkled her nose and James growled. "Why bring her up? I thought we were having fun?"

"Earlier, she threw herself at me again." Tony ran his hands up Amanda's sides to her shoulders. "And her treatment of you in junior year kept running through my head on repeat."

Amanda smiled sadly. "I certainly wouldn't say that was a fun time, but you two had my back. Other than her, cheer was a lot of fun."

"Why would Glenn invite her?" Tony fumed. "It's been, what, six years? And I'm still pissed."

"Maybe she slept with him," James suggested, one eyebrow rising.

Amanda cuddled closer. "Let's just forget about her. I want to have fun with my best friends."

"Sure, darlin'." Tony vowed to keep Carolina's name off his tongue for the rest of the night, but he wasn't sure he should forget about her. She was always up to something and he wanted to make sure he was prepared.

Chapter Ten

Flashback: Sleepovers Can Be Fun

Amanda tumbled across the grass at the first football game of junior year, flipping seamlessly from a cartwheel to a back handspring and ending with an aerial. She landed solidly, heart leaping in her chest at the cheers from the stands. James and Tony were in the front, with all their parents, cheering "Go Amanda, go!" She gave them a wink before flipping her ponytail over her shoulder and rejoining her teammates for the rest of the routine.

Later, in the locker room, a couple of her teammates came over while she was changing.

"Nice flips today!" said Kimberly.

"Thanks," said Amanda happily. "They felt really good!"

"Did you want to come to my sleepover tomorrow night?" asked Carolina, the captain of the cheer squad. "Cheerleaders only."

"Umm, I'll have to ask my parents," replied Amanda. "And I'm lifeguarding until nine. Is it okay if I'm late?"

"No hot date?" asked another girl across the room. Amanda couldn't remember her name. Jennifer, maybe? Or Jessica?

"No, I'm not dating anyone," answered Amanda. She missed the smirks and nudges the girls exchanged as she pulled her shirt over her head.

"Of course you can be late," Carolina said.

"I'll talk to you tomorrow, Carolina. Thanks for inviting me!" Amanda walked out of the change room, a spring in her step, directly into her parent's arms.

"I'm so proud of you, jelly bean," said her father, kissing her on the forehead.

"You looked kick-ass out there!" Tony exclaimed from behind her.

"Weren't you supposed to be watching the football team?" teased Amanda.

"We watched them when you weren't on the field," replied James smiling. "It was hard to look away from your death-defying stunts."

"Meh, that was nothing," Amanda bounced happily. "Pizza? I'm starved!"

"That's our girl," her mom squeezed her shoulders tightly.

Amanda walked up the front steps to Carolina's house and rang the doorbell. When the door opened, she turned and waved to her mom in the car.

"The girls are upstairs. You must be Amanda, the new tumbler on the team," said Carolina's mother.

"Nice to meet you, Mrs. Santorini," said Amanda politely. "Sorry I'm late. I was working."

"Doesn't bother me in the slightest, dear. Up the stairs, last door on the right. You can hear the music from here," Mrs. Santorini smiled.

Amanda walked up the stairs nervously. It was her first sleepover, not counting the ones she had with the guys, and she didn't know what to expect.

"You're here!" squeaked Emma, a freshman, as she opened the door. "I'll be right back. Bathroom!" She giggled and dashed down the hallway.

Carolina opened the door further and grabbed her arm, pulling her into the room. "So glad you made it! How was work?"

"An old man wore a speedo to the pool today," Amanda replied, deadpan.

The girls in the room stared at her blankly. "Ew! Not cool," said Jessica/Jennifer, finally. "I don't want to hear about gross stuff."

"Yeah, like, did any cute boys come in to swim?" asked Kimberly.

"I was guarding Aquafit and the senior's swim tonight," said Amanda. "Nothing exciting ever happens on Friday nights, unless you count asthma attacks as exciting."

Awkward silence, other than the blaring music, fell over the room. *Tough crowd,* thought Amanda sarcastically.

"Should I get into my pyjamas?" asked Amanda into the silence.

"Great idea," said Carolina. "You can put your stuff in the corner here and the bathroom off my bedroom is free now."

Amanda slipped into the bathroom. *Just don't make any more jokes,* she told herself. *They don't react the same way that Tony and James do.* She pulled off her clothes, folding them neatly into her backpack and got into her pyjamas. She was glad she had picked this pair, as they were similar to the ones that the other girls were wearing. An oversized t-shirt, that had once belonged to Tony before he grew out of it, paired with tiny booty shorts that read *I heart Iron Man* on the bum. "Deep breath, let's do this," she said, psyching herself up before she opened the door.

The girls were sitting in a circle on the floor, with a place left for her between Emma and Carolina.

"What game are we playing?" asked Amanda cautiously, putting her backpack beside her pillow before joining the circle.

"Truth or Dare!" exclaimed Kimberly.

"Oh. Yay?" Amanda replied nervously. *At least I have nothing to hide,* she thought.

"Jessica, Truth or Dare?" asked Carolina.

Jessica, Amanda repeated to herself. *Not Jennifer.*

Jessica replied, "Truth."

"Who do you think is the hottest boy in the school?"

"That's a tough one!" laughed Jessica. "I can never decide if it's James or Tony! Amanda, what do you think?"

Amanda, startled, blushed. "Oh, I don't really think of them like that."

"Bullshit! You can't tell us that you've never thought about making out with either of them. Or both!" The girls all giggled.

"No, really I—"

"You've never kissed either of them?" demanded Carolina. "Does that mean that the rumors about them being gay are true?"

"Is it my turn?" asked Amanda, cheeks flushing.

"Amanda, Truth or Dare?" asked Jessica.

Amanda chewed her lip, thinking. The dares might be even worse! "Truth," she said.

"Who has the biggest dick, James or Tony?"

"I don't know!" exploded Amanda. "I've never asked them to whip it out and lay it on the table!"

Shocked, the girls giggled.

"You are bound by the code of sisterhood and cheerleading to tell us the truth!" said Carolina ferociously.

"I honestly don't know!" said Amanda, getting angry. "It's my turn to ask a question, isn't it? Emma, Truth or Dare?"

Emma gulped. "Truth."

"Why are you girls so intent on asking questions about my relationship with James and Tony?"

Emma stared back, wide eyed. "I don't know."

Amanda sighed. "Sorry. I'm feeling a little paranoid." She got up. "You can play on without me. I'll be right back." She walked into the bathroom and sat on the edge of the tub. *Poor Emma. I didn't mean to jump down her throat.* She stood up and looked at herself in the mirror. "Get yourself together!" She splashed some water on her face and then re-entered the room.

"We were about to have a handstand competition!" said Carolina. "You in?"

Amanda smiled with relief. This, she could do. "Hell yes!" She tucked her shirt into her shorts and readied herself beside the other girls in a line.

"Three, two, one, up!" shouted Jessica. She had her cell phone out and was dancing around the five girls standing upside down, recording the competition.

"And Kimberly is down!" announced Carolina.

"Josee is down, and took down Rose with her!" Jessica chortled.

"Amanda and Emma are still up!"

"Not for long!" shouted Carolina, and she yanked Amanda's shirt out of her shorts, letting it fall over her face and exposing her breasts.

Amanda came down hard, bruising her knees on the floor. "How dare you!" she shouted, face crimson. "You are all just... Just..." she seethed, searching for words. "Horrible, two-faced bitches!"

She grabbed her pillow and backpack and opened the door. "See if I ever accept an invitation from you ever again!"

She stomped down the stairs. Mrs. Santorini met her at the bottom of the stairs. "Is everything alright, dear?"

Amanda wiped at her eyes and pulled her cell phone out of her backpack. "May I have a glass of water? I'd like to go home. I'm not feeling well."

She called her parents first. Her dad answered and didn't ask any questions other than the address. Then she texted James and Tony. *Backyard ASAP. Bring your sleeping bags. Dad's picking me up.*

Mrs. Santorini came back with the water, looking concerned. "Did you want to sit down?"

"No, thank you," replied Amanda. She drank the water quickly. "I'll just wait for my dad outside."

"I will wait with—"

"That's not necessary, thank you." Amanda cut her off. "My dad should be close by."

He was. Amanda had barely closed the door when her father drove up. "Please, take me home. And next time I have a brilliant idea to go on a sleepover with girls I barely know, remind me of what a disaster this one was."

"It's okay, honey," said her dad, taking her hand and kissing the back. "It won't always be like this."

"Girls are awful." Amanda sighed. "Give me my boys any day of the week. We're going to sleep in the backyard tonight."

Her dad raised his eyebrows. "You might get cold," he said mildly.

"The guys will bring their sleeping bags and we'll zip up together," said Amanda, shrugging away her father's concern.

Her dad's eyebrows remained raised, but Amanda didn't notice. She was staring out the window without really seeing what she was looking at, her mind trying not to focus on the humiliation she'd just incurred.

When they pulled into her driveway, James and Tony were waiting on the front step. James was still wearing the satin scarf he slept in to protect his hair.

"Look after her, boys," said her father, getting out of the car.

"Of course, Mr. Beyer," replied Tony.

"She's our girl," added James.

Mr. Beyer nodded and went into the house, a gentle smile on his face. Amanda hadn't moved from the front seat. James and Tony exchanged worried glances. What had happened?

"Come on, let's get you to the hammock," said James, opening the door.

Amanda blinked up at them and Tony pulled her out of the car.

"It was awful!" she said and then burst into tears.

Tony carried her to the backyard, Amanda still crying into his bare shoulder. James brought her things from the car and closed the doors behind them.

They flanked her on the king-sized mattress hammock, wrapped in the two sleeping bags. They slowly managed to get the full story out of her, from the bad reaction to the jokes, to the Truth or Dare, and finally to the handstand competition and the aftermath.

"Poor kid," murmured Tony, petting her hair back from her face.

"I can't believe they didn't laugh at Mr. Oppenstein in his speedo! Did you tell them that he is covered in hair and looks like a dancing bear?" asked James, desperately trying to make her laugh.

"No, I didn't get the chance," said Amanda, giggling through her tears. "They already thought I was weird enough."

"Who cares what they think?" demanded Tony.

"*We* don't think you're weird," said James. "And doesn't what we think matter more than what vapid, bitchy girls think?"

"Very true," said Amanda, cheered by the conversation. "Although they did say one thing that made me curious..."

"What?" asked Tony.

"Who is bigger?" she asked mischievously.

For a moment, James and Tony puzzled over what she meant and then blushed furiously. In between them, Amanda started laughing.

"I didn't mean it!" she gasped, between bursts of giggles. "I just wanted to see the look on your faces!"

"I'll forgive you because you've had a difficult day," said James, grinning.

"But don't ask us again unless you want to find out the answer," winked Tony.

"No, no!" she said, now blushing as bright as the boys. "I won't ask again."

Early the next morning, Mrs. Beyer peeped out the kitchen window to the hammock and put her hand to her heart.

She grabbed her phone and tiptoed out the door to sneak a picture.

The sleeping bags were shoved down around the bottom of the hammock. James was lying on his back, his afro barely contained by a satin scarf. Amanda was practically on top of him, her right leg thrown across his pyjama-clad hips, head resting on his bare chest. His hand was on her knee. Tony was wrapped around her, his arm around her bare waist, as her shirt had ridden up a bit in the night. His right leg rested over both her left leg and James's right. James's right arm was stretched over to Tony, and was holding his left hand.

Mrs. Beyer slipped back into the house and showed her husband the picture.

"None of them have dated," he said. "I'm worried about what will happen when they do."

"They'll be fine," she reassured him. "Their friendship will last."

"When they were little, I thought that James and Amanda would grow up and get married," he said sadly. "Now with Tony thrown into the mix, someone is bound to get hurt."

"It's obvious to anyone with eyes that they all care about each other, to the exclusion of everyone else," she replied.

"Have you heard the rumors around town about them?" he asked, his eyebrows raised. "This picture certainly makes them look true."

"Does it matter?" she demanded in return. "They are still best friends, so it obviously doesn't bother them, whether the rumors are true or false. They treat her with respect and love. She couldn't do better."

Outside, Amanda was waking up. She arched her back into a stretch and then stilled. Behind her, Tony was pressing into her ass. She flushed at the hard ridge that pushed into her. Under her leg, James was also hard, and Amanda's face burned more. *I still wouldn't be able to answer the girls about who is bigger, but now I know how big they really are,* she thought to herself. *How am I going to get out of this predicament without all of us getting embarrassed?*

Tony's phone vibrated. Then James's. Both guys woke up, blinking slowly. "Morning, gorgeous," rasped James.

"Morning, handsome," simpered Tony behind her, making Amanda chuckle.

James fished his phone out of his pocket, lifting Amanda's leg out of the way and seemingly undisturbed by his erection. "Who sends texts at six-thirty in the bloody morning?" he yawned, waking his phone up.

Then his eyes went wide. "Shit."

Tony, who had also grabbed his phone, echoed him.

"What is it?" asked Amanda.

"The text," said James. "It's from Glenn. He says, *Thought you should know about this,* with a link to a video."

"Oh God, please, no," moaned Amanda. "How many people got that?"

"Hold on a moment, I'll ask him," said Tony, quickly typing the query: *How many people was this sent to?* They waited with bated breath.

Vrrrr

Tony looked down at his phone. "Fuck."

Amanda groaned.

"Let me see it," she said, motioning for James to hand her his phone. "Maybe it's not as bad as I imagined."

She clicked the link, which brought her to a cloud-share where the video was stored. She pressed play and the video started by showing off her legs, down to her butt, which was clenched tight. Words popped up as the camera hovered on her butt: *Always knew she was a tight-ass!* Then the motion of the camera swung around to the front and there she was, shirt tucked in, upside down. She could see Carolina standing beside her and although she knew what was going to happen, she mentally begged her not to do it again. But she did. The video paused on her naked torso and then words wiggled across the screen: *Amanda: Hot or Not?* The video stopped. Horrified, Amanda closed her eyes and slowly put the phone down.

"This is awful!" she whispered. "Why would they do this to me?"

"Because they're jealous," said Tony simply.

"You didn't see this! They are horrible!" She all but shouted at him.

"No we didn't, and we won't watch it unless you give us permission," said James calmly. "They *are* jealous. They're jealous because you're smart, beautiful, and talented. Plus, you had the balls to call them on their bullshit last night and then you spent the night with two gorgeous male specimens," he gestured at himself and Tony, "while *they* spent the night with a bunch of girls, being mean and nasty to each other."

Tony snorted at the expression 'gorgeous male specimens,' and Amanda huffed a laugh.

"Well, one part's true, at any rate," she said, after James had finished speaking. "You're both gorgeous. And *they* couldn't decide which one of you was the hottest guy in school."

Both James and Tony made faces. "I didn't like them very much before, but now I wouldn't touch them with a ten-foot pole," said Tony.

Amanda sighed and then made up her mind. "You might as well watch it. Everyone else will have by now."

"Are you sure?" asked Tony.

"We're not trying to pressure you into showing us something that was made without your consent," James said seriously.

"I can give my consent now," said Amanda sadly. "That's the important thing."

"I'm trying not to be too eager to see you topless, but I'm sorry, I kind of want to see you topless," said James with a wink.

"All you had to do was ask!" said Amanda playfully as she toyed with the hem of her t-shirt.

"I don't think I could handle the stunning beauty of your naked body in person," grinned Tony, covering his eyes dramatically. "Not before breakfast."

Amanda blushed. "Stop flattering me and watch the damn video."

They picked up their phones and pressed play. When they got to her butt, James scowled. "Don't they know that a proper handstand requires taut muscles in both the ass and the core? Ridiculous."

Amanda smiled at her friend, already feeling better, but still anxious about the big finale. What would they say?

At the end of the video, Tony growled, "If I ever see those girls—what were their names?—I'll tear them to pieces!"

"I don't know," said James slowly. "There isn't anything all *that* horrible in this video." He looked up to see shocked expressions on both Amanda and Tony's faces.

"Other than lack of consent, of course!" he added quickly. "But seriously, look at your body, Amanda." He leaned over so that Amanda could see his screen, too. Tony joined them on her other side. James pointed out each part of her body on the screen as he described it. "Your abs are tight and you've got a killer six pack. Your breasts are..." James hesitated.

"Perfect," suggested Tony dryly. "Spectacular, gorgeous, stunning—"

"Yes to all of that," said James with a grin. "Essentially, you've got the sexiest body possible on display."

"You do have some excellent points, James," said Tony thoughtfully. "This body will fuel my fantasies for months. Years, even! And now I don't even need to embellish." He laid back on the hammock and pretended to jack himself off. "Oh, yes, beautiful. Amanda, mmm."

"Tony, stop it!" laughed Amanda, blushing. Tony stopped, grinning.

"My point, and Tony's, is that you have nothing to be ashamed or embarrassed about. Own it. You've got the most rocking body in the school and now everyone else knows that, too." James kissed her cheek and smacked Tony on the leg. "Ass."

"We got you, love," said Tony. "And now I'm going to text Glenn back and tell him that this video was not made with your consent and that he should tell everyone else that. And if anyone brings it up to you, they will regret it."

James flexed his biceps and grinned. "They will definitely regret it."

"You don't think my breasts are too small?" asked Amanda teasingly. "They aren't really..." She gestured at her chest helplessly. "Much?"

James and Tony openly gaped at her.

"Are you kidding me?" asked Tony in a strangled voice. "And now I'm thinking about your breasts again." He blushed and looked away awkwardly.

"No! And I think that's what Tony's trying to say, too," James said wryly. "Why would you want them to be any bigger? You're perfect!"

"I am so lucky to have you two in my life," sighed Amanda happily. "I love you."

Mrs. Beyer exited the house, carrying a tray with orange juice, eggs, bacon, and pancakes. "Good timing, you're up." She placed the tray on the patio table.

The scent of bacon made Amanda's stomach growl and she patted it. "Hush, tummy. Food will be in you soon."

James rolled his eyes at Tony, who grinned back.

"Last one to the table has to do the dishes!" shouted Tony as they all scrambled off the hammock.

"Thanks for breakfast, mom," said Amanda, stuffing a forkful of pancake into her mouth.

"You're the best, Mrs. B," added James.

"You're welcome. I took the cutest picture of you three before you woke up," said Mrs. Beyer, pulling her phone out of her pocket.

All three of them stopped eating, looking at each other with wide eyes.

"Here you go! Aren't you just gorgeous together?" Amanda's mom gave her the phone and the boys crowded around to see over her shoulders.

Amanda's jaw dropped. They really did look good. "Can I have this picture, mom?"

"Of course! I was going to print one for each of you," said Mrs. Beyer happily.

"No. I mean yes, I want a hard copy, but can I get the digital file today?"

"Sure thing, honey. I'll send it to you right now." Mrs. Beyer took her phone back and hummed to herself as she went back into the house.

"What idea is rolling around in that big, beautiful brain of yours?" asked James quietly.

"*That* is what consent looks like," said Amanda seriously. "Not some sneaky video of girls pulling my shirt off. Can we put this picture online? Today?"

"Are you sure? You know that there are rumors about the three of us at school already," said James hesitantly.

Amanda flushed. "Do those rumors bother you?"

"The rumors either paint James and me as studs or gay. They can't seem to make up their minds," said Tony sarcastically. "But you know what girls get called when they're sleeping with more than one person."

"They've been calling me that for a very long time," replied Amanda calmly. "This won't change anything. The picture will make the rumors about the three of us look like they're true. Does that bother you? I don't give a shit."

"Neither do I," replied James.

Tony grinned. "Give them something else to talk about other than that fucked up video *and* everyone will know you're not to be messed with unless they want to deal with James and me. I like it."

After breakfast and dishes, which they did together, they dashed upstairs to Amanda's computer and loaded the file into a photo editing program.

"What should we say?" asked Amanda. "Hashtag consent?"

"Hashtag consent received?" suggested James.

"Hashtag consent matters," said Tony.

"Perfect," said Amanda to Tony, her fingers tapping at her keyboard. "Save, upload, and... Save. You guys really are the best–to go through this with me."

"What is there to go through?" asked Tony with a wink. "Girls will be throwing themselves at James and me, trying to get a piece of this." He flexed his muscles, still bare from the waist up.

"The pyjama pants ruin the look you're going for, I think," said James, inspecting his friend somberly. "It might be better if you took them off," he added, just before he tackled Tony onto Amanda's double bed.

"Nooo," cried Tony through his laughter. "Amanda would be scarred for life!"

"I'll deal," said Amanda with a chuckle, as she joined James in tickling their friend on her bed.

Chapter Eleven

James

Around midnight, the DJ packed up and people started leaving the party. But James was still feeling wide awake, and so were his friends.

"It feels like nine o'clock!" Tony said, a giant grin on his face. "I'm still on Cali time."

"I'd just be starting to look for a bar in Austin around now," Amanda agreed. "Let's see if Glenn has any other games for us to play, or if he's kicking us out."

As it turned out, Glenn wasn't ready for the party to end either, and he had one last game left for anyone who wanted to stick around.

The twelve of them pulled chairs around the patio rug and Glenn lit the citronella candles to keep the insects away.

"This game is not for the faint of heart," Glenn said, patting a white box in his hands. "I wrote the cards myself based on a version of Truth or Dare I found on the internet." He paused to look around the circle of faces. "To that end, I will insist that everyone hand over their electronic devices. No pictures allowed from this point until you leave my house. Does everyone agree?"

Heads bobbled in agreement, although some of them were hesitant, and Glenn held out a basket to each person in turn. When he got to Amanda, she shook her head. "No pockets, no cell," she said, showing him her skirt.

"Seriously!" Kimberly shouted from the other side of the circle.

"I put mine in my bra," said a girl from the other side of James. She introduced herself as Morgan, Damien's girlfriend.

Amanda shrugged. "I'm not wearing a bra."

"I carry a purse," Carolina said, her nose in the air. "Who knows when I might need a condom or something, right, Tony?"

"Always good to protect yourself," Tony replied noncommittally.

"Speaking of protecting yourselves," Glenn said cheerfully after collecting the last cellphone. "These are going inside the barbeque. It's off, don't worry. But we'll need these." He took out a basket and replaced it with the cell phone one. Inside the new basket was a hill of condoms.

James whistled. "We having an orgy?"

Some of the girls gasped.

"Only if you want to," Glenn said with a wink. "As I said, we're playing Truth or Dare, and the punishment will be removing an article of clothing. You can earn items back, of course, on a successful completion." He looked around the circle. "Anyone want out?"

Kimberly raised her hand. "I think I need more alcohol for this."

"Coming right up. I made jello shots for anyone who stuck around for this. Strawberry and lime." He opened the fridge under the granite countertop and pulled out two trays of little paper shot glasses. "Jellies up!"

"You're spoiling us," Amanda said admiringly, taking one of each color.

"It's all for good fun," Glenn replied with a grin.

"I'll say." Tony took two as well.

James sucked the jello out of his first cup. He was definitely already feeling the buzz from the previous drinks, but a little liquid, or not-so-liquid in this case, courage couldn't hurt if condoms might be needed.

"Who is brave enough to draw first?" Glenn said, taking the lid off the box of cards. He shook it slightly.

"I'll do it," Amanda said, leaning forwards and plucking a card out of the box. "I read it and then answer?"

Glenn nodded. "Or complete the dare, or ask someone else. The card will explain."

"Alright. 'Have you ever fantasized about having sex with your own gender?'" Amanda tossed her hair behind her shoulder. "Well, yeah. I'm bisexual."

Glenn opened and closed his mouth for a second. "Okay then. I think we should pass the box around clockwise. Put your card at the back, draw from the front."

Tony took the box and drew a card. "'What's the weirdest porn you've ever gotten off to?'" He leaned back in his chair and rubbed his chin with one hand. "Weird is kinda subjective, isn't it? How about one I didn't think I'd like because it seemed weird before I watched it?"

The group agreed.

"It was a video of this girl inserting objects inside her ass. They got bigger and bigger, until the last one didn't go all the way in, it was still hanging half out and she was super stretched around it. And then she pushed them all out again." Tony shrugged. "Something about her body expanding around each object as it came out of her... That's what did it for me."

"That's so nasty!" Carolina said, leaning forwards. "Did any of your girlfriends ever do that for you?"

"I think that's a separate question," Tony replied, passing the box on to Josee.

Josee got the first dare of the evening. James watched her crawl around to each chair to get told she was a good girl and get pats on her head like a puppy dog, joining in when it was his turn. She had flushed cheeks, both from the alcohol and the embarrassment.

The box made its way around the circle, Carolina being the first to lose an article of clothing—her shirt—when she refused to do the dare of peeing in a cup and drinking it. James didn't blame her, although he was getting mildly annoyed by all the passes she kept making at Tony. She'd squeeze her breasts together while looking his way, puckering her lips and winking.

James pulled a card out and swallowed hard. "I guess I know what the condoms are for."

"Oooh!"

"What's it say?"

"Read it!"

Clearing his throat, James waited for silence before reading, "'Cock-warm for a minute while blindfolded. At the end of the minute, guess who it is. If you guess wrong, you lose. If you refuse to play, you lose twice.'"

Whoops of glee echoed through the backyard space.

"Are you up for the challenge?" Damien sneered.

James got to his feet and picked up a blindfold. "My only request is that the dude wear a condom. Do you think you could handle my mouth on you?" He looked Damien in the eye and smirked in satisfaction when the other guy broke first. "That's what I thought. Pick the guy." He put the blindfold on, and was completely surrounded by darkness. "Amanda, can you please spin me around and then lead me to my victim?"

Amanda giggled. "Don't worry, I won't spin you too fast."

"We'll move the 'victim' to a separate chair," Glenn said. "Good. Everyone else, hush. Any sound could give away who it is."

"He already knows it isn't a girl," Carolina said, voice grating on James's already frayed nerves. "We should be allowed to talk."

"We'll keep this rule for every blindfolded dare," Glenn said.

"Holy shit," Carolina said suddenly, awe in her tone.

James heard the unmistakable sound of a condom wrapper opening, and then Amanda was leading him around his chair to one behind it.

"Kneel," she whispered. "There's still carpet here."

"Small favors," James said. He felt the hairy knees on either side of his chest and ran his hands up over cargo shorts. *Glenn, Oliver, Ben, and Tony all had cargo shorts on,* he thought to himself. *One eliminated.* His fingers brushed against cloth over the guy's belly as he encircled the good-sized half-hard penis in front of him. *Nobody's lost their shirt yet. That doesn't help. Glenn kept talking as if it wasn't him. Oliver, Ben or Tony?* He opened and closed his jaw a couple times before saying, "Start the clock," and engulfing the cock with his mouth.

The latex made guessing harder, as he couldn't taste the guy and it masked the scent. James concentrated on other senses than sight and taste. He could smell a strong masculine scent, slightly sour from sweat, from the base of the cock. The deep breaths above him sounded calm, almost unaffected, but James knew better. He could feel the cock in his mouth thickening with arousal. *Is it possible that this is Tony?* James thought about it as he hovered in position. *Could be. Ben, unlikely, unless he's changed drastically. He was flinching as much as Damien when I stood up. Oliver? I don't know him well enough to eliminate him.*

"Twenty seconds left," Amanda's voice penetrated his thoughts.

Okay, if I guess Tony and it is him, people will think we have a thing. Do I care? Would he care? If I guess Tony and it isn't him, would he be upset that I don't know him well enough? The cock feels about right, from what I remember seeing of him in quick glimpses. I'm going to guess Tony.

A quiet hitch in breath above him sealed the deal. That was definitely Tony's breathing.

"Five, four, three, two, one," Amanda counted down. "You are relieved from duty, soldier. Who was it?"

"Tony," James said, voice raspy from his throat being stretched. "Can I get something to drink? Latex lingers on the tongue." He made smacking noises with his lips.

"How'd you know it was me?" Tony's voice sounded surprised.

James took off the blindfold. Tony had already tucked himself away, and was holding the empty condom between two fingers. His shorts were tented. "Cargo shorts, no panicked breathing. I wasn't sure, it could have been Oliver, but I know you have a decent-sized cock, so it was an educated guess."

"You sneak a glimpse at me, Jamie?" Tony asked, grinning, his cheeks pink.

"Like you haven't returned the favor," James snorted. "Don't play like you don't know what I'm talking about."

"His size was a pleasant surprise to *me*," Carolina purred.

"Damnit," Tony muttered under his breath.

James huffed a laugh and took another jello shot from the tray as he dropped off the blindfold.

"After that exciting dare, let's see what gets pulled next!" Glenn said cheerfully. "Go ahead, Amanda."

"'Make-out heavily with someone for a minute while blindfolded, hands behind your back. They are allowed to let their hands wander. At the end of the minute, guess who it is. If you guess wrong, you lose. If you refuse to play, you lose twice.'" Amanda stood up. "Yes, I'll play." She headed for the blindfolds.

James glanced around the circle. If he was chosen, he wasn't sure he'd be able to stop at a minute. If he wasn't chosen, he might rip the person's head off. Tony would be the safest choice for everyone.

Unfortunately, Damien was the lucky dude. He smirked at James as he passed by, showing him his middle finger.

"I don't trust him," Tony whispered.

James shook his head. He didn't either.

Amanda was led silently over to the chair Damien was sitting in by Josee, and she straddled Damien's lap. "Ready," she said, and Josee started the timer.

Damien's hands immediately went to her ass, pulling the skirt up, squeezing and manipulating her cheeks for everyone to see. Seemingly bored with that after a few seconds, he slid his hands under her shirt at the front, hiking it up until it bunched under her armpits. The angle the party was watching from didn't give them a view of her front, but James could tell that her breasts were exposed and Damien was groping her. Amanda's knuckles were yellow with tension as she held her fingers behind her back.

James's blood boiled as Damien's hands crept around her back again, grabbing her ass and pulling her into a grind against him.

When Josee called the end of the minute, Amanda immediately yanked her shirt down and got up, revealing Damien's smug face.

"Who did you kiss?" Josee asked.

"Ben or Damien," Amanda replied.

"You've got to pick one."

Amanda shifted from foot to foot, biting her lip in thought. "Ben," she said at last. "I don't think Damien would be so aggressive with his girlfriend sitting right there." She took off her blindfold and cursed.

"All part of the plan, sweetheart," Damien said, swatting her ass as he passed by. "Strip for us."

Amanda glared at his back. Finally she sighed. "Well, everyone's already seen my boobs, thanks Carolina." She stripped out of her shirt and dropped it on the back of her chair. "I need another couple shots."

James couldn't take his eyes off his beautiful best friend. He may have seen her boobs years ago in a video on his phone, but she'd grown up a lot since then, filled out into an adult body with curves he would kill to touch. His jealousy towards Damien grew, because he'd put his hands all over her.

Clenching his hands into fists on his knees, James took a deep breath. "Tony, your turn," he said, passing the box that Amanda had left on her seat.

Tony read the card in his hand and took a deep breath. "I hope y'all are ready for this. 'Masturbate vigorously for a minute without coming. If you come, you lose. If you refuse to play, you lose twice.'"

"Alright, Tony! Put on a show for us!" Carolina purred.

Tony exchanged a glance with James, and it was all James could do to keep from laughing. Who needed telepathy when Tony was broadcasting his feelings so plainly? He'd be able to stop himself from coming because he'd think of Carolina.

"Do you want me to move to the chair or stay here?" Tony asked Glenn as he unzipped for the second time that night.

"Here's fine. Do you need a tissue?"

"Nah, I have better control than that. A minute's nothing." Tony pulled out his cock and stroked it once before spitting into his palm. "Has anyone started the clock yet?"

James was satisfied that Tony was still hard from the cock-warming he'd given him and sat back to enjoy himself. Amanda returned to her seat, tripping a little as she sat down. "You okay?" James whispered to her.

"More than a little tipsy," she replied, staring at their friend's fast-moving arm.

He put a finger to his lips to try to get her to keep her voice down and she copied him, giggling quietly. "More than a little tipsy," she repeated in a stage whisper.

"Water?"

"No, thank you. Not yet, or I'll have to pee," Amanda said. "I don't want to miss anything."

Glenn called the end of the minute and Tony released his cock, swiping at the tip to get the pre that had oozed from it. "That doesn't count, right?" Tony asked, his chest heaving.

"Nope," Glenn replied.

Amanda licked her lips, her gaze fixed on his finger with the drop of white. "What are you going to do with that?" she asked breathlessly.

Tony chuckled. "Why, you want it?" He jokingly offered his hand to her, but she grabbed it and wrapped her little pink tongue around his finger, lapping up the droplet. His jaw clenched. "Apparently so."

"Mmm," Amanda hummed, dropping his hand in his lap.

James felt like he scooped his jaw off the floor. "You're just full of surprises tonight," he murmured under his breath.

Tony passed the box to Josee, who pulled a much tamer Truth card, and tucked himself back in his pants.

Trying to stop himself from staring at Amanda's perky pink nipples topping creamy white breasts, James looked around the circle of familiar faces. Most of them were paying attention to Josee telling them about her latest wet dream, something about Mr. Darcy from *Pride and Prejudice*, but Carolina was staring daggers at Amanda.

The box went around the circle again, more people losing articles of clothing.

James pulled a Truth card. "'Have you ever kissed your best friend?'" He tapped the card against his mouth as he looked to his left at his closest friends. "Does the cheek count?"

"Surely you've done more than *that* with her! You're practically eye-fucking her right now!" Carolina sneered.

"If you think this is eye-fucking, you're sadly mistaken." James shook his head.

"No, the cheek doesn't count," Glenn put in.

"Then no, I haven't kissed either of my best friends." James put the card away.

Amanda shook her head. "No, that's not true. We kissed, remember?"

"You did?" Tony asked, his head tilted to one side like a puppy who'd missed out.

"We did?" James frowned, his brain moving sluggishly as he tried to remember.

"At a birthday party in sixth grade," Amanda prompted. "Although *why* twelve-year olds were playing Seven Minutes in Heaven, I have *no* idea! You hadn't moved in yet, Tony," she said, patting his knee. "It was my first kiss. Yours, too. And we decided—"

"—That kissing each other was just too awkward!" James completed her sentence. "I'd forgotten about that!"

"I'm so forgettable!" Amanda said with a laugh. "Good to know." She pulled a card, but before she started reading it, Glenn interrupted.

"You didn't answer truthfully, James. Lose the shirt!"

"I didn't remember," James corrected. "But I'll go along with it for the game." He peeled out of his shirt and dropped it at his feet. "Go ahead, Amanda."

She was grinning. "'Make the people on either side of you come in one minute or less. If you fail, you lose. If you refuse to play, you lose twice.'"

She looked from one to the other. "You both okay with this? I can take the penalty if you prefer."

"You only have two articles of clothing left," Tony croaked.

Amanda shrugged. "I can earn them back. Yes or no?"

"Yes," James agreed, a little too quickly.

A muscle in Tony's jaw jumped. "Okay."

"Let's get you two settled, then." Glenn directed James to sit in Amanda's seat. He handed both men a tissue with a grin. "Enjoy yourselves."

"I don't want condoms," Amanda said as she settled between Tony's knees. She licked her lips as Tony took out his cock once more, and flipped her hair behind her shoulder. "Don't hold back. I'm on a time limit." She winked. "Get yours out too, James." She slicked up her left hand with a swipe of her tongue.

"Ready?" Glenn waited for Amanda to nod. "Go!"

Amanda licked up Tony's cock like it was a popsicle and Tony's hands clenched on his knees. She moaned and started enthusiastically bobbing her head over him, reaching out for James's cock with her left hand.

"Ohhh, fuuuuuck," Tony groaned, dropping his head back.

James sucked in a breath as she started a smooth slide with her hand over his cock, in time with her mouth. The pressure was a little loose at first, but quickly became tighter as her confidence grew. A little twist at the tip made his cock twitch and leak a little pre and he swore under his breath. "Shit, Amanda," he breathed.

"Gonna come!" Tony warned. "Fuck, Amanda, I—" He groaned deep in his chest as his hips stuttered. "Oh my God!"

Amanda pulled back and some cum splashed across her cheek.

"Shit, sorry," Tony gasped, hurriedly putting the tissue over the tip to catch the rest.

She shook her head with a smile, but said nothing else as she walked on her knees in between James's thighs. Opening her mouth, she let a little of Tony's cum dribble into her hand and used it to slick up James's cock, swallowing the rest.

It was possibly the hottest thing he'd ever had done to him in his life.

And then she lowered her head, her tongue circling the crown, applying suction, bobbing her head down and twisting her hand around the base...

James was losing his cool, and fast. That was the point of the game, of course, but he couldn't help wishing that it could last a little longer, that she could take her time. He could tell that she was really good at this and enjoying it.

Amanda hummed, his cock touching the back of her throat. His balls drew up, ready to release.

"Five, four..."

He looked down at Amanda, her eyes half-closed. He wondered if it was in concentration or pleasure. Her lips were stretched obscenely around the girth of his cock, and yet he couldn't feel any teeth.

"Three, two..."

Everything clenched. He was close. So close. "Amanda," he said, his voice coming out in a reverent whisper.

"One. Time's up."

Amanda pulled away and James gasped from the warm night air wrapping around his spit-slick cock, cool after the heat of her mouth. He bit his lip, trying to stave off the orgasm, but he was too far gone. "Fuck!" he exclaimed, his cock pulsing in his hand.

The first spurt was too violent, missing the tissue and hitting Amanda's chest. The sight of his white cum trailing over her reddened skin—*Red from arousal?* James wondered—lit him on fire within, prolonging his orgasm. He sank back in the chair with a shuddering sigh. "Sorry I didn't make it sooner," he said. "It was not from your lack of skill. I think my brains were just sucked out."

Amanda grinned. "Don't worry about it. I can always earn them back." She stood, undoing the hidden zipper at the side of the skirt and let it fall to her feet. "I would like my chair back, unless you want me to sit on you?" she teased, wiping the trail of cum off her breast with one finger and sucking it into her mouth.

"Don't tempt me," James growled. He tucked himself away as he moved back to his original chair.

He caught a glimpse of her toned ass when she turned around to sit and felt his cock stir to life once more. *Jesus, give me a break,* he thought. *You just got off. Chill.*

Tony pulled a card and read it. "'While blindfolded, someone will spit in your mouth. Guess who it is. If you guess wrong, you lose. If you refuse to play, you lose twice.'" He grimaced. "That's disgusting unless it's a partner. I don't trust you lot." He gestured at everyone except James and Amanda. "I'll lose twice." He stripped off his shirt and then stood to shimmy out of his shorts.

"I'd complain that you're a spoilsport, but with a view like that, it's hard to," Carolina said. "I'll sit on your lap and keep you warm if you need it."

"I think Tony's hot enough as is," Amanda retorted.

The game went around the circle again. Kimberly finally lost, and a disagreement broke out about what she should lose, since she was wearing a dress. The jocks wanted her to take the whole thing off, as it was a single article of clothing, but Amanda argued that she was the only person wearing a dress and should only have to pull it to her waist. Finally Glenn raised his hand. "We will vote. Dress fully off? Dress half off?" He nodded. "Half off it is."

Blushing, Kimberly pulled both straps down her arms to the applause of the rest of the party until her breasts were bared.

"Now everyone's at least a little bit naked," Amanda said, beaming. "I think that's cause for another round of shots!"

Glenn, in only his boxer briefs like Tony, passed around the jello shots while the next few cards were played.

James read his card. "'Have you ever walked in on your parents having sex or heard them having sex?'" He nodded. "Not seen, but heard. I came home early from school in senior year. My last class had been canceled, so I went home. I wasn't expecting my parents to be there, but I could hear them all the way in the front hall. I left immediately, so I have no idea what room they were in, and went to Amanda's backyard to start my calculus homework instead."

"I do *not* remember you telling me this story before!" Amanda exclaimed. "Your parents are so in love. I adore them."

"You would think that." James grinned at her enthusiasm.

"'Do a lap dance for a minute while blindfolded. The recipient may not touch you. At the end of the minute, guess who it is. If you guess wrong, you lose. If you refuse to play, you lose twice.'" Amanda hopped to her feet and headed for the blindfolds. "Pick a fun person for me, please!"

James voted along with the others, and Kimberly was chosen to receive the lap dance. She blushed as she moved to the empty chair.

"Ready, Amanda?" Glenn asked after leading her to the chair by a hand. "Hit it!"

James was mesmerized by Amanda's body gyrating and grinding. She was giving Kimberly the best lap dance he'd ever seen. At the end of it, Amanda guessed correctly, and Kimberly returned to her seat with a flush that traveled down her chest.

Tony was next. "'Make-out with any person you wish for a minute.'" He grabbed Amanda's hand before she sat down after pulling her skirt back on. "Can I kiss you?"

Amanda promptly straddled his lap and fused their mouths together to wild cheering from most of the voyeurs.

This kiss was nothing like the make-out session she'd dealt with earlier with Damien. Tony's hands didn't frantically grope her all over, for one. For another, based on the almost pornographic moans coming from both of them, Amanda seemed to be enjoying herself.

James felt his cock stir to life and shifted in his chair. He frowned. This wasn't going to work. He couldn't watch them and remain unaffected. He got to his feet, intending to grab another shot, but his bladder made itself known the instant he stood up. Everyone's attention was on the two performers, so James crossed the patio and let himself into the house.

It was quiet, remnants of the party strewn across the kitchen. He itched to tidy up, but knew that Glenn had hired a cleaning crew for the morning. The bathroom was in the hallway just off the kitchen. He had to focus to get his erection to go away before he could pee properly, and even then, it felt like he was going to spray the entire toilet seat.

After cleaning up and washing his hands, James stared at himself in the mirror. His eyes were a little bloodshot, but other than that, he seemed to be okay. He returned to the party, noting that the box had moved on to Rose. She was telling an avid audience about getting caught masturbating in residence by her roommate.

"Jealous James returns!" Damien mocked once Rose was done and the box had moved on to Oliver.

James raised an eyebrow. "More like I didn't want to piss myself." He glanced over at Tony, who looked concerned, and gave him a small smile. Tony relaxed with a nod.

By the time the box had made it to him, he'd almost forgotten the name-calling.

"'Finger a girl for a minute while blindfolded. At the end of the minute, guess who it is. If you guess wrong, you lose. If you refuse to play, you lose twice.'" James grinned. "Don't mind if I do!" He grabbed a blindfold and settled himself on the separate chair. "I'm ready."

A few seconds later, he heard two sets of feet approach.

"How would you like her?" Glenn asked.

"Facing towards me, straddling my lap, if that's okay with her." James smiled at where he hoped she was standing. "It's easier the other way, but this gives her a bit of privacy."

A warm body sat on his lap, and James curled one hand over her thigh, holding the left out for her. "Take hold of my pinkie and ring fingers. If I do something you don't like, squeeze them twice. If you do like it, once. Do you understand?"

A small but strong hand gripped him and squeezed once.

"Good girl," James murmured. "Can I touch your body while I pleasure you?" One squeeze. "Thank you."

"You ready?" Glenn asked.

"Is moving her underwear to the side part of the one minute, or can I do it in advance?" James asked.

Glenn chuckled. "Part of the one minute."

"I'm ready."

"Go!"

James wasted no time, his right hand sliding up under the girl's skirt, thumb slipping under the material of her underwear. A slight tug, and it shifted to the side. He ran the tips of his fingers along her slit. "Oh, honey, you're absolutely soaked," he murmured just loud enough for her to hear him. "So turned on. It feels amazing." She squeezed his fingers once when his thumb circled her clit, and he heard her breath hitch. He smiled. "You like that? Good to know." He did it again, his index finger finding her opening at the same time and pressing inside. There was no resistance, only smooth heat pressing in on him. He pulled it out again and joined his middle finger to his first, sliding them both inside her. "You feel amazing. Do you want a third inside you?"

One squeeze.

"Greedy thing. I'll give it to you. Moving my hand up to your breast now." She changed the angle of her grip on him as he found the nub of her nipple. James circled it at the same time as his thumb copied the motion on her clit. Now three fingers were inside her easily, her walls gripping them when he pulled them out, wanting to keep them inside her, filling her. He pumped them a couple times, both circles shrinking until he was pinching lightly on her nipple and rubbing directly over her clit.

She sagged forwards, pressing her forehead to his shoulder, rocking her hips in time to the thrusts of his fingers. He wasn't moving them quickly, not wanting her to come in front of her friends unless she wanted to. The girl whimpered and his heart stuttered.

"Amanda," he said. Not a question. He knew her voice almost as well as he knew his own, despite never hearing this exact quality to it before.

"Oh thank God," Amanda replied. "James, come on, I need more."

"More what? Speed, time—"

"Fingers!" Amanda interrupted. "And the other stuff."

"Ten seconds," Glenn announced.

James squished his pinkie finger in with the other three, his thumb working over her clit. Her body sucked his fingers in as if it was born to do it, the slick sounds his hand was making loud between them. "Come on, Amanda. Are you going to come for me?"

"Five, four..."

"So close," Amanda whimpered.

"Three, two..."

"It's okay, sunshine." James knew she wasn't going to make it. Not this time.

"One. Time's up. We already know that James guessed correctly."

Amanda whined when James removed his hand from her body, covered with her juices.

"I'm sorry," James whispered to her.

She took a couple deep breaths. "That was intense."

James licked a finger and groaned. "Sunshine, I'm always intense."

Amanda giggled and took the blindfold off him. "No you're not."

She danced back to the group, James following her with a full hard-on. Amanda picked up the box and pulled out the next card. Her nose wrinkled. "Okay, this card puts me out. I'm not doing it." She tucked it back in the box and passed it to Tony.

"What was it?" Carolina asked, pouting. "You're not even going to read it to us?"

Standing up, Amanda wiggled out of her skirt. "'Be a free use doll for a minute while blindfolded.'" She hooked her thumbs into her thong and pulled it down as well, stepping out of it completely bare. "That's a step too far for me. Glenn, mind if I skinny dip?"

"Go right ahead," Glenn said, blatantly staring at her. "Kinda wouldn't mind swimming myself."

"Me too," James said, standing and fiddling with the enclosure on his shorts. Tony stood as well.

"Why don't we all go swimming then?" Carolina suggested, getting to her feet. "Is your pool heated, Glenn?"

"Of course." Glenn practically fell on his face trying to step out of his underwear.

"Just keep your heads above water," James cautioned, kicking off his boxer briefs. "If you're as tipsy as I am, remembering to hold your breath when you're under water could be difficult."

Amanda tugged on his hand. "You don't have to be a lifeguard tonight," she said. "Come on!"

James followed her into the pool.

He'd follow her anywhere.

Chapter Twelve

Flashback: Prom Night

Heart thumping in her chest, Amanda watched as first James and then Tony got out of the limo. The noise level from the crowd increased dramatically as the second man exited, and Amanda smirked to herself.

"You good, miss?" asked their driver over the partition that separated the driver's seat from the back.

"A little nervous, but I'm totally fine, thank you." Amanda smiled at him. She scooted across the seat to the door and took Tony's outstretched hand, stepping out of the limo into the bright sunshine.

The babble of the other seniors ceased immediately, a lone hysterical giggle breaking the unnatural silence.

Amanda tilted her chin up and looped her free arm through James's. "I feel like I'm on the red carpet at a movie premiere," she whispered.

"Yeah, except the 'paparazzi' aren't taking pictures," Tony murmured.

Amanda made eye contact with a couple people as they made their way to the amateur photo booth. Most of them didn't look surprised, but the smirk on Carolina's face made Amanda's stomach clench. She'd been on the team for her last two years, and Carolina had despised her. Amanda was sure that the only reason she had been chosen to join the squad was because of her gymnastic capabilities.

The students had started talking again, mingling and casting furtive looks at the three of them.

"Who knew that we'd be so popular," James muttered to the other two, who grinned at him.

"I don't know about you two, but I expected to turn heads in this dress," Amanda said flirtatiously.

Tony glanced behind them. "Yeah, the guys are having a hard time keeping their eyes off you. Can I put my hand on your lower back?"

"Such a gentleman," Amanda said. "Of course you can."

"I was raised properly," Tony said with a smirk. "Here we are." They approached the photo booth. He unlinked their arms and put his warm hand low on her back.

Goosebumps erupted at his touch and Amanda shivered.

"Cold?" James asked, concerned.

"No, not at all." Amanda dropped her arm from his to pick up a tiara prop. "My dress is lower than I realized."

"I'm very aware of it," Tony murmured in her ear, leaning forwards to pick up a pair of oversized glasses.

"Let us know if you're uncomfortable," James whispered on her other side, choosing a fluffy pink feather boa. "What?" he asked the other two, who giggled at him. "It matches my suspenders."

"Alright, but I'm taking the top hat instead," Amanda said, switching her props.

They had fun posing and accepted the sets of pictures that were printed out after they returned the props.

"You'll hang onto mine for me, please, James?" Amanda asked, watching as he put them in the inside pocket of his jacket. "Shall we go in? Find out what sort of seating arrangements they've made?"

"I pulled some strings with the grad committee," Tony said conversationally as they entered the ballroom of the convention center. "Glenn helped with the seating arrangements. We're at a table with some of the softball team and their dates."

"That's a relief," Amanda said. "I was worried they'd put me with the cheerleaders."

Both Tony and James shuddered. "No thank you!"

They double checked the seating chart and were relieved to find that they were at Glenn's table. Their classmates were filtering in behind them, so they moved on to their table to look for their names.

"They might have put us here, but whoever set the table didn't realize we were a throuple," Amanda said, picking up her name card and bringing it around the table to place between theirs.

"A throuple?" James laughed. "That's a good word."

"My mom used it. I like it."

They shifted name cards around the table to fill in her previous spot and sat down.

Tony pointed at a projector screen set up at one end of the ballroom, next to the dance floor and DJ setup. "I guess they'll be showing highlights from the year."

"Oh, that'll be cool," Amanda said, wiggling in her seat. "We were all in a bunch of sports that did well this year. Soccer, baseball, volleyball, cheer, cross country..." She listed off on her fingers as she tried to remember everything. "I feel like I forgot one."

"Basketball," James added.

"Right. That was way back in the Fall, so I forgot about it," Amanda teased.

"You *forgot* about us winning the championship?" Tony gasped, mock-offended.

"Well, you know, it's not like you did anything all *that* impressive," Amanda said playfully.

"I'll show *you* impressive," Tony grumbled under his breath, making her laugh.

"I like the giant glass windows looking out on the garden," James pointed out. "That'll look beautiful during the sunset."

"I'm just glad that the sun isn't directly aiming in at us," Tony said with a wince. "That could be painful."

The other two nodded in agreement.

"Hey, Tony!" Glenn greeted his teammate.

Tony stood up for hugs and smacks on the back as Glenn and the others filed in and sat at their table with them. Amanda and James smiled at everyone from their seats.

"I thought James was your date." Amanda overheard Glenn whisper to Tony. "I put Amanda between two of the single guys so that she'd still be at the table with you, but she could still have fun."

Tony chuckled. "No no, you've got it all wrong. James and I are *her* dates."

"Oh!" Glenn widened his eyes dramatically and Amanda bit back a giggle. He turned to her. "You look beautiful. You're lucky to have two dates tonight."

"I am," she agreed, grinning.

The MC called for everyone to take their seats. "I'd like to call Carolina up to present the graduating class with a video of their time in high school!"

As Carolina walked up to the stage, vibrant red dress rustling with every step, Amanda quietly started panicking. "*She* set up the slideshow?" she hissed at Glenn, who was sitting beside Tony.

"Yeah." His brow furrowed in confusion before he understood. "Shit. She wouldn't do that to you, would she?"

"She might," Tony growled. "Want me to stop her?"

At Tony's honest question, Amanda relaxed. "No. No, that's alright." She sighed. "Most of the people here have already seen the video, and it was last year. Maybe it won't be in it."

"As long as you're prepared for it," James whispered. "We're here for you."

They watched the video, exclaiming happily whenever there was a recognizable moment. A ninth grade picture of James and Tony sleeping on top of each other popped up, to the catcalls of their classmates.

"Damn, you two were so cute back then," Amanda said teasingly.

"What happened?" Tony said in mock-horror.

"You grew up," Amanda replied.

Tony grinned, blushing slightly.

They were in multiple other pictures and videos together, mostly playing various sports or cheering on the sidelines.

And then a familiar bedroom appeared and Amanda sucked in a sharp breath. "Would you look at that? She really *is* going to be a bitch."

"You going to be okay?" James asked softly as the video played through.

The noise level in the auditorium increased as the video neared the end.

Amanda made eye contact with Carolina, who was looking very smug up on stage. "Yeah, I'm fine."

Pandemonium broke out as the last frame of the video stayed up on the screen. The teachers sitting near the back of the room got up from their seats and started heading toward the stage. The others at their table stared at her.

Amanda yawned and inspected her fingernails. "What? Haven't you seen a handstand before?" she said casually, heart thundering in her chest.

James

Tearing his eyes away from the image on the screen, James seethed as he saw the smirk on Carolina's face.

"At least they removed the text," Amanda said with a nonchalant shrug.

James saw right through her act; her hands were shaking. He took one in his and Tony grabbed the other. "Why isn't the video continuing?" he hissed. "This was last year in the fall. There's still two full years to go through!"

Finally, the video continued, with the picture of the three of them that they had put up online the morning after the video. Their addition, *#ConsentMatters* written across their bodies, had not been photoshopped out. Whoops and cheers greeted the image and Amanda grinned. More sports followed and he felt Amanda's grip on his hand lessen. The teachers returned to their seats, but they were whispering to each other.

"I think *someone* is holding a grudge," Tony whispered, and James had to agree.

When the video finally ended, everyone applauded and Carolina curtsied.

She stepped up to the microphone and turned it on. "I'm glad you enjoyed looking back on our high school years!"

More applause.

"I would like to welcome someone very special up to the microphone. Someone who had a starring role in our little movie!"

"She wouldn't dare!" hissed Tony, looking murderous.

"She would," Amanda sighed.

"Everyone put your hands together for Amanda Beyer!" Carolina said, pointing towards her table.

"You do *not* have to go," James said urgently.

"No, I'm fine." Amanda pushed back her chair and stood calmly. "She won't expect this."

"Whatever you say, we're with you," James said.

"Thanks." Amanda smiled at him.

James watched her gracefully walk up to the microphone and greet Carolina.

"Good evening, everyone," Amanda said cheerfully, receiving cheers. She turned to Carolina. "I have to say, I wasn't prepared to say anything tonight. Was there a specific reason you called on me?"

Carolina, James noticed, was looking like a deer caught in the headlights. He smirked and relaxed back in his chair. "Where's the popcorn? I think we'll enjoy this," he said to Tony, not bothering to lower his voice, making the people around them laugh.

Amanda winked at him from across the room.

Carolina must also have heard him, or at least the laughter, because she seemed to regain her composure. "Yes, I thought you'd like to say a few words about the video tonight."

A chorus of "oohs" went up from the audience.

Amanda smiled. "Sure."

James grinned. *This is going to be good.*

"Participating in team sports these past few years has been very rewarding. The friendships I've made will last, at least until we all move on to bigger and brighter futures." Amanda paused, grinning for effect. "I will never forget the championship game for volleyball this year, when we didn't think we had a chance, and then Holly smashed through their defense."

The audience shifted restlessly and Amanda chuckled. "Ohhhh, you meant *that* video," she said in a loud aside to Carolina.

The audience tittered.

Amanda put a finger to her chin and James almost laughed at her dramatics. "But why would you want me to talk about a video that you made *without my consent?*"

There was complete silence. Carolina's face turned red and she reached for the microphone, only for Amanda to pull it out of the stand and walk back towards her table.

"You want to know what *I* think, Carolina?" Amanda asked over her shoulder. Not waiting for a reply, she continued on, "I think that you thought you could embarrass me into leaving tonight if you showed that video. Perhaps then you might have a chance with one of...let me see if I can remember your *exact* words...the hottest boys in school." Amanda stopped walking and turned to face Carolina, who had followed her in a vain attempt to regain control. "Ouch. Your boyfriend probably isn't too happy to hear that. Sorry, Jack."

Carolina looked like she wanted to melt into the floor.

"There's something that you never understood about my friendship with the boys," Amanda said casually, continuing on her way. "They would have left with me." She shrugged. "That picture of the three of us asleep? My mother took that. We shared it together. Consent matters." Amanda reached the table and gestured at James's lap.

James pushed back from the table and she sat sideways on him, putting an arm around his neck.

Amanda winked at him. "But you know what?" She turned to pierce Carolina with her gaze. "James pointed something out to me, once I gave him permission to watch the video." Amanda paused for effect. "I looked *fucking hot*."

Tony whistled loudly and several other guys followed suit.

James squeezed her around the waist. "You're doing great, babe," he said, the microphone picking up his words, to the delight of the audience.

Amanda grinned down at him, caressed his cheek, and stood up again. She walked over to Carolina, standing an inch away. "I'm just glad you chose to go after *me*, who had a solid support structure, rather than one of the other girls." Amanda moved as if to give back the microphone, but then said, "Oh and you're lucky I'm not pressing charges against you for taking a video of my naked body. I was under the age of eighteen at the time, so you just showed child pornography to everyone here." Amanda handed the microphone back to a now ashen-faced Carolina and returned to her seat.

"And that's how you do a mic drop!" Tony chortled.

"That's our girl," James whispered, feeling so proud of her he thought he might burst. "Damn, that backfired spectacularly," he said louder, making the students around them chuckle.

Carolina returned the microphone to the MC without saying anything further.

"After that takedown, who's hungry?" the MC said awkwardly. "Let's eat!"

The food was good, but James ate without tasting much of it; he was so shaken by Carolina's actions. The DJ played quiet music during the dinner.

He noticed a teacher approach Carolina and whisper in her ear. She looked murderous, but as there was no way he could overhear, he was left wondering what was said.

Eventually, the MC spoke into the microphone again. "There's a buffet dessert at the back. Let's get this party started!"

The DJ put on a slow song and called for all the couples to come to the dance floor. Most of their table got to their feet to join the others who were dancing.

James and Tony stood up and waited for Amanda to join them.

"But how...?" she asked.

"Just trust us," said Tony.

James led them to a spot on the dance floor that was a little off to one side and swept her into his arms. After a few steps, he spun her out, and Tony caught her free hand to spin her into him. Amanda fell into his arms with a giggle.

"You two definitely know how to make a girl feel special," she said breathlessly.

Then she was spinning into James's arms again and Tony was right behind her, swaying to the beat with her and James.

She spun in the middle of their little circle to face Tony. "Thank you, both of you," she said. "You're amazing."

Every dance, fast or slow, they danced together, ignoring the stares and comments swirling around them, until Glenn came and tapped Tony on the shoulder at nine thirty.

"It's time," he said mysteriously, before he disappeared down a hallway.

"Tony, what's going on?" asked Amanda, confused.

"I'll be right back," said Tony. "Keep an eye on the garden outside if you want a laugh." He winked before he ran off down the same hallway as Glenn.

"Is he talking about doing what I think he's talking about?" Amanda asked James, her eyes dancing with amusement as he pulled her close.

"If you think the baseball team is going to streak across the garden of the convention center, yes, I think that's exactly what's going to happen," whispered James into her ear.

Amanda shivered as his breath caressed her neck, sending a ripple effect through his body. He loosened his grip on her. *We're best friends,* he reminded himself.

Shouting from outside distracted them from dancing, and they looked up along with everyone else. Outside, naked masked men raced across the garden in the gray evening light.

Everyone inside the ballroom gathered at the windows, shrieking and laughing. Amanda and James continued to dance as they watched over their classmate's heads.

"There's Tony," giggled Amanda. "I hope the others don't know him as well as I do."

"He *is* pretty recognizable, even with a mask on," agreed James, laughter rumbling deep in his chest. "But then, we've seen him without his shirt on way more often than the others."

The men were running back the way they had come, hollering loudly and giving everyone in the ballroom quite the show.

"Well, that should be something to remember."

Chapter Thirteen

Amanda

The water caressed Amanda's body intimately as she swam. She shivered at the sensation, her body still riding high from James's last dare and the alcohol swirling in her veins.

She spotted James and Tony talking as they leaned against the wall, separate from the others splashing each other in the shallow end. James was acting like a lifeguard, keeping an eye on everyone, although he glanced over at her more often than the others. Tony, however, didn't look away from her, meeting her gaze head-on.

Amanda stood when she reached them, the water hitting her middle. The cool night air tickled her warm skin, giving her goosebumps and making her nipples tighten.

"How are you?" Tony asked her, training his eyes mostly on her face.

"I think I need to pee," Amanda replied.

"You think?" James repeated, amusement making the corners of his mouth curl up.

"I'm pretty sure." She swished her arms through the water and then spun in a circle. "But it's so nice and warm here."

"You could make it warmer," Tony teased.

"Ew. I might be drunk, but I'm not doing that." Amanda wrinkled her nose.

"Do you want one of us to go with you?" James asked.

Amanda was spinning in a circle again. "Go with me where?"

The men exchanged smirks. "To the bathroom?" Tony prompted.

"Wow, are you a mind reader?" Amanda asked, jaw dropping. "I was just thinking I had to pee!"

"Maybe drink some water while you're there," James suggested. "I think you're a bit drunker than you realize."

Amanda giggled. "Maybe I am. I'm having trouble following the conversation and I want to kiss you." She cocked her head, her smile vanishing. "Why did we never get together?"

James bit his lip. "I'm not sure that's a conversation we should be having right now."

"Why not?" Amanda frowned. "It's because you don't want me, isn't it?"

"Sunshine—" James started, but Tony cut him off.

"Didn't you have to pee?"

"Right." Amanda gave each of them a hug and made her way to the stairs at the end of the pool. Several people tried to pull her into their game, but she begged off, managing to keep her thoughts on her task despite the difficulty.

The wet slaps of her feet on the concrete left grotesque footprints behind her. She took a towel from beside the sliding glass doors and dried off, not wanting to leave wet spots in the house that someone might slip on. She draped the towel over the back of the chair she'd sat in for the game and then entered the silent house.

It was almost creepy, how quiet a house could be when you could hear shouts of joy from the backyard.

Amanda found her way to the bathroom. It was a relief to finally empty her bladder. She must have been holding it longer than she thought. She washed her hands and headed back to the kitchen where she grabbed a fresh glass and filled it with water.

She leaned against the counter as she drank it slowly, looking out the kitchen window at the back garden. She couldn't see the pool from this angle.

"Hey," said a voice from behind her.

She whirled, surprised, and saw Ben entering the kitchen from the dining room. "I thought you were outside," she said.

"Nah. I needed a break. You know, I think you look even better than you did in high school." He didn't meet her eyes as he said that, keeping them fixed on her body.

"Thanks," Amanda replied. She took another sip of her water. "How have you been, Ben?"

He shook his head, a slight smile on his face as he took a few steps closer. "Come now, that's not how you repay a compliment, is it, Amanda? I say you look smoking hot, you're supposed to return the favor."

"Maybe she needs to be reminded of her place."

Amanda's head whipped to the left to take in the speaker of the new voice. "Damien," she greeted him. "Where's Morgan?"

Damien shrugged. "Still in the pool."

Suddenly Ben was much too close. "See, Damien and I, we were wondering how it could possibly be that you never hooked up with Tony or James."

"But after seeing how James reacted to you and Tony making out—"

"And Tony's reaction to James fingering you open—"

"We came to the conclusion that they're jealous of each other." Damien was now standing on the other side of her, boxing her in.

"But we think that you need two guys to make you feel good." Ben's fingers flicked her nipple and she arched into the sudden pleasure.

"That card you pulled at the end of the game is super hot. But one minute just isn't enough time to be a free use doll, don't you think?" Damien asked, his breath hot on her neck. His hand was flat on her belly, traveling down, down, down...

Amanda's head was spinning from the alcohol and unexpected proximity of the two guys. "No—" she protested.

"We didn't think so either," Ben said encouragingly. His hand was back on her breast, cupping and teasing at the sensitive nipple.

Damien's hand had reached its destination. "Fuck, you're dripping wet. You want to be fucked real bad, don't you, doll?"

"No!" Amanda shouted, her muscles finally reacting. She tossed the water in her glass into Ben's face, momentarily blinding him, and threw the glass itself at Damien. She didn't wait to see what happened to either of them, running past Ben to get out of the kitchen.

"Bitch!" Damien screamed.

"It wouldn't take long. We're naked already," Ben growled, knocking things to the ground as he chased after her.

Amanda pulled out a chair from the breakfast table and left it behind her, hoping to slow Ben down long enough for her to get the glass door open.

It worked, surprisingly.

She ran out into the warm night air directly into James and Tony's arms. "What's going on? Are you okay?" Tony asked.

"I want to go home," Amanda sobbed, pressing her face into his chest.

A low rumble from James. "What happened?"

"They tried to..." She couldn't continue, a full-body shiver taking over her.

Tony hugged her tighter. "You're safe now," he murmured. "Is this okay? Am I making you uncomfortable?"

"I have never felt so safe," Amanda reassured him.

"Let's get dressed," James suggested. "I think it's time we went home. We've all got orientation tomorrow."

Tony raised his eyebrows. "Sunday?"

"Dude, it's been Sunday for hours. Orientation is Monday," James teased.

Amanda pouted. "I don't wanna get dressed."

Tony chuckled. "You don't want to be arrested for public indecency, do you?"

"Do I look indecent to you?"

"You're gorgeous. Not the point," James said firmly, pulling on his shorts.

"I don't want to put my thong on. It's not comfortable." Amanda crossed her arms.

"Then don't. Put on your skirt," Tony suggested.

"Fine."

They got dressed quickly, the men retrieved their phones, and they left after saying quick goodbyes.

Amanda skipped a little on the walk home, each hand held securely by one of her best friends. "This is a beautiful night," she said happily.

"Did you want to talk about what happened?" James asked softly.

"I threw water in Ben's eyes and the glass at Damien." Amanda shrugged. "I didn't like them touching me, and I think they thought we were still playing the game. At least I want to believe that, because the alternative is a lot to process."

"That's our girl," Tony said, giving her hand a squeeze.

"We won't let them be alone with you again," James growled. "And no more of that game. I didn't like how Damien groped you during that first dare."

"He pulled my shirt up," Amanda said. "He probably would have stuffed his fingers inside me if he'd had the room."

"I'm glad he didn't," Tony replied, voice tight.

"You didn't grope me nearly as much," Amanda said thoughtfully. "Why? I wouldn't have minded."

"I didn't ask first," Tony said after a long pause.

"I'm glad that you got the fingering dare and not one of the other guys," Amanda confided in James. "And that I was chosen. You're really good at it."

"Thanks," James said with a chuckle.

"I didn't get to come, though." She pouted. "Damien said I was wet and wanted to be fucked. I didn't want *him* to do it, but if one of you asked, I wouldn't say no."

Her house came into view as they rounded the corner.

"We're home!" Amanda said happily, not noticing the silence from the men. "I don't want to sleep inside. Can we sleep on the porch?"

"Sure," Tony replied easily.

They quietly climbed the stairs, trying not to wake her parents, and tiptoed into her room, where the guys had put their overnight bags on the spare bed.

Amanda immediately started stripping, dropping her clothing into the laundry basket. "Where's my underwear?" she asked. "Did I leave it behind?"

"Here," Tony said, pulling it out of his pocket. "You gave it to me."

"Right. I forgot." She tossed it in after her clothes and opened her pyjama drawer, pulling out a pair of boxers and an oversized t-shirt.

"Is that mine?" James asked, pointing to the shirt.

She turned so he could see his name across her back. "It's your camp shirt from high school." She pulled on the boxers. "And these used to be Tony's before he grew out of them." She left them still changing and tiptoed downstairs and out the back door. She dug through the outdoor storage bench and pulled out a light comforter, climbing onto the giant hammock bed with it and curling up in the middle.

The guys joined her not much later.

"Where do you want us?" James asked.

"One on each side of course," Amanda said with a yawn. "I want cuddles."

Their weight and warmth on either side of her soon pulled her into sleep.

Amanda's eyes shot open two minutes before her alarm went off on Monday morning. She turned it off and hopped out of bed, stretching the back of her thighs by bending and putting her hands flat on the floor. She moved through her routine slowly, waking up each muscle group one by one. After five minutes, she was wide awake and ready to start the day.

She changed into her uniform, a black one-piece bathing suit under black shorts and a red muscle shirt with the white word *Lifeguard* emblazoned across the chest. She tucked her socks in the waistband of her shorts, grabbed two hair elastics from her dresser, and dashed down to the kitchen.

"Morning sweetheart," her dad greeted her while frying bacon on the stove. "Do you have time for breakfast?"

She inhaled happily. "For one of your breakfast sandwiches, I'll make time." She hopped onto the island in the middle of the kitchen and chose an orange from the fruit bowl.

"Are you getting a ride over with James, or are you walking?" Mr. Beyer flipped the bacon with a spatula.

Her stomach did a little flip along with the bacon at the mention of her friend's name. "The three of us are going to drive over this week for orientation, since there'll be plenty of parking. Once the camps start next week, not only will there be a lineup of parents dropping their kids off, but the complex will be open to the public again. We'll be walking then."

"Sensible," her dad said. "I never expect anything less from you three."

Her stomach twisted like the orange peel now dangling from the half-unpeeled fruit in her hands. Would he say the same if he had seen the three of them at Glenn's party on Saturday night?

The mental image of her two best friends naked and hard dissipated as the sick feeling in her stomach rose up. They had spent the day together yesterday, relaxing and recovering from their massive hangovers, completely ignoring the elephant in the room.

Granted, they'd all been *massively* drunk.

But she loved them with all her heart. She wanted them desperately. And they'd treated her the same as always.

They must not feel the same way as me, she thought, pulling a segment out of the orange and popping it in her mouth. *That's okay. They don't have to.* She took a deep breath in through her nose. *At least they're being gentlemen about it, not rubbing my actions in my face. I can't imagine that they would do that.*

"Can you get the plates?"

"Sure thing." She slid off the counter and crossed the kitchen to the appropriate cupboard. *James was just being his sweet self, saying those things to me while he was playing with me. My drunken brain just added meaning where there wasn't any. And that kiss that Tony and I shared, while amazing, was just a kiss.* She shivered. Her memory of that kiss was muddled, just like the rest of that night, but she'd thought she'd seen more than just lust in Tony's eyes when she'd pulled away. *I just imagined it. He would have brought it up yesterday if it was real.*

"Everything okay?" her dad asked.

"Hmm?"

"You've been staring into that cupboard for a while. Are we out of plates?"

Amanda blinked and laughed. "Sorry. Lost in thought." She grabbed three plates and brought them over to the stovetop.

"I'll say! I thought I'd have to send out a search party for you."

"Dad!"

"Do you need lunch today?"

"No. Thank you, though. We get free food at the cantina in the complex all summer."

Her dad whistled. "Nice."

The front door opened and closed, Tony's voice echoing through the hall. "Amanda! Ready to go?"

"Oh, shoot!" Amanda glanced at the clock on the stove. "I forgot they have us starting half an hour earlier today!"

Her dad handed her the breakfast sandwich. "Bite," he advised, scooping up the other half of her orange and putting it in her free hand. He tucked her water bottle in the crook of her arm. "Go."

"*Fanks,*" Amanda mumbled around her bite of sandwich. She hurried down the hall to the front door, where Tony was shifting from foot to foot.

He chuckled when he caught sight of her. "A little behind?" he said. "Not often I'm ready before you."

She shook her head at him. "Don't get used to it," she said, once she swallowed her bite. "Help?"

Tony took her water bottle and dropped it in her bag. "What else?"

"Shoes?"

"Sure, Cinderella." He knelt and held her running shoes open for her to slip her feet in, tying the laces with a double knot just the way she liked.

"Payment?" She offered him a bite of the breakfast sandwich.

He took a small-ish bite, a smear of ketchup lingering on the corner of his mouth.

Before she thought about her actions, Amanda reached out and wiped it off with her knuckle. The look in his eyes nearly took her out at the knees.

She swallowed hard, wondering if she was reading too much into the normal interaction. Then she looked at her hand. "Shit, I don't have napkins."

Tony chuckled, the tension between them broken, and bent to pick up her bag. "Wipe it on the sandwich. Come on, James is waiting for us."

He gestured for her to leave with a bow, closing the door behind him. His long legs ate up the distance between her house and James's.

Amanda trailed after him, eyes still focused on the ketchup on her finger. She glanced around. Nobody was watching her. She lifted her knuckle to her mouth and licked the ketchup off, feeling like a teenager with a crush. She sighed and took another bite of her breakfast sandwich, picking up her pace as she crossed the street.

"Your chariot awaits," Tony said, holding the back door open for her.

"How come I'm in the back?" she asked.

"Because I'm holding the door for you." He cocked an eyebrow up, waiting for her to argue.

"I call shotgun on the way home," she said, ducking into the car.

"Sure thing, darlin'," he drawled. "Do you need help doing up your seatbelt?"

She dropped the half-orange onto her lap. "I'm fine, thank you."

"Now that we're done with the chivalry, shall we get this show on the road?" James asked from the driver's seat.

The trip to the sports complex barely took ten minutes, but she knew the walk next week would take over half an hour. She didn't mind; it meant she got uninterrupted time with her best friends.

"Tony! Over here!"

"Do you have a fan group?" Amanda said, leaning on the hood of the car as she carefully separated a segment of orange from the rest.

Tony stuck his tongue out at her. "If I do, you and James would be the only ones I'd want on it."

"Aww, muffin." Amanda grinned at him and popped the orange in her mouth. "You know I'm your biggest fan."

He flipped open his sports sunglasses, sliding them on as he squinted towards the building to spot who was calling him over. "It's Glenn, Oliver, and the guys. I'll see them later during orientation."

Amanda's stomach flipped. "The guys, meaning Damien and Ben?"

Tony made a face. "Yeah."

"Don't worry, you don't have to go anywhere near them," James said, flanking her.

"Unfortunately not true," she said with a sigh. She offered the last piece of the orange to James, who took it without using his hands. Her nerves sang when his lips brushed her fingertips. To distract herself, Amanda pushed off the car and took her bag from Tony. "I can handle them just fine." *Now that I'm not drunk as a skunk,* she thought to herself as they headed towards the front doors of the building.

"You can," Tony agreed, exchanging glances with James that she pretended to ignore. "But we've got your back if you need it."

Her heart fluttered. "Thanks. I know I can always count on you two."

"Tony!"

"What am I, invisible?" James murmured for only her to hear.

Amanda nudged him in the ribs. "You don't want *her* calling out for you," she said, recognizing Carolina's high-pitched whine.

"I forgot that she'd be here too," Tony groaned. "Can I ignore her?"

"You can try." No sooner had Amanda spoken before Carolina appeared on Tony's free side.

"Isn't it cute when couples match?" Carolina asked Tony, gesturing at James and Amanda's matching lifeguard uniforms. "It's too bad we're in different departments. Do you think I'd make a good coach, and then I can wear royal blue with you?" She plucked at the front of her white blouse.

"We're not a couple," James said quickly.

Amanda's heart sank into her stomach. *He jumped on that fast. Is he so against people thinking we're together?*

"All the coaches have been hired," Tony said in a monotone.

"Well, I'm sure there could be room for one more!" she simpered, catching hold of his hand.

He shook her off. "I'm not in charge of hiring. Besides, were you ever involved in running a sport?"

"I was captain of the cheer squad for two years," Carolina retorted, flipping her hair behind her shoulder.

"When they put in a cheer camp, you can apply for the position. Good luck."

"That's a great idea!" Caroline clapped her hands. "I'll mention it to my father. I'm sure he'd be willing to add it to the camps we offer." She pulled her cellphone out of her purse, slowing her pace as she did so.

In unison, they picked up their pace.

"I forgot her dad was the owner," Tony hissed.

Amanda patted his arm. "It's okay. You can't be perfect all the time."

Tony snorted, sliding his glasses on the top of his head as they entered the building. "She really shouldn't be in charge of impressionable youth."

"No kidding," James muttered.

"Every camp has at least two counselors. They'll have to hire someone else too," Amanda tried to be reassuring. "I'm not sure who they could get who wouldn't already have a job, but if they can't get someone, the camp won't happen. It would be a liability."

"That helps," Tony admitted. "I really don't want to see her any more than I'll have to with her working at the front desk."

They made their way through the big complex to the staff room, where they signed in with the appropriate person and chose their shared locker.

There was a bit of confusion when they all put down the same locker number, as it was standard to only share between two people.

"If you won't allow us to put three names down, I just won't have a locker, and I'll put my things in with the guys," Amanda pleaded.

"You could share with one of the other lifeguards," the administrator tried, pulling out the list of names. "There are several who haven't arrived yet."

Amanda shook her head. "No, thank you. I will be sharing a locker with my friends."

"She can share with me," Carolina pronounced grandly as she swept into the room.

James subtly rolled his eyes.

"Well, that's one way of making sure she has a locker all to herself," Tony muttered.

"You can put whatever locker number you want next to my name," Amanda told the administrator. "I won't be using it."

They walked from the common space into the locker room, which had benches in between the rows of multicolored metal lockers. There were ten individual changing and shower rooms with lockable doors around the perimeter for the staff to share. The toilets were in a separate room on the other side of the common space, with full doors instead of flimsy public restroom stalls.

"I love working here," Amanda said dreamily, hooking her bag on one of the hooks inside the locker.

"It's certainly a sweet set-up," James agreed. "Are you sure you want to share with us?"

"A little late to ask me that now, don't you think?" Amanda replied, bumping her hip into his. "Even with Tony's stinky shoes, I would rather share with you guys than anyone else."

"Hey, not fair!" Tony complained. "I'm running around outside for hours. It's not my fault."

"You can share with me, Tony," Carolina offered as she entered the room. "I would never complain about your scent getting all over me."

Tony visibly shuddered. "No thanks."

"That you think I'm complaining just shows how little you know me," Amanda said tartly. She turned her back on the girl, dismissing her. "Are we outside or inside first?"

"We're with the entire team outside for obstacle courses first thing," James said, grabbing her sunscreen.

"Right, of course." She held her hands out for him to squeeze the lotion onto her palm.

"I'm so lucky that my father agreed to the cheer camp," Carolina said, inserting herself into their conversation. "And they had a spare counselor shirt in my size!" She started unbuttoning her blouse. "I get to hang out with you guys all week!"

"Carolina, there are change rooms for you to change in privacy," Amanda said.

"Oh, I don't mind," she replied with a wink at Tony.

Tony's jaw clenched. "*I* mind," he said quietly. "There are other people here, and they didn't sign up to be subjected to someone changing in front of them."

Carolina huffed, but she scooped up her blue T-shirt and stomped over to one of the changing rooms.

"This is going to be a long summer," Tony sighed.

Chapter Fourteen

Flashback: First Day of School

Tony's heart thumped loudly somewhere in the vicinity of his throat the closer they got to school. Amanda and James were talking about their teacher, repeating what previous students had said about her.

"I've heard she's a hard-ass…"

"But she really cares about what her students learn…"

"Lots of homework every night…"

"Gives us responsibility…"

Tony swallowed nervously and reconsidered the position of his heart. It was in his stomach, and his breakfast didn't like it there.

He was jolted from his thoughts at the feeling of Amanda threading her arm through his. He dragged his eyes away from the pavement near his feet and focused on his friends. They were looking at him expectantly.

"Sorry, I spaced out," he apologized. "What?"

"We'll make it through this year together!" repeated Amanda. "We'll make seventh grade the most fun ever!"

"Rah, rah, rah?" chanted Tony sarcastically.

But James and Amanda latched onto the chant enthusiastically, dragging him along with them until he couldn't help but join in. Amanda's sunny smile was infectious and Tony felt his fears settle. It was nice to have friends.

"Anthony, would you answer the question on the board?" Mrs. Callaghan asked after lunch.

Tony felt himself slipping back into his old habits from before his adoption, his stony face falling into place. "No," he snapped. The shocked and surprised expressions on the faces of his friends only made him feel worse, and he deepened his scowl.

"If you take that attitude with me, young man, you'll find yourself staying for detention every afternoon this week!" The teacher reacted instinctively to the tone and attitude, which only succeeded in making things worse.

"Fine by me," snarled Tony.

"Well, that escalated quickly," whispered James to Amanda, who was sitting between the two boys.

Tony grumbled to himself, thinking, *Fine friends* they *are, not even sticking up for me. Stupid teacher, singling me out.*

Exchanging furtive glances, Amanda and James bent to their work and ignored the whispers of their classmates.

Tony heard the whispers and they made him grumpier than ever.

"Why would *they* choose to sit with *him*?"

"Who talks back to the teacher on the first day of school?"

"He thinks he's so tough..."

Tony shrank into himself, every second making him feel worse. The disdain coming from the room felt like it would smother him.

The final bell rang and the students thundered out of the classroom. Amanda and James made no move to leave their seats.

"You two may go," said Mrs. Callaghan sternly. "Anthony and I have some things to discuss."

"It's Tony," said Amanda, her voice shaking a little. "And we're not going to leave him here alone."

"Go away," said Tony sullenly.

Amanda drew in a sharp breath. Tony winced internally, but didn't look up from the scarred desktop. He knew that he had made her cry.

James growled. "You don't get to talk—"

"No!" Amanda shouted. Her chair squeaked across the floor as she pushed it back from her desk. "No!"

Startled, Tony looked up at Amanda. She was standing over him, fists clenched in fury, face red as she tried to control her tears.

"You do not get to treat our friendship like it's *nothing*! You don't get to treat our school or our teacher like they mean nothing! I don't know what happened to make you all growly and angry all of a sudden and I *don't care*!" Her voice was rising in volume and she squeaked on the last words. "We are your *friends* and I'm going to *sit* on you until you tell us what is *wrong* with you!"

Cooperatively, James yanked Tony's chair out from under his desk. Amanda plopped sideways onto his lap and, twisting her body, wrapped her arms around his shoulders. James hugged both of them from behind the chair. Tony sat rigidly in his seat.

"This is rather uncomfortable, so you'd better spill soon," said James, after a minute of silence. Amanda tightened her grip.

"Whatever happened, was in the past," said Mrs. Callaghan gently. "Your friends care an awful lot about you, Tony, and I think you owe them, at least, an explanation."

Tony's mind was racing. Was it what happened? What the teacher had said? What the kids had been saying at lunch? He didn't know what to say, but he knew where to begin. He forced himself to relax.

When his arms came up to encircle Amanda, she burst into tears. "Hey, you're getting my shirt wet," he said dryly.

"You deserve it," she sniffled.

Tony took a deep breath and said, "I was in foster care in Austin. For a long time. No one wanted a kid who got into trouble. But I got into trouble because no one wanted me. It's easier to act tough all the time when there's nobody to care about you. Then the Carlsons came along and they took a chance on me. But I was still going to the same school and everyone expected me to be the same. It's...hard...to leave a pigeon-hole. I kept getting into trouble. Instead of returning me to foster care, they home-schooled me last year. And then Mr. Carlson got a job at the university here, where he'd grown up, so we moved across the country. They thought...hoped...that a new school would help."

Amanda had stopped crying, but she still sniffled occasionally.

James loosened his hold on him and stood up. He kept one hand on Tony's shoulder.

Tony kept going. Once he'd opened his mouth, it was like he couldn't stop. "I met you guys." He readjusted Amanda on his lap. His left leg was falling asleep. "And I couldn't believe my luck. You accepted me, without knowing anything about me. You let me work and play with you every day this summer. I heard what the other kids were saying about you two at lunch. You've never invited *anyone* to do that before. Who was I to interrupt your perfect lives? Everything just...it all just felt like too much. Too good to be true. So I guess I started pushing you away and it started with reacting like my old self with you, Mrs. Callaghan."

He looked over Amanda's head at the teacher. She was looking thoughtful.

"I'm sorry I acted out. I'll try to be better." He put one hand on James's and rested his cheek against Amanda's hair. "For them."

"I think we can come up with a signal for when you're feeling overwhelmed," said Mrs. Callaghan kindly. "Put your hand on your head and I'll give you the bathroom pass to go and take a breath."

Tony smirked.

"Just don't abuse the privilege, or I will revoke it," she added with a firm smile.

"I won't. Thank you," said Tony.

"Don't thank me; thank your friends."

"You guys are more than I deserve," said Tony fervently, as he squeezed Amanda around her shoulders and held James's hand tightly.

"Yes, we are," announced Amanda with a sniff.

"Just talk to us next time," said James with a chuckle. "We aren't going anywhere." He gave the back of Tony's head a gentle smack. "I already told you that we weren't friends with the other kids, that you fit where no one else did. Now you get it?"

"Yeah, now I get it," Tony said sheepishly.

Part Two:

Middle of
Summer

Chapter Fifteen

Tony

Tony was awake.

He didn't mean to be. It was sometime before sunrise, based on the thin sliver of light on the horizon.

Blearily, he glanced across the large mattress swing to where James would usually sleep, but of course he wasn't there. He was returning from Boston later today with his parents, who brought him with them to sign the paperwork on the house they'd bought.

Tony shivered with happiness. He couldn't believe his luck. The Lavallee's had decided to buy the house as an investment property, and they were letting the three of them live in it in the fall. James's name would be on the paperwork, in case anything came up suddenly, but his parents were the real owners.

Unfortunately, the lawyer couldn't see them until the end of day on Friday, so they'd driven up after lunch, and had chosen to stay overnight in the city.

Meaning the sleepover that the three of them had planned ended up being just he and Amanda.

She was currently plastered against his side, head resting on his chest, legs interwoven with his. He didn't think she could get any closer without crawling inside his skin.

He finger-combed her hair away from her face, tucking it gently behind her ear. *I am so in love with this woman.*

It had been difficult to keep that to himself over the first half of the summer. Ever since Glenn's party, when he'd had a taste of what it could mean to be hers, he'd been dying to tell her that he wanted her.

But he and James had talked after she'd fallen asleep that night, and had agreed to let her lead. And she had never brought it up. There had been flashes of heat and a hefty amount of flirtation, but Amanda had never come right out and talked about what had transpired between them that night.

He was almost ready to throw caution to the wind.

Almost.

Amanda moaned and rolled her body against his, grinding her pelvis against his hip, and suddenly he knew exactly what had woken him up.

Now fully awake, Tony tried to decide whether he should wake *her* or just hope that she would stop.

He *really* didn't want her to stop.

Except she didn't know what she was doing.

Who she was rubbing against.

Amanda shifted in her sleep, moving more on top of him, and ground harder against his hip bone. The shift had moved her face into the crook of his neck, her hot breath fanning over his ear.

He could hear every noise she made. Every breathy moan, every whimper.

It was going to make him want to do something he shouldn't.

At this point, he was rock hard, and her gyrations had shifted the waistband of his boxers down. Something had moved her own boxers too, because he could swear he was feeling her juices rubbing directly onto his skin.

Clenching his hands into fists, he looked up at the overhanging roof as if it could offer him salvation, or at least an answer of how to get out of this alive.

No answer came, so he cupped her shoulder in one hand and whispered, "Amanda?"

"Oh God, Tony," she groaned, pressing her lips against the sensitive skin of his neck.

Hearing his name on her lips, said *like that*, almost made him come on the spot. "Amanda, wake up," he said a little louder, mentally kicking himself for not letting her rut to completion on him.

"But you feel so good," Amanda mumbled. "Need you."

His jaw clenched. "You can tell me all about it in the morning. I need to pee."

"Promise?" she said, not sounding any more awake.

"You can tell me anything," Tony said.

"Good." She rolled onto her other side with a yawn. "Love you."

"Love you too." Tony leaned over to kiss her shoulder and then climbed out of the mattress, hoping he didn't jostle it enough to wake her entirely.

Once on his feet, he padded into the silent Beyer house, maneuvering his way easily even in the dark. He left the bathroom door open since nobody was home, and pulled his boxers down, raising an eyebrow at his penis. "Seriously, dude?" he muttered. "Asleep means no consent. Give it a rest."

It took him a while to soften enough to be able to pee, but eventually he managed it. On the way back outside, he paused to grab a drink of water in the kitchen, watching Amanda through the window, a sliver of the rising sun falling across her legs through the vine-covered trellis.

She's so beautiful, he thought, his heart clenching. *I'm so lucky to have her in my life. I don't want to screw up our friendship.*

He briefly considered finding somewhere else to sleep, but knew Amanda would be upset if she woke alone. Screwing up his courage, he re-entered the backyard and retook his position on the mattress.

She instantly gravitated towards him, backing up until he was spooning her, and hummed happily in her sleep.

Tony didn't think he'd fall asleep with her warm body pressed against his, but exhaustion won out, and his eyes closed. Soon he was fast asleep.

When he woke up again, he was alone on the bed, the sun fully risen and shining directly in his face.

He groaned and draped his arm across his firmly closed eyes.

"Oh good, you're awake!" Amanda said cheerfully.

The bed dipped and swayed as she climbed on.

"Open your mouth," she said playfully, straddling his waist.

"You know, it's a good thing I trust you," Tony complained, voice raspy with sleep, but obediently opened his mouth for the berry she held against his lips.

"Of course you trust me," Amanda said, patting his cheek while he chewed. Then she grabbed his hand and pulled him halfway to sitting. "Come on, I made fruit granola yogurt cups. Then we can go for a swim!"

"Yeah?" The thought of food perked him up a bit and he cracked his eyes open. "Did you happen to make coffee as well?"

"Of course I did!" Amanda said, kissing his forehead. "I've already had a cup."

"I can tell," he said dryly.

Tony followed her to the patio table, stretching his arms over his head to work out the kinks in his lower back. "I think I'm getting old."

Amanda gasped from her seat. "Don't you dare! You're only a month older than I am. Does that mean I have to start complaining about my hips or something next month?"

"You will never grow old," Tony said, dropping a kiss on the top of her head before pulling out his usual chair, the metal scraping over the patio stones. "Any interesting dreams last night?" he asked out of habit, and then froze, his spoon halfway to his mouth when he remembered what, exactly, she had been dreaming about.

"I dreamt about swimming," Amanda said, stirring her cup.

"Swimming or drowning?" Tony asked. "Very different connotations."

"Quite so," Amanda replied, nodding gravely. "Swimming."

"That's a relief."

"Agreed. What about you?" she asked.

Tony blushed. "I'm not really sure what my dreams were about."

"Then why are you all red?" Amanda teased.

Because I can't stop thinking about you moaning in my ear and grinding on my thigh, he thought. "Great coffee," he said, changing the subject, not smoothly in the slightest.

"So evasive. Don't worry, I'll get it out of you eventually," Amanda said confidently before sticking her spoon in her mouth and humming contentedly.

"Wanna bet?" Tony said with a smirk.

"So there *is* something!" Amanda declared triumphantly.

"I deftly changed the subject once. Want to watch me do it again?"

Amanda burst into laughter, nearly falling off her chair with the force of it. "*Deftly!*" she gasped out, and then she was off again, laughing so hard that she went silent.

"You're going to get hiccups," Tony said, amused.

Amanda nodded, but kept up her silent laughter, tears streaming from her eyes.

"It really wasn't that funny."

Now she shook her head and gasped grotesquely for air.

Tony chuckled. "Now you've done it."

"I *hic* know! *hic*" Amanda managed to say, rubbing her sternum after each hiccup. "The way *hic* you *said* it! *hic*"

Tony smiled to himself as he scraped the inside of the cup, getting the last of the yogurt. "I'm going to get into my swimsuit," he said, standing up and gathering empty dishes to bring into the kitchen. "After I put these in the dishwasher, of course."

"Oh, you don't *hic* have to do that!" Amanda protested.

"This is practically my house too. Don't treat me like a guest," Tony said firmly.

Amanda followed him into the kitchen, her dishes in her hands, and leaned against the counter while she finished her yogurt.

Tony kept stealing glances at her long, tanned legs while he rinsed the dishes and put them in the dishwasher. He nodded at the bowls that had held the chopped fruit. "There are still some strawberries."

Amanda peered into the bowl. "It seems like a waste to put these in a Tupperware." She fished one out and held it to Tony's lips. "Open up!"

He maintained eye contact as he took the slice into his mouth, letting his tongue drag along the pads of her fingers a little longer than he probably should have. But if he hadn't, he might have missed the flash of arousal on her face, the widening of pupils in her blue eyes, or the way her breath quickened. *My crush may not be as one-sided as I thought!* Tony's heart leapt.

He picked up a strawberry slice of his own. His heart pounded as he wavered in his decision. *Give it to her, gauge her reaction? Or steal it for myself and cut the tension?* There was still one slice left in the bowl, so he decided to be playful. He held it out for her, but just as she leaned forwards, he popped it into his own mouth and smirked at her.

"Hey! No fair!" Amanda slapped him lightly on the bicep. "I gave you one!" She scooped the last one out and ate it, glaring at him as she chewed.

Tony laughed. "I can cut more if you want them." He put their dishes in the dishwasher. "Ready?"

"More after swimming." Amanda said decidedly. She patted his bare chest. "Sunscreen for both of us first."

"Since you're already in your swimsuit, you get the sunscreen and I'll meet you out back," Tony suggested.

He'd left his spare clothes, including his bathing suit, in the little office just off the kitchen, and changed quickly. "Hey, when are your parents getting home?" he asked, joining her on the back porch.

"Not until Monday. Wanna stay over tonight and tomorrow too?" Amanda asked, her big blue eyes looking up at him pleadingly. "I'm so lonely without anyone here!"

"I'll have to run home for a change of clothes," Tony said, tapping his chin in thought.

"It's *so far away*," Amanda teased, handing him the lotion.

"It is. I might need a ride." He accepted the bottle of sunscreen and squirted a generous amount into his palm before rubbing his hands together.

Amanda let out an unladylike snort. "I'll get James to give you a piggyback when he gets here." She lifted her hair, pulling it up into a messy bun with practiced twists of the elastic she had around her wrist. "Don't forget—"

"The tops of your shoulders. I know. I remember." Tony winced. At the beginning of summer in high school, he'd thought she'd gotten them, and she thought he had. She'd had blisters for two days. He started there, gliding his hands over freckled shoulders and up her neck. Then he worked his way down her back, over her shoulder blades and ribs to the edge of the bikini bottoms.

"You know," Amanda said, almost breathlessly, "my bathing suit shifts while I'm wearing it. You need to get the skin just underneath the material as well."

Tony swallowed hard. She'd never asked for this before, always rubbing it in herself. Hesitantly, he slid his fingertips under the edge of the material, feeling the swell of her ass, the dip in the center, and the swell on the other side. "Your hiccups are gone," he said, more to distract himself than to have a conversation.

"Yeah," she replied. "I drank water upside down in the kitchen before I came out."

"That always works for me."

"Can you do my legs, too?" she asked, her voice barely above a whisper.

Tony wordlessly reached for the sunscreen bottle and got onto his knees behind her. He could smell the oils from the lotion on her skin, the leftover pool scent that never fully left spandex no matter how many times it was washed, and something else...something sweet and earthy that made his mouth water.

He started at her left ankle, working his way up smooth, shapely calves, around her knee, and up her strong thigh. She spread her legs a little when he got higher, and the unknown scent hit him again. His hands twitched as he realized he was smelling her arousal. *Ohhhhh fuck!* He bit his lip hard and forced his hands to remain steady. *Don't be a dick. You're just putting sunscreen on your best friend. She's not propositioning you. Get yourself under control!* He avoided the area near the material of her ass, because part of that area *was* her ass and he wasn't sure how far she was going to take this.

Switching legs, he grabbed the sunscreen again, squirting more into his palms. The second leg was the same as the first, although the mouth-watering scent was more prominent now that he was aware of it.

"You need to get under the material there, too," Amanda murmured.

"You're going to have to show me where," Tony said, proud of his voice for not cracking. He may have gone through puberty many years ago, but *Amanda* was asking him to touch her *ass*!

"Not at the front, but everywhere else," she said calmly, gesturing.

Tony bit his lip again. He placed his hands on the sides, getting under the strings, and slid down over her ass, trying not to think about where his hands were at that very moment.

"You're doing such a good job," Amanda purred. "Do you mind doing my face and arms as well? I'll get even coverage that way."

"Sure, Amanda." He got to his feet and moved in front of her. "I'll do your face first."

With careful hands, he brushed the stray wisps of hair off her face with the back of his knuckles and then applied sunscreen on her forehead, down the bridge of her nose over the smattering of freckles, onto her cheeks, and along her jawline to her chin. He moved down her neck, careful not to press hard on the delicate skin of her throat, and made the mistake of glancing into her eyes. Her pupils were completely dilated with desire.

"Arms," he ordered, his voice hoarse. She placed one hand and then the other in the center of his chest as he coated each arm with the lotion.

"Your turn."

Tony nodded and handed her the bottle.

"Sit so I can get your shoulders, neck, and face."

He obeyed and tried not to focus on the feeling of her small hands rubbing the lotion over his body. She dug her fingers into the muscles in between his shoulder blades and he couldn't stop the moan that escaped his lips.

"Feel good?" Amanda asked.

"Yeah," he replied.

"You made me feel really good, so I thought I should return the favor."

"You don't have to," he murmured.

"I want to."

He wondered if they were still talking about sunscreen.

"Stand please."

Her hands were getting closer to the edge of his swim trunks and he closed his eyes, trying to think of the least sexy things possible.

She stopped and moved to stand in front of him, continuing her application of sunscreen across his pectorals. "Arms," she instructed.

He gave her his left, and she placed his palm against her sternum, the sides of her breasts brushing against his outer fingers every time she moved. Tony studied her face; she was entirely focused on getting the sunscreen into his body. Once she reached his hand, she grasped his other one, replacing the first. Tony very carefully thought of his grandmother's apartment and how it always stank of lavender and kitty litter.

Finished with his arms, Amanda moved back to his torso, applying firm pressure as she rubbed over his ribs. He appreciated that she wasn't trying to tickle him, not that it would have registered in his brain as a tickle at that point. She moved further down his abdomen, under his belly button, and through the trail of hair that led under his trunks.

His breathing quickened. *She can't possibly not notice the effect she's having on me,* he thought.

"Is it alright if I get the skin under your waistband?" she asked quietly.

"Yeah," he replied, just as softly, and was rewarded with a smile.

She slipped her fingertips under the front of his waistband and he gritted his teeth at the gentle pressure she applied as she moved across his lower abdomen. Rather than walk around him, she wrapped her arms around his waist to continue the circuit, bringing their faces close together.

"What are we doing?" Tony asked under his breath.

"Putting on sunscreen." Amanda winked at him.

"Amanda," he growled.

She shivered against him and her eyes glazed over with lust.

"Why now? Why today? We've put sunscreen on each other before and it was never like this," Tony pressed, both needing to know the answer and dreading it.

"Like what?"

Tony raised an eyebrow and pressed a hand low on her back, bringing her hips into contact with his.

Her eyes widened and a little moan escaped her lips.

"I ask you again, why today?" Tony's voice rumbled from deep in his chest, so low he barely recognized it.

"I was tired of walking on eggshells," Amanda whispered.

Chapter Sixteen

Flashback: Swimming

"I hate summer colds!" pouted Amanda. "Poor James."

"I think it's more of a flu," corrected Tony. "He's spending most of his time either in the bathroom or sleeping."

"Whatever," stated Amanda flatly. "He can't come out and play with us, and I hate it."

"What do you want to do?" asked Tony, feeling sad that she was disappointed to only have him to play with.

"James has the best ideas for games," Amanda sighed. "It's too hot to think."

Tony looked sadly at his sandals. "We could...it's not a game, but we could do James's chores for him. Make it easier on his parents to look after him?"

Amanda brightened considerably. "With both of us working, it will hardly take any time at all, and then we can relax in my pool!" She hugged Tony tightly. "Great idea!"

Once a week, all three twelve-year-olds had chores to do around the house, including mowing the lawn and weeding the garden. Amanda and Tony had done their own chores the day before when James first felt sick, but he hadn't felt up to it and slept the whole day.

Tony started the lawn mower and Amanda bent over the front garden. In next to no time, they switched both jobs and yards, with Amanda mowing and Tony weeding the backyard.

In under an hour, the yard was spotless. Tony and Amanda gave each other a high five before racing across the street to get changed and into the pool.

Once they were bobbing on pool noodles, Tony asked, "So...how long have you known James?"

"All my life!" exclaimed Amanda. At Tony's skeptical look, she elaborated. "Seriously! Our moms met in prenatal classes. For breathing during labor, or whatever. And they really hit it off. James was born about two months before me, so our moms kept in touch and started enrolling us in baby classes and playgroups, and they chose times that worked for both of them."

"They lived across the street from each other, but didn't meet until prenatal classes?" asked Tony. "That's funny!"

"Oh, sorry, no, James didn't live across the street at that point. They moved there when he was about a year old, I think. Mr. and Mrs. Lavallee liked this neighborhood and the schools, and so when the people who used to live there told my parents that they were thinking of selling, they suggested they sell to the Lavallees! We've been in the same classes for everything ever since." Amanda beamed happily.

"Everything?" teased Tony. "I'd love to see James in tights."

Amanda laughed. "Okay, not everything. He didn't take ballet with me. But we did try a hip hop class together. He was *much* better than me. We also finished all our swimming levels together. We're going to be lifeguards once we're old enough. He considered joining gymnastics with me, but he preferred soccer and the classes were at the same time."

"I would love to play soccer," said Tony wistfully.

"You should try out this year!" said Amanda excitedly. "James would love to have someone to practice with! I'm going to try out for the school volleyball team. And cross-country this fall. James said he wants to do that with me. You should, too! It'll be fun! We'll go to meets together and we can train in the neighborhood on the weekends. We can start training now! I mean, once James is better."

Amanda got so excited that her noodle escaped from between her legs and hit Tony in the forehead. He blinked water out of his eyes and saw Amanda laughing in front of him.

"Think that's funny, do you?" he asked, still unsure of his new friendship. He found his old habits of acting tough slipped out of his tight control most often when he felt like people were laughing at him.

"Yes, I do!" giggled Amanda. "What are you going to do about it?"

Tony put on a fake scowl, hoping that this was the right tactic, and swam-stalked towards her, leaving his noodle behind.

"Uh oh!" gasped Amanda between giggles. She swam backwards unsteadily. "What are you going to do?"

"Teach you a lesson. No one laughs at Tony Carlson and gets away with it!" Tony grabbed Amanda around the ankle, yanked her towards him, and started tickling her ribs.

Amanda shrieked with laughter and squirmed to get away. "Nonono!" she gasped. "Laughing *with* you! Not *at* you!"

"Do I look like I'm laughing?" growled Tony, trying to hide his grin and failing miserably. It was impossible not to smile when Amanda laughed.

"You'd be laughing more if I was tickling you, too!" Amanda squeaked, trying to get her fingers between their bodies to get at his ribs.

She caught him right at his most ticklish spot, and he let out a loud laugh that ended on a high squeak. He released Amanda, embarrassed.

"Why did you stop?" asked Amanda. "I didn't even have to beg!"

Tony flushed and turned away.

"Come on, what was it?" Amanda asked, concerned. She tried to swim around him to see his face.

"Just drop it!" He squeaked on the second word, and then his voice dropped. He hid his face in his hands.

"Ohhh." Amanda drew out the word slowly. "Tony, your voice is chang-ing. Is that all?"

Tony nodded, still not looking at her.

Amanda threw herself at his back, wrapping him up in a tight hug. "You're my friend, Tony. Don't worry about it." Amanda let go. She glanced down at her budding breasts and flushed. "My body is changing and doing weird things too. I'm going to need you to not freak out on me when stuff happens to me."

Tony tentatively looked up at Amanda. She wasn't laughing at him. She looked a little upset, and Tony thought he knew how to fix that.

"Friends?" he asked, holding out his hand.

"Forever!" she said gleefully, and launched herself at him in a full body hug, ignoring his hand and knocking them both over in the water.

Chapter Seventeen

James

Still buzzing with the excitement of signing the paperwork for his first house, even if it was technically his parents who owned it, James leapt out of his parent's car the instant his dad put it in park in front of their house.

His mom chuckled at him while she followed him. "Excited to tell the others?" she said, her voice carrying up the stairs.

"What gave me away?" James called back down. He dumped his overnight bag into his laundry, refilling it with clean clothing. "We're staying at the Beyer's while Amanda's parents are away, okay?"

"If you feral kids get hungry, you're more than welcome for dinner," his dad said, poking his head into the room on his way past. "Just give us a couple hours warning to prepare the banquet."

James laughed. "Fair." He quickly changed into his swimsuit and tossed his bag over his shoulder. "Love you!"

"Love you too!" his parents echoed.

Taking the stairs two at a time, he was out the door and across the street less than five minutes after arriving.

I wonder if Tony's even up yet? he thought with a smirk. *Depends on how loudly Amanda moves around, I suppose.*

Thinking about his friends invariably made him think about Glenn's party at the beginning of summer, and how good they had been together. He and Tony had been patiently waiting for Amanda to bring up the topic, but she hadn't yet and he was getting desperate. *I think it's time,* he thought. *If she shuts down, I'll drop it, but I have to try. I love her, and I need her to know that.*

As for Tony...

One declaration of love at a time, he thought, taking a deep breath.

He let himself into the backyard by the side gate and strode around the house to the back just in time to hear Amanda moan softly. The sound went straight to his cock, and the sight of his best friends pressed together sent more blood pulsing south.

"I ask you again, why today?" Tony's voice rumbled.

"I was tired of walking on eggshells," Amanda whispered. "I kept thinking I saw something in your eyes, but I wasn't sure..." She pushed away from him to face the patio doors.

James could see a tear streak down her cheek in her reflection, so he spoke up. "Wasn't sure about what, sunshine?"

Tony jumped and Amanda let out a little squeak as she whipped around.

James tossed his bag onto the mattress and leaned against one of the pillars. "Why are you crying?"

"I wasn't trying to force myself on you!" Tony exclaimed, his face bright red. "I'm sorry!"

Amanda shook her head. "Stop." She blinked her eyes rapidly. "Ugh, I've got sunscreen on my hands and can't wipe these tears away!"

"Allow me," James said, and brushed his thumbs gently under each of her eyes. "Better?"

"Yes." She swayed towards him and pressed her forehead against his shoulder. "I wasn't sure what to do."

"Do about what?" Tony asked, half-sitting on the edge of the table.

James ran his hand lightly up and down her back. Her breath was tickling his chest, but he didn't want her to move.

Finally, she said, "Why am I so terrified to talk to you? It never used to be like this."

"Spit it out! I'm imagining the worst over here," Tony exclaimed, exasperated.

Amanda stood up straight. "It's nothing bad. I hope. I just..." She took a deep breath. "Don't think any less of me?"

"Sunshine, you can't change our opinions of you that easily." James leaned against the pillar again, sticking one hand in the waistband of his swim shorts.

Her eyes tracked the movement for a moment, glazing over, before she gave herself a little shake. "I wasn't sure what to do about what happened at Glenn's party."

"Glenn's party?" Tony repeated.

"Yes," Amanda confirmed.

"What do you mean?" James asked cautiously.

"Well, why didn't we talk about it?" Amanda asked, flailing her arms and pacing a step or two. "We woke up the next morning and just...pretended like nothing happened!" She came to a stop and wrapped her arms around herself. "I felt so vulnerable."

"Vulnerable?" James repeated, staring at her intently. "Why?"

"I had been acting so—I climbed all over both of you when I was naked and drunk!" she exclaimed.

"You had also been assaulted in his kitchen and publicly groped without your permission," Tony pointed out. "It was a wild night, not all of it good."

"And when you didn't bring it up, I—we didn't want to force you to relive some potentially scarring memories," James added. "But we can talk about it. We certainly don't think less of you for anything that happened that night."

"Definitely not," Tony rushed to reassure her.

"That's not—" Amanda cut herself off and sighed. "Thank you. I'll try to figure out a different way of saying what I'm trying to say." She looked past Tony to the sunscreen bottle and smiled.

James swore he saw a lightbulb click on over her head. *What are you up to?* he thought.

"I saw a post on Tumblr the other day," Amanda said, lifting her eyebrows. "It raised the point that women's and men's nipples were essentially the same, and that it was ridiculous for Tumblr to ban female-presenting nipples when male ones were perfectly fine. There was an example of a trans man who had posted a post-op photo that didn't get flagged, but all his pre-op ones were. What are your thoughts on that?"

"I'm all for all nipples being free," Tony said. "But I can't help it if I find the ones with a bit of meat behind them sexy."

Amanda nodded thoughtfully and tilted her head at James. "Then James would be sexy to you? Because he has some solid pecs."

James flushed at being inspected by his friends. "I swim a lot."

Tony opened and closed his mouth a couple times. "Well, yeah. I would say that James is sexy," he said, a blush creeping up his cheeks.

"Thanks, man," James replied with a shy grin.

"Should he have to cover up?" Amanda continued.

"No, definitely not," Tony said immediately.

"I'm just following this to its logical conclusion here, but if James is sexy and doesn't have to cover up—" Amanda smiled innocently "—then neither should I."

James's jaw dropped.

"What?" squeaked Tony.

Tugging on the strings at the back of her top, Amanda shrugged and said, "Tony didn't get a chance to put sunscreen on my front. Can I get some help with that?"

And then she lifted the top over her head and threw it at the mattress.

It hung evocatively over the bag James had so casually tossed there a few minutes ago.

"Am I going to have to do this myself?" Amanda said, stalking over to the table to get the sunscreen.

"No!" James said quickly.

Tony snatched up the bottle.

"I'll do it," they both said at the same time.

James met Tony's eyes, and a swift understanding passed between them. *Let Amanda lead. We'll follow her anywhere.*

"Here," Tony said, holding the bottle upside down to squirt some lotion into James's hands.

He tried to figure out the least sexy way of putting it on her, just in case they'd been reading her wrong. He decided to start on her stomach, wrapping around the sides of her ribs and down over hard muscle to the slightly softer lower belly. He moved back up again and Amanda put a hand on his wrist.

"Under the material, please," she breathed, a light flush on her cheeks. "In case it shifts while I swim."

James swallowed hard. Eyes on her face, he let his hand be moved back down her belly and slipped his fingers under the string over her left hip bone. He moved across her body, trying to keep his breathing even, although he almost failed when she closed her eyes and her breath hitched halfway through. When he finished, he rubbed the lotion on her belly into her skin, the sides of his fingers grazing the swells of her breasts.

Once he had finished, Tony took over, pulling Amanda to stand between his legs facing him so he could paint the upper part of her chest.

James picked up the bottle and squirted a little more into his palms. He moved behind her, his hands hovering, hesitating. "Are you sure— Okay, then."

Amanda had grabbed him by the wrists and put his hands directly on her breasts. "Make sure to get everywhere," she said, tipping her head back to look him in the eyes. "Be *extra* thorough."

"Fuck," Tony muttered under his breath, sliding his hands down to join James.

"Ohhhh," Amanda groaned, leaning back against James's chest, pushing her breasts further into their hands.

Their fingers brushed against each other, slippery with lotion, lighting up his nerves and making his mind go fuzzy. Her skin was so soft, her nipples hard from desire, and he couldn't believe she was letting him touch her like this.

"We should probably put some sunscreen on James too, don't you think?" Amanda asked breathlessly after a few moments.

"Yeah, okay," James said reluctantly, pulling his hands from her enticing body.

Now it was his turn in the middle, his friends slicking his skin with lotion until he was coated from head to toe.

"Last one in the pool is a rotten egg!" Amanda shrieked, and then she was off, running down the lawn to the edge of the pool. Her messy bun bounced on the top of her head.

"She's seducing us," Tony said dazedly. "She's got to know how this is affecting us, right?"

"I mean, it's pretty obvious," James said, adjusting himself in his swimsuit.

"Hey, are we good?" Tony asked, putting a hand on James's shoulder. "You seem a little tense."

"If Amanda actually feels that way about us, either one of us or both of us..." James blew out a sharp breath. "I'm terrified about how our friendship will change."

"Would you rather not find out?" Tony asked.

James nudged him with his hip. "Some things are worth the risk, right?" He averted his gaze in case Tony saw the depth of his feelings for him as well. *I'm not ready to change everything quite so drastically all at once.*

"I'm just along for the ride." Tony spread his hands, walking backwards towards the pool. "I hope I don't have to get off this rollercoaster too soon."

"Good metaphor," James said, following him.

"Don't get all teacherly on me now," Tony scoffed, rolling his eyes. "Don't you have to go to school for that first?"

"I have to have an aptitude for teaching first," James teased. "And who better to practice it on than you two?"

"Oh yeah?" Tony chuckled. "You going to *school* us?"

James's smile turned wolfish. "If you need it."

Tony's eyes widened in what James hoped was pleasant surprise.

"Watch your step," James advised, and Tony turned around just in time to not bang into the fence around the pool.

"Took your time getting here," Amanda said, floating peacefully on her back. "What were you talking about?"

James wasn't sure if he should avert his eyes from her bare breasts or not. They were enticingly above the surface of the water, pink nipples drawn in tight from the breeze blowing across them. He wanted to feel them again.

"You," Tony said, slipping into the shallow end of the pool.

Righting herself, Amanda beamed at him. "What about me?"

"Where do you see this," James gestured between the three of them, "going?"

"I think I might have a better question," Tony interrupted. He reached out for Amanda's hand. "What did you dream about this morning?"

Amanda blushed. "The three of us were swimming in this pool, except we were all naked, and we weren't exactly swimming."

James grinned and joined them in the pool. "Talk about a literal *wet* dream."

She splashed water at him, barely reaching his chest. "Tony was in front of me and we were making out, and James, you were fingering me from behind." She shivered, her eyes glazed with lust. "Tony woke me up before I could come."

Tony groaned. "Darlin', I wish I could have let you grind yourself to completion on my thigh this morning, but I'm not sure I could have kept my hands to myself if you had. And you were asleep! No consent happened."

"Oh." Amanda frowned. "I'm sorry. I wasn't really awake enough to realize I had done that to you. Can you forgive me?"

"Forgive?" Tony spluttered. "I'm not asking for an apology! I meant that *you* couldn't consent!"

"Amanda," James tipped her head up by her chin. "Is this a new fantasy? Something to try on for size?"

Her expression changed to one of hurt. "Do you really think I'd do that to you? Either of you?"

"Today just feels a little out of left field," James said. "Like you're horny and we're convenient."

Amanda gasped, pulling her chin out of his fingers. "I'll have you know I've been crushing on you both for literal *years*. Do you know how much courage—" She broke off, clenching her jaw. Her eyes flashed angrily. "If you don't feel the same way about me, at least treat me with respect and tell me that to my face instead of insulting me!"

"Sunshine—" James started, but Tony cut him off.

"Why didn't you say something after Glenn's party? Sure, we were all pretty drunk, but that kiss we shared was the best thing that's happened this summer." He tugged her close, cupping her face in his hands. "I think what James was trying to say is that we're concerned that this is a little sudden and he wants to know where we stand with you."

"I might be a little emotional right now," Amanda whispered.

"Understandably," Tony said cheerfully. "Take your time."

"Why didn't either of *you* say anything after Glenn's party?" she countered his question. "Also, you know how I feel about you, but you still haven't told me anything about your feelings. I'm feeling really vulnerable here."

"I'm in love with you," James blurted out. When his friends stared at him, he shrugged. "How's that for vulnerable? I didn't say anything after the party because I was afraid."

"How are you so sure?" Amanda asked, reaching her hand out for his.

"Do you remember when I went to Costa Rica with Nicolas for Christmas?" James asked her.

She wrinkled her nose. "It was just last year. That was the worst Christmas ever."

"Yeah, it was." James smiled shyly. "Because I wasn't with the people I loved. Amanda, you're my forever. I'll work every day to prove myself to you." He kissed her knuckles, smelling the chlorine salt on her skin. "You don't have to say it back now. I know you'll come around eventually." He winked.

"You are ridiculous," Amanda informed him. "Of course I love you. That was actually the most confusing part for me. I'm in love with both of you, and I have been, well, since senior year of high school at least. I just didn't realize the depth of my love for you until Crystal."

Tony narrowed his eyes in thought. "You brought her home for Thanksgiving sophomore year?"

"Junior year," Amanda corrected. "Yeah. She wanted commitment, and all I could think was that if I said yes to her, I'd hardly ever see you two again. I don't know how this is going to work, the three of us, but there's absolutely no way I could ever choose between the two of you. You each have half my heart."

"Leaving none for you," James said quietly.

"I'll have yours, I hope. And yours?" She tilted her head questioningly at Tony.

"God, yes!" he exclaimed fervently. He flushed and covered his face with one hand. "I tried to get you out of my heart while I was in San Francisco, but I only ended up hurting Wendy instead."

Amanda pressed a shaking hand to her lips. "Oh no. I'm sorry. She was a sweetheart."

Tony's shoulders slumped. "Yeah. I called myself every name in the book over it. She forgave me anyway." He dragged his hand down his face until he could look at them. "She said she understood that true love always wins."

"I feel so selfish," Amanda whispered. "Why do I deserve two wonderful men when—"

"Stop that," James said harshly. "It's not about deserving anything." His voice softened. "It's about love; who we *choose* to love. And it just so happens to be you." The water swirled around him as he stepped closer to her. "Sure, it's unconventional—" Tony snorted and James ignored him

"—but with our families on our side, we can make it through anything. As long as we're together."

"Pretty words. But how is this going to work? You know, logistically?" Tony asked, biting his lip.

"By this, you mean relationship?" Amanda shrugged. "I have no idea. Something, something–communication is key?"

James chuckled. "To be honest, I don't see things changing all that much. Just, maybe talk to us instead of keeping things bottled up inside?"

"I can try. Does this mean you *do* want me? I wasn't sure because you never brought up what happened at the party, and I'm just me, you know. You've seen me at my worst! Why *would* you want me?"

"Okay, first of all, you've seen us at our worst too," Tony said, pointing between himself and James. "And we're hot stuff." He waggled his eyebrows suggestively.

Amanda gave his shoulder a push, toppling him backwards into the water. He came up grinning and shook his hair, splashing them.

"I'm going to set the record straight here." James swallowed hard. *Why was it so hard to say, when it seemed like everyone was on the same page?* "I want you. Desperately. I've been hard since I got here, and it's not likely to go away because you look so fucking hot without a top on that it's taking all my willpower to keep my eyes respectfully on your face. I can barely keep my hands off your body. Just say the word."

"*James!*" Amanda whimpered, swaying towards him. "Yes."

"Yes to what?" James asked, hardly daring to hope.

"Yes to everything!"

"Being both my girlfriend and Tony's? Me touching you? Be specific."

"All of that!" Amanda threw herself at him, and he caught her instinctively.

His hands found her waist and moved up her body. Hardly daring to breathe in case this was an illusion or a dream, he cupped the weight of her breasts in his hands, running the pads of his thumbs over the nubs of her nipples.

"Yes," she breathed, arching into him.

James let go and cupped her head in his hands. "I'm going to kiss you now," he said.

"Good!" Amanda said and then moaned.

Glancing down, James saw that Tony had taken over where he had left off, wrapping his arms around her from behind and working her nipples into stiff peaks with twists of his fingers. Satisfied that she was being taken care of, James bent down and kissed her slack lips, parting them further with his tongue to taste her. She moaned into his mouth, clinging to his shoulders as her hips gave little stilted rolls against his.

"Wow," James gasped. He looked over her shoulder into the eyes of his other best friend. Seeing the arousal in them matching his own was a heady experience. Amanda groaned between them, drawing his attention. "What do you want, Amanda?"

"I want you to make me come while I'm kissing Tony," she said. "Use your fingers on my clit. I'm so close already, it won't take long."

"Fuck, Amanda, you don't have to try to sell me on the idea. Turn around."

Tony took over, bringing his hands up to her head, taking out the elastic holding her hair up and let it fall in wet clumps around her shoulders. He buried his fingers in her hair and tilted her head. "I've been imagining this for a month and your hair was always down. Can I kiss you, Amanda?"

"If you don't, I might do something drastic."

"More drastic than letting us rub sunscreen all over your body?" Tony teased.

"I think that worked out *very* well, don't you?" She cocked an eyebrow up at him. "Tony, please!"

Tony didn't waste any more time. He bent the scant inch to press his lips against hers. She opened to him instantly and he delved into her mouth, their tongues visibly tangling. Her short nails dug into his shoulder blades and he hissed, pulling back slightly.

She chased his lips, leaning forwards and pressing her ass against James's rock hard cock, making him groan.

If kissing her had been amazing, watching her kiss his best friend was even better. He slid his hand between them, feeling the ridge of Tony's hard cock against the back of his hand as he slipped under the spandex of her bikini bottoms.

The fabric was constricting, limiting his movement in his quest to find her clit. Amanda's hips jumped when he found the little bundle of nerves, and he circled around it once or twice, nuzzling her exposed neck when she tilted her head to get a better angle in her kiss with Tony.

"Can I undo these?" James murmured, his free hand tracing the little bows over her hip bone.

Rather than answer him, she yanked at the bow herself, the tie coming undone in seconds and the material sagging off her body.

Given more room to work with, James ground the heel of his palm over her clit, fingers delving deeper to plunge into her opening. He held her tight between his hand and body, her hips giving little stilted rolls as she searched for more friction. Her movements kept rocking his hand against Tony's cock.

James had to close his eyes, completely overwhelmed by sensations. The slick heat of her sex was almost too much for him. *How am I going to manage fucking her if I'm on the verge of coming just from fingering her?* "Oh my God, Tony, you have got to feel this," James murmured.

Tony's hand quested downwards, joining his, and James moved out of his way, letting him feel how hot she was for them. Tony groaned deep in his chest, a rumble that made James's cock twitch.

James returned to her clit, rubbing over and around it with different pressures to see what she liked best. Tony's wrist was pressed against the back of his fingers, thrusting in and out of her as she rocked her hips back and forth, frantically searching for her release.

The water around them rippled with waves from her movements.

James kissed behind her ear and scraped his teeth over the shell, making her shudder in his grip. He massaged her breast with his free hand, pinching and pulling lightly at the tight peak of her nipple.

Amanda's body tensed between them, arching her back with a whimper and a muffled cry that Tony swallowed with his mouth. Both men stopped the movement of their hands as she vibrated with her climax.

"Fuck," James breathed. "That was so fucking hot."

Tony pressed his forehead to hers, both of their chests heaving for breath. "Do you believe we want you now?"

A small hand groped James's hard cock and he groaned, a sound that was echoed by Tony.

"Well, I suppose I can believe it when you're both this hard just from getting me off," Amanda said cheekily. "But I'm still not absolutely certain."

"What do we need to do to prove it to you?" James asked, his voice husky with barely contained desire.

"I think a thorough fucking will put my mind at ease."

"Get out of the pool before I bend you over the wall and take you right here," James growled.

"What makes you think I wouldn't want that?" Amanda demanded, pressing her ass back against his cock.

"I'm sure you would, you little hedonist," James teased lightly. "You would have loved it if Tony and I had fucked you in front of everyone for the first time at Glenn's party. Call me a romantic if you like, but I want to take my time taking you apart piece by piece before I put you back together again."

"Dude," breathed Tony, his pupils dilated with desire.

It took all of James's energy to keep his hands from reaching for his best friend over Amanda's shoulder, to know what his lips tasted like, to share his breath.

"Is that what you want?" James whispered, unsure if he was asking just Amanda or both of them.

"Yes."

"Then let's get out of the pool and shower this sunscreen off so that our mouths have free reign over our bodies." James pulled at the ties around her other leg and lifted the dark blue material into the air. "After you, sunshine," he said with a wink.

Amanda tossed her wet hair over her shoulder and walked through the water to the stairs. "I don't have a problem being naked in front of you two. You're the ones still in your bathing suits," she taunted over her shoulder.

The water sluiced down her curves, her hips swaying enticingly as she exited the pool.

James caught himself staring. It wasn't until Tony started moving that James was knocked out of his stupor and hurried to join his best friends on the pool deck.

Amanda had already started the shower and was standing under it, rubbing her hands down her body and over her breasts. Tony was struggling to take off his bathing shorts, the material clinging unhelpfully, and his cock getting in the way. James chuckled, even though he knew he wouldn't be in any better shape once he started his own process.

Joining his friends naked in the shower was as overwhelming as he'd thought it might be, both from the skin-on-skin sensations and the memories of his first time with Nicolas.

Another first day of school, James thought, taking another pull at his beer and staring into the bottle morosely.

This past summer had been particularly difficult, and it wasn't hard to figure out why; Tony had stayed in San Francisco to take more classes during the summer term. Having one third of their trio gone had unbalanced them, and he and Amanda had had to cool off from fighting with each other more than once.

He drummed his fingers on the bartop absentmindedly, staring at the writhing bodies of the dancers in front of the DJ station.

"Hey, man," said a slightly accented voice. "Mind if I sit here?"

James, drawn from his thoughts, looked up into blue eyes. "Be my guest." As the man sat down, James studied him. Red hair, shaved at the sides and long at the top, fell over his forehead. Freckles covered every inch of his skin. His shoulders filled out a sky blue golf shirt, which tapered to a narrow waist holding up beige pants.

"I couldn't help but notice you from across the room," said the man. "Are you here as support for your friend, or for yourself?"

"Just myself," said James, a corner of his mouth quirking up in a lopsided grin. He lifted the bottle to his lips again.

"Nicolas," he said, extending his hand out to James.

"James." He shook the outstretched hand. "You a student?"

"At Boston U, majoring in Architecture," confirmed Nicolas. "You?"

"Same, studying ECE. I'm surprised we haven't bumped into each other on campus before this," responded James. "Where are you from? You have a great accent."

"I'm from Montreal. My family is French." He ran a hand through his hair, pushing it off his face, only to have it flop back over his forehead again. "I was recruited for the swim team here, and they had a good Architecture program, so I took it."

"Swimming?" James gave him an appraising look. "Fly?"

Nicolas grinned, and dimples appeared in each cheek. "How'd you guess?"

"Your body proportions suit fly well. Broad, muscular shoulders, narrow waist. It's pretty obvious." James flushed. "That was rhetorical, wasn't it?"

"No, I was curious." Nicolas smirked, taking a drink from his own beer. "You swim?"

"Not anymore. I used to. I'm a lifeguard, so I see the swimmers practic-ing. It's something you pick up on after a while," replied James.

Nicolas nodded thoughtfully. "I guess you see a lot from the deck." He took one last drag from his beer before setting it down. "I've got practice first thing in the morning, so I had better go. Can I give you my number?"

James made up his mind quickly. "Let me give you mine, too. I'd like to get to know you better." He handed his phone over, and typed his information into Nicolas's cell.

"Nice meeting you," said Nicolas, with a wave goodbye.

"Talk to you soon," replied James, smiling.

Not long after Nicolas had left, James received a text.

Can you cover my shift at the pool tomorrow morning? 6-10 am Please!!! – Jordan

James sighed and checked his schedule. No class until 12 on Fridays.

You owe me pizza. – James

The next morning, James was at the pool early. He had butterflies in his stomach, and hadn't been able to eat breakfast. A bagel was waiting for him in the pool office once he went on break.

The coach was setting up the lane ropes, so James went to help her, rather than pace a hole in the tiled floor. Guarding the swim team was easy money. The university only had one guard on duty to cover their asses in case of an accident, and with the quality of the swimmers and the coach, there was rarely anything to do. However, it meant that there was nobody there to help distract him from his nerves.

What is up with the nerves, anyway? said James to himself. *We chatted for what, fifteen minutes? Hardly long enough to get to know one another.*

He caught a glimpse of red hair as he knelt to attach the last lane rope, and it dropped into the water. "Ah, damn it," he muttered to himself, watching the heavy hook drag the end underwater.

"James?"

He looked up from his position at the edge of the pool, up and up, over the very tight navy speedo and muscled body, into Nicolas's face.

"Fancy seeing you here," he said, getting to his feet and flashing a grin. "Just a sec, I've got to go get this." He whipped his guard shirt over his head and was about to kick off his sandals when Nicolas stopped him with a hand on his shoulder.

"Not that I don't appreciate the view, but I'm sure you don't want to stand around in wet trunks for the next hour until they dry," he said. "Allow me." He slipped into the water and waded to the end of the rope, hauling it over to the wall. He hooked it in easily and turned the crank to tighten it, muscles working.

James put his shirt back on, smiling to himself. "Thanks. Just so you know, I'm totally stalking you."

Nicolas looked up at him from the pool with a grin. "I wondered about that. How many strings did you have to pull to get this shift?"

"So many," chuckled James. He watched as Nicolas lifted himself effortlessly out of the pool, water running in rivulets down his body. Suddenly, his throat was dry. He swallowed hard.

"Nice to see you again so soon," said Nicolas with a wink. "Do you want to grab breakfast after practice? Or do you have a longer shift?"

"I'm covering for a friend until ten. When is practice over?" asked James.

Nicolas put his hand dramatically over his heart. "I don't know if I can wait a whole half an hour for your shift to end. I might die of starvation first!"

James raised an eyebrow at his antics. "Take your time in the shower, and you won't even notice your hunger."

Nicolas grinned, dimples appearing. "Oh, I'll be hungry if I take my time in the shower," he said suggestively, eyebrows raised. "Just not for food."

"Maybe a plate of sausage will change your mind?" teased James with a wink.

"Nico!" called the coach. "Get your skinny ass over here!"

Nicolas turned back to James. "Gotta go. But I do like sausage," he said as a parting shot over his shoulder.

James watched him walk away. "Well, this is certainly going to be interesting," he thought with a grin.

Throughout his shift, James felt his eyes being drawn to the rhythmic motion of Nicolas cutting smoothly through the water. His elegant body moved powerfully through the difficult strokes with ease, James noted admiringly.

When practice ended, Nicolas made a detour to walk past James.

"Impressive," James said casually.

"Fly isn't all that difficult if you practice enough," laughed Nicolas.

"I was talking about your stamina," replied James with a wink.

"Hoo boy," replied Nicolas, fanning himself with a grin. "We'll find out if you can keep up. See you in half an hour!"

"Damn, how does he always manage to get the last word?" James asked the wall. "I kind of like it." He grinned and started to remove the lane ropes from the pool to get it ready for the open swim.

After cleaning up her equipment, the coach came over to say goodbye to James. "You interested in our Nico?" she asked, curious.

"God, was I that obvious?" asked James, his face heating up.

"No, not you!" she laughed. "But Nico hasn't been this relaxed in a while, and he never talks to the guard on duty." Her eyes narrowed. "He also had some record fast times today. Do you want to come to our meet next weekend? If he performs this well when you're watching him in practice, I want to see what he's like in a competitive setting."

James shifted uncomfortably. "Why don't we see how the first date goes, before I start promising his coach I'll come to meets?"

"Oh! Sorry, I didn't realize just how new this," she gestured between James and the changing room, "was." She started to walk away before turning around again. "Don't break his heart." She glared.

"Gotcha, coach." James saluted her.

"Smart ass." She smiled, and then walked away.

By the time James removed all the lanes, and put away leftover flutter boards and pull floats, the guards for the open swim were in the pool office.

"Hey man, thanks for covering for me this morning," said Jordan.

"You gave me enough warning this time," teased James. "When are they going to hire freshmen to cover the last minute shifts?"

"I heard they're holding interviews this week." Jordan grinned. "That means overtime while we put them through their paces. You sure you don't want to come back to work for us?"

James shook his head with a smile. "The city pool gives me the hours I want and doesn't try to get me to take shifts during my classes. You know how hard I had to fight with management that first year."

"That's the difference between you and me," pointed out Jordan. "I don't care if I miss my classes."

"Yeah, and I've got the grades to prove that it's worth it to go," stated James flatly. "Speaking of going, I'm heading out now. Have fun!"

James slipped into the guard's changing room, quickly stripped off his bathing suit and guard shirt, and got dressed. He was out in two minutes, hopping slightly as he fought with the heel of his left sneaker. "See you around!"

"Where's the fire?" asked Jordan, curious.

"I'm meeting someone for breakfast," replied James.

"Someone?" Jordan's eyebrows rose.

"Yes," James replied abruptly. "Bye!"

Nicolas was waiting outside the door, leaning against the wall. "Do you like bagels?"

"Who doesn't like bagels?" asked James with a laugh. "Come on, my stomach is about to eat itself, and *I* wasn't breaking my record times all morning."

"Did Coach say that?" asked Nicolas, his face lighting up. At James's nod, he said, "Sweet!"

They walked to Aesop's Bagels, bought themselves a stack of different flavors, and stocked up on cream cheese and peanut butter. They found a table and two chairs in a quiet corner and sat down to enjoy their breakfast.

After practically inhaling two bagels, Nicolas took a deep breath. "Well, that's better. To be honest, I had breakfast already this morning. At five thirty. But working for three and a half hours at top speed means that I need to eat again before lunch."

"I'm not surprised!" laughed James. "And I'm glad to hear that you didn't work out on an empty stomach." He hesitated, adding, "Since we're being honest with each other, I didn't eat breakfast until after you arrived at the pool, because I was nervous to see you again."

"I thought I was hallucinating when I saw you at the pool this morning, that I had conjured you up from my fantasies," confided Nicolas. "If I had known that you were going to be there this morning, I probably wouldn't have been able to sleep last night. Why didn't you tell me?" he asked.

"I was asked to cover for Jordan about two minutes after you left me last night. I considered texting you, but thought that might be weird," James admitted.

Nicolas nodded. "Ah, that makes sense. Do you usually guard at Boston's pool?"

"No, I work at a city pool. Better hours."

"Ah. I hear that." Nicolas pressed a fold into his paper napkin. "I'm going to be blunt here: do you see this going anywhere?"

James bit his lip and averted his eyes.

"What is it?" asked Nicolas. "I may not know you very well yet, but that is a universal symbol of 'I have something to tell you, and you might not like it.' So spill."

James rolled his eyes. "I am not used to people reading me so easily! Well, other than Tony and Amanda." He took a deep breath. "It's not a long story, but there's history," he warned.

"I'm listening," replied Nicolas calmly, as he spread peanut butter on his third bagel.

James paused for a moment, collecting his thoughts before he began. "Amanda, Tony, and I grew up together. We were always really close." James smiled wryly. "I've been in love with Amanda since I was old enough to know what that meant, and Tony not much later. Nothing ever happened between any of us, though. And now Tony's in San Francisco, and Amanda's in Texas..."

"And you're here," Nicolas finished softly.

James sighed. "Yeah. Tony didn't come home this summer, and I missed my best friend. I was pretty down last night, but you sat next to me. And then you flashed those dimples at me, and I couldn't resist."

Nicolas finished chewing the bite of bagel he had taken. "Wow," he said, finally. "So are you seriously exploring your options, or are you biding your time until you get up the courage to tell your friends about your feelings?"

"I am quite serious." James winced. "I understand if it's too much for you. I want to explore my life outside of them, see if there's a way for me to find love somewhere new. But I thought it was best to fill you in on my situation as early as possible, to avoid heartache for both of us."

"I only have one question," said Nicolas.

"Just one?" muttered James under his breath.

"Yes, one." Nicolas grinned, and then sobered. "Do you honestly think that you'll be able to fall in love with someone else when you've been in love with them for so long?"

"I sincerely hope so."

"I appreciate your honesty," said Nicolas thoughtfully. "I'd like to think about it for a while, if that's okay with you?"

James nodded. "Of course," he replied quietly. "Your coach invited me to your meet next week. Maybe you could let me know by then, so that if your answer is yes, I can support you?"

Nicolas rolled his eyes. "There you go, being all sweet and supportive, and making me want to forget about thinking it over." He grinned. "You are a dangerous man, James."

"So I've been told," James growled darkly.

An answering flare of arousal lit Nicolas's eyes, and his breath caught.

James stood. "I hope your answer is yes. Text me when you know. But I have to leave now, or else we'll end up wrapped around each other, and that doesn't give you any time to think about it." He gave a slight bow. "Goodbye, I hope to see you soon."

He walked through the doors and into the crisp fall air. The noise of the city echoed around him. Clenching his fists, he stood for a moment, collecting himself. After several deep breaths, he felt like he could move again, and took a step. Suddenly, he felt a hand on his shoulder. He spun, to see Nicolas standing before him.

"Yes," whispered Nicolas.

James thought his heart had stopped beating. He stepped forwards and cupped Nicolas' face. "Yes? Are you sure?"

"Yes, I'm sure," he replied. He turned his head slightly to press a kiss on James's palm, keeping his eyes fixed on the other man's face while he did so.

Letting out a shaky breath, James leaned in. His eyes dropped to Nicolas's mouth, who licked his lips. "Fuck," said James, as he threw caution to the wind and molded his mouth to Nicolas's.

Nicolas groaned and wrapped his arms around James's body, one hand sliding up to curl around his shoulder, and the other sliding into the back pocket of his jeans to cup his ass.

Dazed, James pulled back slowly. "Holy shit." He whispered, before he brought his lips back to the other man's, echoing the sounds that he was emitting. James allowed his body to be pulled closer by Nicolas, and felt like his eyes would cross from the pressure on the front of his jeans. One of his arms slipped around Nicolas's shoulders, holding him tightly against his body.

Nicolas slid his tongue along James's and let him bite his lower lip. With a gasp, he opened his eyes to stare into James's dark ones. His pupils were almost completely dilated with need. Nicolas shifted his hips a tiny bit, and closed his eyes at the feeling of James's hard cock pressing against him. A low groan escaped his throat.

"I think," James rasped. "I think we should continue this very pleasant discussion after dinner. I have to get to the other end of campus for class. Do you have one today?"

Nicolas blinked slowly, obviously gathering his scattered thoughts. "Yeah, at three. Are you asking me out on a second date today?" He grinned.

James kissed him twice quickly, once on each dimple, before replying, "If it's not too presumptuous, can I cook you dinner at my apartment?"

"Only if you're dessert." Nicolas winked.

"Oh, you are most definitely going to be my dessert," growled James.

"Good God," Nicolas whimpered. "You make me hot."

James took a deep breath, trying to regain control of his straining cock. "As much as I want to continue making out with you," James teased. "I should probably get going, or I'll be late." Reluctantly, James let go, and felt Nicolas do the same.

"See you tonight," said Nicolas.

"I'll text you my address," promised James, as he hurried to his class.

Nicolas pushed his chair back from the table. "Oh my God, that was delicious," he moaned, and rubbed his stomach. "Where did you learn to cook like that?"

"My dad taught me," said James. "All three of us, actually. Amanda makes the best bread, Tony has a knack for sauces, and I was pretty good with spices."

Wrinkling his nose, Nicolas sighed. "It's going to take some getting used to, you talking about them."

"I'm sorry," apologized James. "I'm not going to stop, though. They are my best friends."

Nicolas shrugged. "I think I'm just feeling insecure. I can get possessive."

"What can I do to help you feel more secure?" asked James seriously.

"Be patient with me?" Nicolas grinned. "It's a lot to get used to all at once."

James nodded. "That, I can do. Would you like to move to the couch? I'll just clean up these dishes."

"Oh no, I'm not letting you clean up as well as cook." Nicolas shot to his feet and picked up his plate. "I was raised with manners."

Relaxing with a smile, James sat back down. "I won't argue with you there. The dishwasher is beside the sink."

In no time at all, the table was cleared, and they headed to the living room to sit on the couch.

"What sort of shows do you like to watch?" asked James, flicking on the TV.

Nicolas laughed. "Anything on HGTV. I always get the best ideas watching those shows, and then I can incorporate them into whatever project I'm working on."

"I swear I've watched every episode of Income Property ever made." James smiled. "I think Amanda has a thing for the host."

"Who doesn't?" Nicolas rolled his eyes. "He knows what he's doing and looks good doing it."

"Point." James smirked.

They settled down to watch House Hunters International.

"Where would you live, if you could move anywhere in the world?" asked Nicolas after a few minutes of silence.

"Costa Rica, I think," replied James thoughtfully. "They have made great strides in renewable resources. And the views are pretty spectacular. What about you?"

"New Zealand," Nicolas answered promptly. "They have amazing weather year-round, epic surfing, and no animals are going to kill you. The scenery is nothing to sneeze at either."

"New Zealand is definitely on my bucket list to visit. I honestly can't see myself living anywhere but here–or maybe Canada–for long. Somewhere near my parents, to make it easy to go home for holidays and special occasions," said James.

"I probably wouldn't live there long," said Nicolas. "There are too many other places I want to visit in the world. I don't want to stay in one place for too long."

"We seem to be on very different tracks of life," said James wryly.

"Hey, don't worry about that now." Nicolas grinned. "We're young! A lot can happen in one year."

James's eyes darkened. "A lot can happen in one day," he drawled.

Their eyes connected, James watching the redhead beneath half-lidded eyes. He wet his lips, suddenly dry, and saw Nicolas focus on his mouth. He could hear his heart pounding in his ears. "What are you waiting for?" he rasped.

In a flash, Nicolas was on top of him, pinning him to the couch, bodies flush against each other. "Permission," he growled. "Do you want me to kiss you?"

James gasped for breath. He was so turned on, everything had a haze of purple around the edges. "I want you to do so much more than that," he groaned. Reaching around Nicolas's body, he grabbed his ass and ground their pelvises together.

James's eyes closed at the sensation before tipping his head up to claim Nicolas's mouth. Both men moaned, and James thrust his hips against the man above him, provoking a gasp.

"Want you closer," begged Nicolas. His hands pulled at James's t-shirt and James sat up to yank it off before helping Nicolas take off his.

James smashed their mouths together again. Their tongues slid against each other, dancing in and out. Nimbly, James undid the button and zipper of his jeans, Nicolas copying him.

As one, they stood up and shucked their pants. They stood in front of each other in their boxers, breathing heavily, pupils dilated, and very aroused.

Slowly, Nicolas reached out and traced a path down James's pectoral and down to his abdomen, where he slid his fingers over each dip and groove of muscle.

"Fuck," whispered James. He sat down on the couch and Nicolas climbed on top of him again, straddling his hips. His hands combed through Nicolas's hair, pulling his head down to kiss him.

Nicolas laced his hands in James's hair and rocked his hips. James ran his hands down his body to grope his ass over his boxers, applying pressure at each thrust.

"James," groaned Nicolas, panting against his mouth. "This feels so good. You're going to make me come."

"Good," growled James. He slipped one hand under the other man's boxers onto his bare skin. "I want you to come for me."

"Oh God." Nicolas closed his eyes.

James kissed and bit down the column of his throat. The grip on James's hair tightened, making James groan with pleasure. Their shafts rubbed against each other in exactly the right way, and Nicolas tensed. "James!" he cried as he came. "Yes, God, yes, James!"

Feeling the other man fall apart in his arms set James off, and he groaned into Nicolas's throat as his release rocketed through him.

"Holy shit," gasped Nicolas.

"That was intense," panted James.

"Well, we knew we had sexual chemistry," said Nicolas with a grin.

"And now we have proof," James said with a chuckle.

Nicolas leaned down to press a quick kiss against James's lips. "Definitely worth giving this a shot."

Chapter Nineteen

Amanda

"Since we're getting close to the point of needing to know," Amanda gasped, her body writhing between the two men while they stood under the shower, "I should mention that I've got an IUD and haven't been with anyone in a year. I was tested after the breakup with Crystal, and everything came back negative."

"That's good to know." James kissed down the column of her throat before bending and sucking a nipple into his mouth. "I'm negative too."

Tony ground his cock against her ass and squeezed her breasts. "Me too. Are you sure you want to go bare?"

"If I can't trust the two of you, who *can* I trust?" Amanda scoffed. "I want to feel you, both of you. This has been a long time coming."

"*Fuck*. You have no idea," Tony groaned. He spun her around, claiming her lips for a heated moment. "Can I eat you out?"

"Here?" She blinked, surprised.

"Is there somewhere else you'd rather be?" Tony asked. "As long as I can get my tongue on your clit within the next five seconds, I'll be happy."

Amanda giggled. "Impatient, much?" Her head was spinning from the attention of both men. James had taken over grinding against her ass, and hands were everywhere on her skin. "So am I."

Tony grinned at her and dropped to his knees. "James, support our girl when her knees collapse, won't you?"

"With pleasure," James said. "Spread your legs. Give Tony access to that pretty little pussy."

"That mouth!" Amanda gasped, more turned on than she could ever remember being in her life. With Tony's guidance, she draped one knee over his shoulder, making room for him at the apex of her thighs.

"Next time, I'm going to take my time to memorize every inch of you," Tony said in between delicate little flicks at her clit. "But today, I have absolutely no patience, so I'm going to get right to the honey." He buried his face between her thighs, tongue delving deep into her channel to lap up her juices.

"Oh God," Amanda whimpered, her hands clenching into Tony's hair. She was torn between leaning on him for support and pulling his head tighter to her body.

Luckily, James made the decision for her, wrapping his arm firmly around her waist. "Don't worry, I've got you, love," he murmured in her ear. "What do you need?"

"More. Just...more of everything!"

"You'll have to be more specific than that," James said with a chuckle. "Come on, use your words."

"You're so mean to me," Amanda whined, her hips rolling in short bursts of movement.

"Yup. So mean. Tell us what you want us to do to you in filthy detail," James said, biting gently on the shell of her ear.

"I want—" She broke off with a groan, Tony's tongue whipping rapid-fire across her clit. "So close!"

"Tell us how to get you there," James repeated.

"I need you inside me," Amanda gasped. "I need to be filled up."

"I can do that," James said. "Bend forwards, give me a bit of room to work with here."

Anticipation wriggled inside her as she felt James back up a bit, and then she felt him at her entrance. He pressed inside her, filling her, but something wasn't quite right...

His cock pressed against her ass again, and she realized he'd stuffed her with his fingers.

"Up on your tiptoes," James said. "You're tall, but I don't want to hurt you when I stand upright again."

Wobbling only slightly, because James was still supporting her with an arm around her waist, she rose up. Tony followed, suckling hard on her clit. James pressed on the front wall of her channel with the flat of his fingernails, and she choked on a cry, her nerves firing signals of overwhelming pleasure. Her toes—the ones in the air behind Tony's head—curled hard. Her back arched and she came, harder than she could remember ever coming in her life.

"Tony, Tony," she gasped, trying to push him away from her over-sensitive clit. "Too much."

"I didn't think that phrase was in your vocabulary," Tony teased, sitting back on his heels. He held her calf, not letting her put her leg down, and kissed her ankle. "This is better than my wildest dreams."

"You can say that again," Amanda said shakily.

"Are you okay with continuing?" James asked, his finger slowly sliding in and out of her. "Can we make you feel good?"

"Yes. Yes to everything," Amanda said. "But..."

"But?" Tony asked.

James stopped moving his fingers.

"Can we go lie down on the hammock? I want to ride one of you."

"Any preference?" James asked, kissing behind her ear.

Amanda shivered pleasantly. "How about a race? Whoever gets to the hammock first gets to be ridden."

"And second place?" James asked, grinding against her.

"I haven't thought that far ahead yet," Amanda said.

Tony chuckled. "Sounds like all three of us are winners no matter what."

"That's the idea."

James removed his fingers slowly and Amanda whimpered at the loss. "Can you stand?"

"Yeah, I'm good."

"Good," he echoed. "I should get a head start. Tony's faster than me on a normal day."

"All's fair in love and—" Tony broke off with a frown.

"Sex?" Amanda finished for him. "On your marks, go!" She giggled at the guys for having to hold their cocks in their hands, the lack of support and weight of them fully erect painful while running.

"Yeah, because you don't have to hold your boobs when you run," Tony called back to tease her.

"I'm not running," she said, sauntering slowly to the covered porch. "Who won?"

"Tony did," James admitted readily. "Get that sweet body over here and relieve some of this tension."

She leaned against a support post and admired the two men stretched out on the hammock before her. "You're sure about this?" she asked hesitantly. "You're sure about sharing me?"

"More sure than anything I've ever been of in my life," Tony said firmly. "Come here and let us show you how much."

"We'll need lube," Amanda said, gesturing at the door of the house.

"Bedside table?" James asked, shifting into a seated position.

"Yes," she replied, not surprised that he knew her that well.

"You won't even notice I'm gone." He got smoothly to his feet. "Or maybe you will, since you won't be able to ride him until I come back." James winked at her.

Tony groaned and stared up at the roof. "*I'll* miss you."

"Aww, schmoopikins! I didn't know you cared!" James teased, blowing kisses at Tony while crossing the patio to the door.

Amanda couldn't stop laughing. "Don't worry, Tony. I'll make sure you forget that we're waiting for him." She crawled onto the hammock beside him.

"How are you going to do that?" Tony asked, reaching out a hand for her.

She ignored it and continued her slow pace up the mattress. "Oh, you know... I'm thinking of sitting on your face."

Tony's eyebrows rose. "That would definitely distract me," he said breathlessly. He grabbed for her wrist and she moved it away.

"But my mouth feels so empty." Amanda pouted. "I'm not sure what to do about it."

"*Amanda!*" Tony groaned. "Get your sexy little ass up here before James gets back and we can both have a little snack."

"Coming." She turned and swung her leg over his chest, backing up until he grabbed her hips and pulled her down.

"Not yet you're not, but you'd better hang onto something," he rasped.

"Is that a hint?" Amanda sassed. But then his mouth connected with her clit, his lips wrapping around the tiny bundle of nerves and sucking hard. "Oh, *fuck*," she muttered, her hips bucking down involuntarily and hitting his chin with her pubic bone.

It was hard to concentrate, but she managed to focus on his bobbing cock in front of her face. Her mouth started to water when she caught sight of the bead of pre-cum about to drip off the head and ducked down to lap it up.

Tony groaned, the reverberations buzzing through her nerves.

The salty musk coated her tongue and she savored it for a moment before attending to her task in earnest. Her entire focus narrowed to his cock, the slide of the weight of him in her mouth, the spongy texture of the head as it rubbed over her soft palette, the scent of the dark curls covering the base that she buried her nose in over and over...

She was shaken from the almost hypnotic trance by the toe-curling orgasm that swept through her. Tony's cock fell from her lips as she gasped and whimpered, her nails digging into his thighs.

"That's it, sunshine," James crooned. "Take your pleasure. Ride his face."

His dirty talk practically caressed her body, goosebumps spreading over her skin. When the aftershocks ended, she sagged over Tony's body. "I'm not sure I can move," she mumbled into his muscled thigh.

"I can lift you," James offered.

"Sounds good. I want Tony inside me." Amanda wiggled her hips a little.

"Come here." James rolled her into his arms, cradling her for a moment before flipping her around until she was facing Tony properly. "I'm going to lube you up now."

Amanda cuddled into Tony's arm, tilting her chin up to fuse their mouths together. She could taste herself on his tongue. Her shiver of pleasure from the kiss redoubled in intensity when James pressed a finger inside her, stretching her carefully.

"You feel so good," James groaned, slowly rocking his fingers into her. "You're dripping for us."

"I think..." Amanda gasped, coming up for air. "I think some of that is due to Tony's enthusiasm."

"Yeah it is," Tony drawled. "You taste so good, I couldn't stop drooling." He ran his hands down her back to cup her ass, grinding her against his cock. "Are you ready?"

"Yes." She tilted her hips far enough forwards to notch his head against her opening.

"Hang on, I haven't lubed Tony up yet," James cautioned. "Can I?"

"Don't make it weird, man. You've had my cock in your mouth," Tony said dryly.

Amanda felt James bumping up against her slick folds with the back of his knuckles.

Tony blew out a sharp breath across her shoulder, closing his eyes and tipping his head back. "Okay," he croaked. "I think that's good."

"All set," James said in agreement, twisting his hand around to drag over her clit before he pulled away.

Amanda stared into Tony's eyes as she reached between them to grip his slick cock in her hand and aim it properly. The flecks of gold, green, and hazel mesmerized her for a moment, his pupils dilated with desire. The head of his cock breaching her, stretching her, brought her back to the present.

Tony's hands rested passively on her hips, not exerting any pressure downwards, but they twitched and his short fingernails dragged over her skin for a moment before he flexed and it stopped.

"I'm not made of glass," Amanda said breathlessly. "I won't break if you're a little rough with me."

"We're still learning each other," Tony replied. "I'm going to be cautious for a while."

"Not too long, I hope." Amanda settled at the base of his cock, her eyes closing gently as she got used to the feel of him deep within her. He twitched and she hummed happily. "I like it rough sometimes."

"Good to know," Tony said, his voice strained. "Are you going to move? You're so tight."

Amanda clenched her inner muscles and a muscle in his jaw jumped. "Your mouth looks distractingly kissable," she said, leaning forwards and pressing a tiny kiss to the center of his sternum right over an inky black flower. Kissing her way up to his collarbone, which she bit lightly, she reveled in the bruising grip he had on her hips. Traveling higher, she finally reached his mouth, nibbling on his lower lip before darting her tongue into his mouth to tangle with his. Their breath mingled as they moved their lips together, her hips rocking with slight movements that made him shift within her, the weight of him heavy in her pelvis.

"God," he groaned. "This is beautiful torture." One hand left her hips to cradle her head, his fingers snagging in her wet hair as he tilted her head to the side. "Please," he whispered against her lips.

Amanda pressed their foreheads together, eyes meeting once more, and breath mingling in the infinitesimal space between them. "Is this okay?" she asked quietly.

"Yes. Anything. Everything. Amanda, I love you," he replied, running his hand over her hair.

Suddenly, she felt like she had to blink back tears. Everything that had happened between the three of them had led them to this moment, to having sex—no, making love with—her best friends in the world. Slowly she lifted her hips, Tony's cock dragging along her inner walls, her nose bumping against his as they kept eye contact, and then she dropped.

A moan exploded from her, Tony hitting a spot deep within her that she had never been able to find on her own.

At the same time, Tony shouted, "*Fuck!*"

"Oh God," Amanda rasped, her throat dry. "This is so much more than I expected."

"Sorry," Tony said. "I can put on a—"

"No, not *you*," Amanda clarified. "This. Us. Being together." She reached out for James and felt her fingers wrapped up in his bigger hand. "Emotionally."

"Well, physically, I think I'm going to explode if you don't move again," Tony drawled. "I feel like a teenager here."

Amanda giggled a little breathlessly, and felt more like herself. "Yeah, alright." She let go of James and propped herself up a little higher, bouncing her hips up and down on his cock. Her breasts swung freely from the motions.

Tony started helping her move, pulling her down harder and harder on each successive thrust. "You make me so hard," he grunted. "I'm going to come soon."

"So am I," she gasped. "Yes Tony, come inside me. Paint me white."

"Fuck," he muttered, his hips thrusting up on each downwards stroke of hers. "What do you need to get you there?"

"A little more," she pleaded.

"I got you," James said unexpectedly, pressing up against her back. His arms wrapped around her waist, his fingers playing over her clit like a virtuoso on a piano.

"Oh, *God*," she cried, and then she was exploding into a thousand tiny pieces, only connected to the Earth by the feeling of her men touching her body.

Her arms gave out and she collapsed onto Tony, lungs fighting for air.

"That was amazing," Amanda gasped. "I've never felt a connection like that before."

James slipped his hand from between their bodies and moved to sit beside them.

Tony pressed a lazy kiss to her temple. "Waxing poetic already? We're not half done with you yet."

"James, I want you to love me," she said, twisting her body to look at him. Tony helped her slide off of his softening penis, both groaning at the loss of contact.

"I already love you," teased James, curving a hand over her hip.

"I want you to *make* love to me," corrected Amanda, smiling, rolling onto her back beside Tony. "You know what I mean."

"I think we should have a snack first. I've got some news that I've been dying to tell you since I got here."

"Really?" Amanda stretched her arms over her head, intrigued. "What is it?"

James didn't say anything for a moment, staring at her body with a slack mouth.

Tony nudged James with a foot. "Dude."

"Sorry." James gave himself a shake. "It's hard to believe I'm not dreaming. Seeing you laid out in front of me like this is more than a little distracting."

"I can think of three solutions to your problem," Amanda said.

"Only three?" Tony muttered under his breath.

"One, you make love to me now and then tell us your news, two, I get dressed so I'm not a distraction, or three, you tell us the jist of your news and *then* we fuck our brains out." Amanda grinned at him.

"You're not getting dressed anytime soon," James growled. "I want you naked as long as possible."

"Agreed," Tony chimed in.

"The paperwork for the house is all signed," James said quickly.

"Oh!" Amanda clapped her hands in delight. "That's awesome! I'm excited to move in!"

"We'll be living together." James crawled up her body, nuzzling her breasts as he passed them. "And I can't wait to christen every single square inch of space with the two of you." He hiked one of her knees up around his hips and slid into her, Tony's spend easing his passage.

"Oh God, that feels good," she gasped.

"So tight," James gritted through his teeth.

"Didn't believe me?" chuckled Tony, lying on his side beside them.

"Oh, I did," replied James. "But it's another thing to feel her for myself." He slowly drew back and re-entered her, his powerful legs flexing.

"Oh James, keep doing that," moaned Amanda. "Oh God!" Her eyes flew open wide when the spot he hit made sparks shiver through her nerves. "Do that again! Right there! Oh, fuck yes!" she cried out.

"The noises you make," James said admiringly. "I could live off the sounds of you in ecstasy."

"Now look who's being poetic," Tony teased.

"It'll be your turn next," Amanda said, turning her head to look at him. He was slowly stroking his cock, already half hard again and her mouth watered. James pressed his mouth to the column of her neck, tongue laving over her pulse point up to a spot behind her ear that made her whimper.

"To be poetic?" Tony asked.

"That too," she mumbled, tipping her head back up to accept James's kiss on her lips.

They kissed her differently, she noted distractedly. Tony was all about the long strokes of their tongues, and James spent more time on her lips in a gentle rhythm that was counter to the snap of his hips.

I wonder what it would be like to watch them kiss each other? she thought, and mentally shook the idea away. *Don't push. Just because they love each other doesn't mean they're in love with each other.*

James ground his hips against hers and she gasped again. "Stay with me, sunshine," he murmured. "What do you need?"

"I think I need to be fucked on all fours," she said.

A slow grin spread across his face. "Hell yeah." He pulled out the next second, flipped her over, and was back inside her before she had the chance to miss him.

Amanda shouted her pleasure into the hot afternoon air as James continued to pound into her, his balls slapping against her clit. He kept up a ferocious pace, sliding in and out of her more and more easily with each successive pulse.

Her walls tightened. She could feel her orgasm's approach like a wave crashing into shore.

James groaned. "Don't come yet, Amanda. Hold onto it, wait for me."

Amanda writhed underneath him, her arms giving out as she fell onto her elbows.

"Fuck, Amanda, come now!" he growled.

She could actually see the muscles in her arms shaking, she came so hard. She couldn't hold herself up any longer, and crashed onto the mattress, turning her head to the side so she wouldn't squish her face.

"Wow," breathed Tony into the silence. "Watching you lose control like that is damn sexy." He brushed his fingers along Amanda's back, lingering on her ass. "It might be a good idea to refuel a bit before the next round."

"I suppose," Amanda mumbled. "As long as I don't have to get dressed."

"Never," both men said at once.

Amanda chuckled. "Then you two aren't allowed either."

"Fine by me. Better access," Tony said, lightly tapping her ass.

James pulled out and she groaned at the loss.

"You are going to end up making a mess," James said.

"I'm not sure I care about that right now," Amanda retorted. "Every muscle in my body is so relaxed."

"You'll care later," Tony pointed out. "Hang on."

The mattress hammock swayed as he got off, and then again when he returned.

"Lift your hips," James said.

"I can't move."

Tony chuckled. "Here, I'll spread my towel out, and we'll roll her onto it."

"I'm a sushi!" Amanda chirped as they rolled her onto her back.

"It's a good thing I love you," James said dryly.

"You've known me my whole life," Amanda replied, stretching her arms over her head and arching her back. "Why would I curb my weirdness now?"

"Your weirdness only makes you more perfect for us," Tony said, skating his fingertips over her tummy.

Amanda shook her head sadly. "I'm glad you feel that way. Not everyone did, and it hurt."

James frowned. "Who?"

"It doesn't matter."

"Crystal, wasn't it?" Tony said.

"She's not a bad person," Amanda defended her absent ex. "She was just...not the right person for me."

"People," James corrected firmly. "We're yours for as long as you'll have us."

Amanda beamed up at them. "Forever then."

Chapter Twenty

Flashback: Crystal

Amanda slid the last textbook into place on her bookshelf and pulled out her phone to take a picture of her dorm room.

"Finished unpacking," she muttered under her breath as she typed. "Third year, here I come. Are you ready for me?" She posted it to her Instagram and had two comments before she'd sat on the foot of her bed.

Tony had written, *Just a little "light" reading* and James had added, *I know where to buy my next doorstop.*

Amanda chuckled to herself and opened the video call app to find the call for the three of them. "I'm guessing neither of you are as on top of things as I am," she said when it connected and she could see her best friends.

"Definitely not," Tony said. "I got into SF two hours ago. I barely made it into my dorm."

"You didn't even bother putting the sheets on the bed before lying on it," James teased.

"I was too tired! My flight left ridiculously early this morning!" Tony complained.

"It was a long flight," Amanda consoled him. "Don't rest too much or you won't sleep tonight."

"Yes, Mum." Tony rolled his eyes.

"I'm about halfway done," James said. "The bus to Boston wasn't too bad, but navigating the station with my luggage was a nightmare. I think every student arrived today."

"I bet. I'm thinking of going out tonight." Amanda bit her lip. "Do you think I should? Maybe I shouldn't."

"Go for it!" Tony exclaimed, sitting up in bed. "You work so hard during the rest of the year."

"You deserve a night of fun before bending to the grindstone," James added. "Maybe someone on your floor will want to go with you."

"That's a good idea." Amanda opened her tiny closet and flipped through the hangers. "What do you think about this one?" She pulled out a black halter mini dress and draped it against herself.

Tony whistled. "Hot stuff."

"What he said," James said with a grin. "But only if someone else is with you."

Amanda waved her hand at the screen. "I'll be fine. Thanks for your concern. I was thinking of heading to the gay bar just off campus. It's like a block and a half from my dorm, very well lit. There's a hot new DJ tonight, according to the announcement I saw in my lobby, so I'm sure I can convince someone to join me."

"Not to be repetitive, but if you're dressed like that, anyone will say yes to going anywhere with you," James said.

Amanda blushed. "You think so?"

"Are we in the habit of paying empty compliments?" Tony demanded.

"Thanks guys. I should get ready. It's getting late."

"Have a great night."

Hanging up with the guys was always difficult, but that night seemed harder than most. She wished they were here with her, that she was going out to dance with them instead of strangers.

Tony's whistle echoed in her mind once the dress was on. The neckline plunged low between her breasts, revealing her tan line. She and James had been working at the city pools that summer, teaching teenagers how to be lifeguards in between guarding stints, and half the time they'd been outside in the bright sunshine. She'd tanned well, her usually pale skin a light brown. However, she'd been wearing a modest one-piece, so the tanned skin stopped halfway down the neckline of her dress.

She shrugged. Nobody would be able to see it in the dark club anyway.

She picked strappy shoes with a low heel and buckled them on before grabbing a clutch for her phone, keys, and money for cover.

The common room was busy with other students, several of whom were dressed to go out. Amanda swallowed down her nerves and approached a small group of people who looked to be about her age.

They welcomed her instantly, and when she suggested the club, they agreed and headed out.

The line outside the club was fairly short, and after waiting for a few minutes, they were let inside.

The pounding beat settled in Amanda's heart, making her hips and feet move before she'd even made it to the dance floor. She let the music flow through her, half closing her eyes as she danced.

"Mind if I dance with you?" a girl shouted near Amanda's ear.

She had hazel eyes framed by thick black glasses, her brown hair short in a pixie cut with a flower hair clip as decoration.

"Sure," Amanda replied with a smile.

"Come here often?" the girl said, placing a hand low on Amanda's hip. Then she made a face. "I'm sorry, that was a terrible line."

Amanda chuckled. "I don't mind. I haven't been here since last year after exams ended, and I don't really come all that often during the school year."

"Just checking, but university, right?" the girl said cautiously.

"Yes, I'm a junior," Amanda reassured her.

"Phew!" The girl made an exaggerated motion of wiping her brow. "I graduated a little over two years ago now. I work for the city with trauma patients."

Amanda was impressed. "After only two years?"

"I have a supervisor," the girl said with a smile. "My name is Crystal, by the way."

"Nice to meet you," Amanda replied, giving her name in return.

The song changed to a slinky beat and the dancers around them started grinding against each other.

"Is this okay?" Crystal asked, moving closer to Amanda and putting one leg between hers.

Amanda looked down into Crystal's eyes and bit her lip nervously. "I don't really know what I'm doing."

"Do you want to?"

The other girl's waist was petite under her fingers, her thigh firm between her legs. Amanda swallowed hard. "Yeah, I think I do."

Crystal grinned and Amanda's heart skipped a beat. The shorter girl trailed her fingers up Amanda's body to cup the back of her neck, pulling her head down. "I think you know how this part works, yeah?"

Amanda nodded, her breath coming faster. Before she over-thought it, she ran one finger over Crystal's mouth before tilting her head and brushing her lips with hers. They were as soft as they looked. Crystal begged for entry, and she opened to her. Amanda felt dizzy from the overload of emotions swirling through her body. They broke apart with a gasp.

"Whoa," said Crystal. "You sure know how to kiss."

Amanda raised a hand to her tingling lips. "So do you."

They danced together for a few more songs, lips joining often. Crystal discovered that if she licked Amanda's collarbone, she would shake slightly. Amanda found that Crystal was sensitive just behind her ear.

"Did you want to come back to my place?" Amanda said shyly. "I'm beginning to feel indecent."

Crystal grinned at her. "I was wondering when you'd ask. I'm down."

"Great." Amanda grinned at her for a moment until she realized the other girl was waiting for her to lead. Giving herself a shake, Amanda grabbed Crystal by the hand and led her off the dance floor. Passing by one of the girls she had come with, she shouted, "I'm heading out. See you later!"

"Later!" the girl said, waving at her while sipping from a blue drink with a straw and umbrella.

The silence outside was almost oppressive after the pounding beat of the club. Amanda took a deep breath, missing the salty air of the Atlantic.

"Are you having second thoughts?" Crystal asked quietly.

"Nope! Just relaxing. I think I was tense in there."

"A need to perform?" Crystal suggested before making a face. "Sorry. Sometimes I can't turn off the therapist."

Amanda chuckled. "It's okay. I'm not used to being around a lot of people, unless they're about waist height."

"What's your program? Something with kids?"

"Oh, no. I'm around kids all summer because I'm a lifeguard. I'm studying business management."

"That's a switch!"

"Eh. I need an underwear job, you know?"

Crystal laughed. "An underwear job? Like working for Victoria's Secret?"

"No!" Amanda joined in her laughter. "It's just something we say at work. Spandex is not great to wear all day, and wet spandex is worse. So we talk about one day in the future when we'll get a job where we can wear underwear instead of a bathing suit."

"I see." Crystal's eyes twinkled with mischief. "What kind of underwear do you like to wear?"

"Uh, I, ah, it's not the sexiest," Amanda hedged.

"We're heading back to your dorm to do a little more than make out, right? I'm probably going to get to see your underwear." Crystal swung their hands between them. "To be honest, I'm more interested in what's underneath them."

Amanda swallowed hard. She'd known what this invite meant, but having it stated like that was making her nervous. "I normally wear cotton bikinis, but I've got a beige thong on tonight," she whispered.

"How riské," Crystal said with a wink.

"This is me," Amanda said, gesturing up at the building they were approaching and ignoring the butterflies in her stomach.

"Hey...look at me." Crystal pulled her to a stop under a streetlight. "We don't have to do anything you don't want to do. You want to make out, that's amazing. You want to strip down and grind on each other until we come? I'm good. And I'm always down to go down. You set the limit."

Feeling like she couldn't quite catch her breath, Amanda squeezed Crystal's hand. "Thanks. I...that all sounds hot. I don't think I can move another step until I kiss you again."

"Yeah?" Crystal smirked and backed up against the pole, pulling Amanda with her. "Then kiss me," she said, tipping her head back.

Feeling bold, Amanda slid her knee between Crystal's legs. "You're beautiful," she said, caressing the other girl's cheekbones with her thumbs.

Crystal's lips parted on a light gasp, and Amanda swooped down to scrape her lower lip with her teeth. "Come up to my room. I'm gong to kiss you until you can't breathe, and then I'm going to fuck you with my tongue until you can't walk," she whispered in Crystal's ear.

Crystal let out a tiny whimper. "Yeah, sounds good to me. Please touch me, Amanda."

But Amanda pulled away, showing huge restraint in her opinion. "Are you as eager as I am? As *wet* as I am? Because if I touch you now, we'll get arrested for public indecency."

"Fuck," Crystal panted. "I really hope your room is close." She grabbed Amanda's hand and pulled her towards the door.

"We'll make it," Amanda said with a chuckle. She was grateful she didn't have to fumble with keys–the main door unlocked with a fob and her dorm room with her thumb print.

"High tech," Crystal murmured, pushing Amanda against the back of the door. "I wasn't super into it before this, but it's kinda sexy watching you do that. Now touch me, Amanda." She said her name like a caress.

"Where?" breathed Amanda.

Crystal shivered. "Start with my breasts," she replied. She tugged on the bow at the base of her neck, and her shimmery black shirt fell forwards, exposing her to Amanda's greedy eyes.

Hardly daring to breathe, Amanda cupped both in her hands and ran her thumbs over the nipples. Crystal encouraged her with a moan. Feeling bolder, Amanda rolled the tiny nubs between her finger and thumb. When Crystal gasped, she pressed her mouth to the other girl's. Amanda massaged her gently, memorizing the feel of her satin skin under her palms.

"That feels good," groaned Crystal.

"Let's get you out of these clothes," Amanda said, sliding her hands between the shirt and checked skirt.

"Only if you strip too," Crystal said.

"Okay." Amanda flushed, nervous to be naked in front of someone she'd just met.

Fabric fluttered to the floor, abandoned by the girls as they stripped to their underwear.

"This is so sexy," Amanda said, tracing the edge of Crystal's lacy black thong. "I didn't realize how good it would look."

"What do you mean?" Crystal asked, walking over to Amanda's bed and perching on the foot.

"I told you I don't have sexy underwear. I didn't really think about how it would look from the other person's perspective."

"Come here," Crystal said, leaning back on her elbows.

Amanda swayed her hips a little more than necessary as she crossed the room to stand between Crystal's legs.

"You're stunning," Crystal whispered. "Underwear doesn't change a thing; it's just the packaging." She reached up and ran her fingertips over Amanda's breasts, making the younger girl shiver. "We should get more comfortable." Dropping her arm, she shifted up on the bed, stretching out as if she belonged there.

"If underwear is the packaging—" Amanda crawled over Crystal and nuzzled her lower belly "—can I unwrap you now?"

"You were one of those kids who peeked at their Christmas presents, weren't you?" Crystal teased.

"Never!" Amanda sat up straight with a gasp. "I loved the surprise. But I tried to guess what was in them based on the shape. My parents swapped boxes with my friends' parents so we wouldn't be able to tell. I almost cried when I unwrapped a box with a remote control car."

"What was actually in it?" Crystal asked, cocking her head to the side.

"A Barbie camper van," Amanda said dreamily. "But then my friend was really confused when he opened his present!"

Crystal chuckled. "That would be a surprise for a boy if he hadn't put it on his wishlist."

"So can I?" Amanda asked again, skating her fingers up Crystal's legs. The smooth shave made her shiver. "Your legs are like silk."

"I'll give you the name of my moisturizer," Crystal murmured. "Yes, go ahead."

Biting her lip, Amanda curled her fingers around the skimpy elastic and pulled down. She moved slowly, revealing Crystal to her greedy eyes. "You're so pretty," she breathed, backing off the bed as she pulled the thong off Crystal's feet and draped it on the edge of the bed.

Crystal blushed. "Thanks."

Amanda crawled back onto the bed, pushing Crystal's knees apart. "I've never seen a pussy up close before," she admitted.

"Am I an experiment?" Crystal asked hesitantly, her hands restlessly skimming her stomach.

Shaking her head, Amanda said, "No, I know I like women. I've kissed them before. I've just never gone this far with a woman before." She traced her fingers along Crystal's outer lips.

"With a woman. You've been with a man?"

"I'm bisexual," Amanda said. "I'm also not a virgin."

"Virginity as a concept is highly overrated," Crystal said flatly.

"Oh thank God, I completely agree!" Amanda said enthusiastically. "Can I continue?"

"Do you have protection?"

"I grabbed a handful of protective stuff from the school LGBT center. I might have a dental dam in there," Amanda said. "I put it all in a box in my top bedside drawer."

"I'll look. I'm nosy like that," Crystal said. "Besides, I don't want you to stop touching me."

Amanda smiled. "Go ahead." Her fingers dipped slightly, floating over the outer edge of the other girl's thin inner lips.

"You are such a tease," Crystal gasped. "Touch my clit, *please*!"

"Where is that?" Amanda said, playing up the teasing. She spread Crystal further, mouth watering when she saw how wet she was. She ran her fingers through the wetness, spreading it around. "This looks like the right spot." The nub at the apex of her lips slipped under her fingertips, hard with arousal. "How nice of you to pierce it. Makes it easier to find."

Crystal, whose hips had jolted when Amanda had rubbed her the right way, could only moan as she dug through the box of condoms.

"Does the piercing feel good? Can I tug on it a bit?" Amanda asked, curious.

"Yes, and a bit. Here!" She tossed a packet down between her legs.

"Strawberry scented?" Amanda read. "Sounds delicious." She opened the dental dam and spread it over Crystal's sex. "Where to start?" she hummed. She didn't give Crystal time to answer, putting pressure around her clit, sliding her lips back and forth before fastening her mouth around the tiny button and fluttering her tongue over the piercing.

"Oh my God, Amanda!" cried Crystal, her thighs shaking under Amanda's arms. Her back bowed up.

Amanda grinned, humming appreciatively at the noises Crystal was making. She rubbed her fingers over her opening through the wet latex.

"You're making me come!" Crystal groaned. "Ohhhhh, Amanda!" Crystal reached up and grabbed onto the top of Amanda's headboard, knocking her stuffed bear off the side of the bed.

"Wow, that was hot," Amanda breathed, discarding the square of latex in her garbage at the side of the bed. She crawled higher up Crystal's body and pressed their torsos together. Nuzzling into the girl's neck, short hair tickling Amanda's nose, she mouthed at Crystal's skin, tasting salt and perfume.

"That was amazing," Crystal said weakly. "Your turn."

"You can take a moment to recover first," Amanda said, mouthing closer to Crystal's earlobe.

Crystal shivered. "I'm going to finger you."

"Sounds fun."

"Understatement." Crystal pulled away, pushing Amanda onto her back. "But first, I need to worship these breasts of yours."

"They're not much," Amanda said dismissively.

"Wait until I get through with you. Then you'll see that they're perfect."

Sensations washed over Amanda as Crystal thoroughly took her apart and put her back together again. Overwhelmed, it felt like all she could do was breathe.

Crystal cuddled up with her again, wiping her sweaty hair off her face. "Watching you come is my favorite thing in the world."

Amanda smiled and joined their lips together. "Want to sleep over?"

"I feel like I'm in middle school, phrased that way," Crystal said with a laugh. "But sure, I can stay the night."

"Good. Bathroom's just down the hall. I don't have a spare robe, but I can grab you some loose clothes?"

"Thanks."

They brushed their teeth—Crystal using her finger—and used the toilet before heading back to the room.

Amanda scooped her bear off the ground and dusted him off. "Sorry Teddy. There you go," she whispered to him, placing him gently on her end table.

"Do you still sleep with your stuffed animal?" Crystal asked, a strange tone in her voice.

"Sometimes," Amanda said with a shrug. "Usually only if I'm feeling really homesick. My grandfather gave him to me on the day I was born. He's been through a lot with me." She crawled into bed and held up the sheet. "You coming?"

She thought she imagined the momentary hesitation before Crystal joined her readily enough.

"Do you want to grab coffee with me some time?" Amanda asked shyly, tracing her fingers over the delicate bones in Crystal's wrist. "See if we can build a connection that's beyond sexual?"

"I'm willing to see where this goes. We'll exchange numbers in the morning."

"Great." Amanda snuggled deeper into her pillow and drifted off to sleep.

Chapter Twenty-One

Tony

"There's a platter of fruits and cheese in the fridge," Amanda directed. "Tony and I cut and arranged them last night because we figured we wouldn't want to be out of the pool for very long today."

"Brilliant," James said. "I'll grab it. You," he pointed at Tony, "keep her occupied." He winked.

Tony's heart felt like it goddamn *fluttered* in his chest at that wink. "I can think of a few ways," he said, skimming his hand up Amanda's body to cup a breast. His hand was so big, he covered her completely.

"Good man," James said before disappearing into the house.

"Don't worry," Tony said, dropping a kiss on her shoulder. "I'm not going to get you too riled up before we eat something to get our energy back."

"I wasn't worried," Amanda said, arching her back so her breast pressed into his palm. "And I'm already riled. Can you take the edge off?"

"Darlin', you're going to kill me," Tony groaned, his cock throbbing in anticipation at being inside her again. "How about I tongue fuck you to orgasm again?"

Amanda squirmed. "Are you sure you want to?"

"Didn't you like it?" Tony half sat up in alarm.

"I loved it," she reassured him with a hand on his arm. "I'm just spilling over with both your and James's cum and I wasn't sure you'd be okay with that."

"Oh." Tony's cock twitched at the idea of tasting James. "It doesn't bother me in the slightest."

"Yeah?" Amanda's pupils dilated with desire. "Can you please?"

"Please what?" Tony asked, feigning ignorance. He bent his head and drew her nipple into his mouth.

"Please suck my clit," Amanda gasped.

"You say the dirtiest things," Tony said admiringly, a slow smile ticking up the corner of his mouth. "Happy to oblige you." He gracefully flipped himself into position between her knees and hauled her ass up into the air. "But I'm not going to take it easy on you."

"I expect nothing less," Amanda said breathlessly.

"Good girl," Tony rumbled, hiking her thighs over his shoulders and fastening his lips around her clit.

"Oh *God*," she moaned, her hands flying to support herself, her shoulders pressing awkwardly against the mattress of the hammock.

"Give me a taste," James rumbled from behind Tony. "I've been dying for her."

Tony lifted his head long enough to say, "Then get over here." He propped Amanda up higher, delving his tongue inside her and tipping his head far enough back that James could join him in feasting on her pussy.

The taste of the three of them mingled on his tongue and he groaned, his hips stuttering in the air for a beat, and then James's cheek was pressed against his nose.

Hot puffs of air hit his face from James, near enough that if they tilted their heads just right, they could messily kiss each other. Tony slammed his eyes shut, hoping that would help, but it only heightened his other senses.

"Fuck, I'm going to come untouched," he muttered.

James growled, "Come in our girl."

"Amanda?" Tony gasped.

"Yes!" she moaned.

Needing no further permission, Tony dropped her onto her back and slid home just in time to pump another load inside her. "God," he whispered, tipping his head back, his chest heaving for breath.

Amanda whined, "So close!"

"Let me," James said, nudging Tony out of the way.

"Anything else needed from the kitchen?" Tony asked.

"Yeah, I couldn't grab the glasses for the juice," James said, arranging himself between Amanda's thighs. "But you don't have to go right away. Get your legs under you first."

"I'm okay." Tony got to his feet, trying to ignore the sounds of James slurping his cum out of their girlfriend. His cock twitched weakly and he shook his head with a slight smile. *Relax, bud,* he mentally told himself. *You'll be back out there soon enough.*

He took his time, going to the bathroom to relieve himself before grabbing the glasses James had left out on the counter. He could see his friends through the kitchen window, the muscles working in James's back as he continued to eat Amanda out. Her cries of pleasure were loud enough that he could hear them through the glass.

His cock throbbed again and he couldn't stop the chuckle that escaped him. "Is it possible to die from too many orgasms?"

Walking back outside, he handed the glasses to James, who was now sitting beside a splayed-out Amanda.

"Pass me the tray?" James asked, gesturing at the table.

The large weighted tray contained everything else they needed for their snack, but Tony removed the pitcher of lemonade before moving it. His hands weren't steady enough for that.

James gave him a knowing look, which Tony returned with a shrug and a smile.

"Want something sweet?" James said to Amanda as Tony joined them with the pitcher.

"I could go for salty-sweet," Amanda purred, obviously eyeing James's hard cock bobbing against his hard stomach.

"Food first," James scolded her playfully.

Tony selected a strawberry and held it up for her. "Do you want it?"

She nodded eagerly and opened her mouth.

"Close your eyes," Tony ordered. When she obeyed, he brought it to her lips, letting her take a tiny bite of the tip.

"Mmm, Tony, it's going to drip," she protested, her brow furrowing.

Tony chuckled. "I'm counting on it." He caught a drip in his free hand and brought the berry to her nipples, circling around them and getting them sticky with juice.

"Lean back against me," James rumbled, pulling gently at her shoulders until she lay against his chest.

Tony followed, prowling over her. He gave her the berry and latched onto her breast, sucking up all the juice he'd spread over her. He scraped his teeth over the tight buds gently and she gasped, hands flying up to hold his head in place.

"Harder!" she whimpered, hips thrusting up, searching for friction. "Ahhh!" she cried out, fingernails digging into his scalp.

Cock twitching back to life, Tony flicked his tongue over the bud clenched between his teeth, making her writhe underneath him.

"Fuck, yes, need more!" she whined. "James, I need you inside me now!"

"We'd knock the food over," James said mildly.

"Then use your fingers!" Amanda begged. "Please!"

Tony felt James's fingers questing between their bodies, brushing against his hardening cock, and fought the moan that threatened to escape.

Amanda moaned instead. "Yes, James. Another one. Stretch me, come on!" She loosened her grip on Tony's hair and he relaxed his jaw, changing to a delicate suckle that had her thrusting against his leg, James's fingers hard against his thigh. "Fuck, Tony, that feels so good!"

For a few minutes, the only sounds were her heavy breathing and the slick squishing of James's fingers as he worked them in and out of her body.

"Another!" Amanda gasped. "James, come on, I'm not going to break."

"If I put another in, I'll be fisting you," James rasped. "I don't want to hurt you."

"Oh God, *yes*," Amanda exclaimed, arching her back. "Yes, put your fist in me. Let me take it."

"*Fuck*," whimpered Tony, releasing her breast to press his head against her sternum. "That's so fucking hot."

"Get the lube, Tony," James ordered. He pulled his fingers out of her, dripping with her juices, and spread her legs, draping them over his knees to hold them apart.

"Can I change my mind?" Amanda asked, panting.

"Of course," James said immediately. He shifted to close her legs, but she put her hands on his to stop them. "Are you alright? Did I hurt you?"

"I'm fine. Not hurt." Amanda reached behind her back to run her fingers over James's hard cock. "I want to sit on you while we eat."

James groaned, dropping his forehead against her shoulder blade. "Yeah, that sounds like delicious torture. You promise you'll eat? You keep distracting me."

Amanda giggled. "It wasn't me this time, it was Tony."

Tony shrugged. "Guilty as charged."

Amanda sank down over James's cock, her head back against his shoulder and legs spread wide over his thighs.

The dark of James's cock surrounded by the pink of Amanda's lips made a beautiful picture, one Tony wished he could immortalize.

"You look amazing like that," Tony said, his voice barely a rasp. He cleared his throat. "Lemonade?"

"Yes, please," Amanda said, only a tiny catch in her voice.

"You?" Tony asked James, meeting his eyes. There was a fire within their depths that made Tony's heart stutter.

"I don't think I'll be able to eat like this," James ground out through a clenched jaw. "Make sure she does."

"Yes, sir," Tony said with a mock salute. He started pouring a glass for Amanda.

James tilted his head, a smirk playing over his lips. "Don't call me 'Sir' unless you're ready to find out what that really means."

Tony's hands shook a little and a splash of lemonade fell down onto the towel that had been under Amanda. *I'd forgotten that James had joined a BDSM club with Nicolas,* he thought. He put down the pitcher and gave Amanda the glass with a lowered gaze, half-afraid of looking at James again in case he read too much on his face.

"Hey," James said, and Tony's eyes flew up unbidden. James looked embarrassed. "I wouldn't do anything without complete consent, yeah?"

"I know that," Tony was quick to reassure him.

"We're good?"

"Yeah, we're good," Tony parroted, feeling silly. "Cheese?" he offered to Amanda.

"Brie on a ritz, please," she said.

He got it for her before repeating the process for himself. He looked up at James again, quirking an eyebrow in question, but James shook his head. "I'll eat when you two are fucking again."

Tony chuckled. "Sure, man."

"I was hoping I could make another request," Amanda said, biting her lip.

"Anything," James replied.

"I want Tony to suck on my clit while you're inside me. I want him to make me come while I'm stuffed full of you and then after we're finished eating, I want to be fucked so hard that I pass out from pleasure."

James chuckled. "I will certainly give it my best shot. Tony?"

"Hell yes!" Tony croaked. His mouth watered; not only would he be feasting on her clit, but James's cock and balls would be right in his face. He would have to resist the urge to travel down from her pretty pussy and lick at his best friend. *Platonic, ha! Not on my part.*

He latched onto her clit, alternating sucking and flicking his tongue, and hummed, pleased, when Amanda's hands found their way into his hair again. His chin moved as he played with Amanda, rubbing against James's sac, and Tony had to anchor his hips to stop himself from rutting into the mattress, he was so overcome by desire for both of his friends.

"She's getting close," James rumbled and Tony shivered at his tone.

Tony redoubled his efforts, burying his face in her body. He was soon rewarded; her fingers clenched in his hair and her body shook under his onslaught.

"Fuck," James growled, head thrown back. "Fuck, that's tight."

"Too much, too much!" Amanda pulled Tony's head back. "Oh my God!" She sagged against James.

"Still good with the plan?" Tony gasped, resting his forehead on their thigh. He felt it quiver.

"No, I need to be fucked right now!" Amanda panted.

"Okay." Tony pushed the tray to the edge of the mattress and got to his feet, moving it to the table.

James pushed Amanda onto all fours on the mattress, rising up on his knees behind her. "You are so kinky, our perfect little girlfriend. Up for anything, aren't you?" He snapped his hips into her, punctuating each word with a sharp thrust. "Does it feel good to be fucked? Is this what you want?"

"Yes, yes, *yes*!" Amanda cried, her voice muffled by the mattress as she buried her face in it.

"Fuck," James muttered, his jaw clenching so hard Tony heard it creak. "This feels too good. I'm going to come."

"Not yet. I'm so close! James!"

"Shit," gasped James. He pumped his hips a few more times, but Tony knew he'd reached orgasm and Amanda hadn't yet.

"Tag in?" Tony said.

"Yeah. Damn, I'm sorry Amanda." James looked embarrassed.

"Don't be sorry," she said dreamily. "Come on, Tony. Give it to me." Amanda wiggled her ass in the air.

Tony couldn't look away from her gaping pussy. "You're so turned on," he murmured, running a finger around her loosened muscles. Tony was getting the beginnings of an idea. "Can I make a suggestion?"

"Does it involve me orgasming?" Amanda demanded petulantly.

"Most definitely. You were begging for James to fist you earlier."

"Are you suggesting what I think you're suggesting?" James interrupted, gaze pinning him in place.

Tony swallowed hard. "I might be. Would you be up for that?"

James stared at Tony.

"It's okay if you're not. We don't have to—"

"I think that would feel fucking amazing," James interrupted him.

"Can you fill me in?" Amanda pouted. "I'm feeling empty."

"Not for long, if you want to do this." Tony took a breath and explained, "If we can stretch you enough to take a fist, then you could take both of us."

Amanda's jaw dropped. "You'd both be fucking me at the same time?"

"Only if you want, of course," Tony said quickly.

"Oh fuck, yes!" Amanda wiggled her ass again. "Get to stretching me!"

James chuckled and smacked her ass. "Stay relaxed and it won't take long. Tony, would you like the honors?"

"How long do you think it'll take before you're back in business?" Tony asked, his gaze flicking down to James's softened cock.

"Not long, if I'm watching you stretch her open," James said.

"Why don't you lie on your back, darlin'," Tony suggested. "You'll be on your knees when we take you, so let's give them a break."

Once Amanda was settled, Tony slid three fingers into her, scissoring them easily. "Oh, we have fucked you good," he murmured appreciatively. "Feel how well you take me. I'm going to give you my pinky now. Yes, just relax. You're doing great." Tony thrust a couple times, feeling her muscles loosen. "Okay, I'm going to go a little deeper, up to the last knuckle. You'll feel a stretch... Oh, fuck, baby, you're taking me so well." He twisted his hand, curling his fingers up, making her hips jolt. "Feel good? You okay?"

"Feels so good!" Amanda groaned, her hips rocking slightly. "Give me more!"

Tony curled his thumb against his palm and slid his hand deeper into her body. He thrust a few times before attempting the widest part of his palm, hardly daring to breathe. "Fuck, Amanda, your body is amazing. Are you ready for this? Relax, darlin'." His free hand rubbed a loose rhythm over her clit and then he was inside her. Tony stared, slack-jawed, at her body wrapped around his wrist. His cock twitched. "Damn..."

James whistled quietly. "Fuck, that's amazing."

"Are you going to *move*?" Amanda whimpered, her legs moving restlessly. "Feels so full!"

Tony twisted his wrist, pulling out until the widest part of his palm was stretching her. Slowly, he curled his fingers into a fist and pushed back in.

Amanda came, her back arching and a flood of juices drenching his fist.

"Fuck," Tony whispered, pulling out again. There was less resistance now, her body accepting the width of his knuckles. He traced the outer edge with the fingers of his free hand, loving the clenching of her muscles around him. "I think she's ready for us." He looked up into James's dark eyes. "You good?"

"I am so ready."

"Who's under?"

"You. I'll guide both of us in." James kept his gaze on Amanda as he said this, but Tony could see his cheeks darken slightly.

"Guys, I want you in me!" Amanda begged, drawing their attention back to her. "Tony, lie down."

It took some creative positioning, but they managed to organize themselves; Tony on his back, Amanda straddling him, James behind her.

Amanda kissed him while Tony felt the large hand of his best friend grip his cock. Amanda's hips lowered until she was flat against him and suddenly there was another cock against his own.

His eyes rolled back as he felt her opening against his head, and then he was squeezing in, James's cock pulsing in tiny thrusts to help ease their passage.

"You good, darlin'?" Tony asked Amanda, who was breathing hard into his shoulder. His eyes met James's and his breath caught; James looked so powerful and sexy.

"Feels great. Intense. Connected. Love you both!" Amanda spoke in short bursts in between shallow breaths.

"We're going to start moving now, okay?" James said in a strangled voice. Amanda nodded vigorously.

Tony flexed his glutes, the motion shifting his hips enough that he could thrust in and out of her. He could feel James giving a long, slow thrust that blended well with his own rhythm.

Their eyes met again over Amanda's shoulder. James leaned closer and Tony's heart rate picked up a notch. *He looks like he's going to kiss... Her shoulder.* Swallowing his disappointment, Tony wiggled his hand between his body and Amanda's, sliding down until he could massage her clit with short flicks.

"Tony, James, I'm going to come!" Amanda gasped. "Fuck... I'm close. It's so much, I—" She cut herself off by biting into the meat of Tony's shoulder, her body tensing and shaking between them.

Tony felt James's cock pulse, warm liquid flowing over him, and then he was coming too, spilling inside her. "Wow," breathed Tony. He was panting for breath, feeling like he'd just run a marathon. "That was intense."

"So good," murmured Amanda. "Definitely not an every time thing. Special occasions only."

Tony chuckled, feeling James twitch within her. "Graduation, Fourth of July, Halloween, Christmas?"

"Don't forget the first day of living together," Amanda said, burying her nose in his neck. "Brilliant idea, that was. Can't wait." She chuckled slightly, the motion making her twitch around him. "We're never going to be clothed at home, are we?"

"I like undressing you too much for you to always be naked," Tony teased.

"How do you know that?" Amanda challenged. "I believe I stripped my own bikini today."

"Mostly," James added with a chuckle.

"If it means getting my hands on you, I'm going to like it," Tony said simply.

"Aww," Amanda said, melting on top of him.

"Not to ruin the moment, but I need to pull out," James said between gritted teeth.

"Boo," Amanda mumbled. "Go ahead." Her sharp hiss of breath accompanied James's movement, and then he was flopping down beside them.

"You're amazing, you know I think that, right?" he murmured, running a hand down her back.

His eyes flicked over to Tony's face for a moment, and Tony felt his cheeks burn. *Was James talking to him too?*

"My parents invited us over for dinner tonight," James continued as if Tony wasn't having a crisis right in front of him. "In case we didn't want to cook."

"Hmm, not cooking, but having to put on clothing," Tony said thoughtfully, squeezing Amanda's ass and making her squeak.

"Eventually your refractory periods will catch up to you," Amanda teased.

"You should go pee," James advised her.

She pouted. "I don't want to feel empty." She wiggled on top of Tony, his cock still buried inside her.

"I can get you a plug later," James said, tucking a strand of hair behind her ear. "But for now, safety first."

"I think we should go to your parents," Amanda said, pushing herself upright with what looked like great effort. "If we stay here, we'll forget to eat. As much as I'd rather stay naked, I need food."

"I'll text Dad," James said, reaching for his phone.

"Are we telling them?" Tony asked quietly, watching the combination of fluids gush down Amanda's leg. There was a puddle of sticky mess on his pelvis that he needed to wash off.

"Telling them what?" James asked distractedly while typing.

"I'm not keen on keeping you two a secret," Amanda said, pausing at the door into the house. "You're my boyfriends, right?" She sounded unsure of herself.

James and Tony exchanged glances. "Yes," they said in unison, and nodded at each other.

"I know it's unconventional, but our parents love us. They raised the three of us together. I doubt they'll have an issue with this," James said, pointing between the three of them.

"That's a relief." Amanda beamed at them. "I'm going to shower and change. Can one of you grab my bikini from the pool and hang it, please?" She disappeared into the house.

"Was that an invitation to join her?" Tony asked, eyebrows raised.

"I get the feeling that if she was going to invite us, she would have said so," James said, his phone back in the pocket of his pants. "I'll get her suit. You've got..." he indicated his belly with a wave of his hand. "Hang on, don't move."

He tossed Tony a roll of paper towels. "I think I'll head home to have a shower too," Tony said, making a face when the towels didn't do much more than spread the mess around. "Then I can put on something that includes a shirt."

James grinned. "I don't mind, but I'm sure my parents would appreciate it."

Tony found himself flushing again. *Is James flirting with me?* So much had changed already that afternoon, he wasn't sure he was ready for more. And what if he was reading James wrong?

"How do you feel?" James asked him quietly.

"In love, sore, lucky, amazed, happy," Tony said, matching his volume. "Take your pick. You?"

"Yeah, that sums it up," James said with a chuckle. "Did you feel like a third wheel at all?"

"Never. You?"

"Nope." James reached out and squeezed Tony's free hand. "I really think this will work. I love you, man."

"Love you too," Tony replied, heart aching to tell him that it was more than platonic. But if James didn't feel the same way, it could ruin everything.

At work on Monday, Tony felt like he was flying. He couldn't stop the grin that kept stretching across his face at inopportune times, and his kids were starting to notice.

"Tony, what are you smiling about?" asked Dan, one of his regulars.

"He looks like he's in love," said Brinn, another regular.

Am I that obvious? he thought, shaking his head. "If you have time to be speculating about my private life, then you're not focusing on your drills hard enough."

A chorus of groans met his words.

"What's this?" Tony put his hands on his hips. "I thought you were here to get better at soccer. Is that not why you're here?" he added sarcastically.

"I'm here because it was the only place that could take me all day," piped up a new kid. Tony hadn't quite caught all the new names yet.

"Well, while you're in my care, you will learn soccer drills. And at the end of the week, if you can score a goal on me, I'll buy all y'all ice cream."

An excited cheer went up.

"Notice I said 'if'," Tony clarified. "And you definitely won't manage it if you don't practice. Are we clear?"

"Yes, coach!"

"It's no wonder you're their favorite," Glenn murmured out of the side of his mouth while they watched the young teens dribble their soccer balls around cones.

"Because I bribe them?" Tony chuckled.

"Because they never notice when you distract them from questions about your personal life." Glenn snapped his head towards the field and raised his voice. "Amber! Watch the person in front of you, not your feet!"

"Nah, I think it's because I let you yell at them, and then I gently guide them afterwards."

"Sneaky bastard." Glenn stared out over the kids for a moment. "Mo, go around *each* pylon, no skipping!"

Tony jogged over to the end of the obstacle to greet the kids that had just finished. "Good job," he said, giving out high fives. "Way to focus." Once all the kids and Glenn had joined him, he went around to each kid, letting them know how they could improve.

"Tonyyyyyyyyyyy!"

"What the—" Tony cut himself off when he noticed expressions of delight on his charges' faces. "—heck?" he finished mildly. He took a deep breath, closing his eyes to find his calm before continuing his instructions to the kids. "Okay, try to apply what I've told you on your way back to the start. Once you get there, take a water break."

"How do you keep all that in your head at once?" Carolina purred, trying to latch onto his arm.

"By doing my job," Tony growled, shaking her off. "Is something wrong with one of your kids?"

She shrugged. "How should I know?"

Tony rolled his eyes. "Because it's your job? Now let me do mine." He jogged over to Glenn, his good mood almost ruined.

"Dude," Glenn said admiringly as they walked alongside the field.

"She's only chasing me because I'm not giving in," Tony grumbled. He shuddered. "She's not my type."

"Your type being..." Glenn prodded.

"Someone I enjoy being around." There went his grin again, breaking across his face without his permission.

Glenn chuckled. "You finally knocked boots with her, huh?"

Tony made a face. "Who says that?"

"Tossed her salad? Had some horizontal refreshment? Played with the kitten? Filled the cream donut? Conquered the fortress?"

"What?" Tony had to stop walking, bending over to put his hands on his knees as he spluttered with laughter. "Dude! You're killing me. What do you do, research that sh—stuff for your degree?"

"Yes, of course. I got my degree in linguistics, you know."

"I can't tell if you're joking or not," Tony said, narrowing his eyes at his friend.

Glenn shrugged. "Chicks dig witty banter, and linguistic chicks have big brains. They loved the word play."

"You do you, man." Tony clapped him on the back. They got back to the kids, who were sitting on the grass, drinking their water.

"Was that your girlfriend?" they chorused as if they had practiced.

Tony pinched the bridge of his nose above his sunglasses. "You kids aren't going to let this go, are you?"

"No," they replied, grinning.

"I am only going to talk about this once, so listen up." Tony waited until he had everyone's attention. "That woman is not, and never has been, my girlfriend. If that rumor ever got back to my real girlfriend, she'd be hurt. I don't want that, do you understand me?"

"Who *is* your girlfriend?" Joe piped up.

"Does she work here?" Mel asked.

"Is she gorgeous?"

"You deserve the best."

"I didn't realize I was that interesting," Tony drawled. "I thought you were here to get better at soccer, not start a gossip magazine. No more questions. Mo, you did much better this round." Once again, he gave each kid a compliment and a tip on how to improve. "We'll switch up the drill this time. Short sprints!"

Everyone groaned.

"I guess I'm definitely going to win at the end of the week. No ice cream for you."

While the kids were running their sprints, Glenn punched Tony's shoulder. "You distracted me too, you little shit."

Tony shrugged. "I've never made a habit of talking about my partners."

Glenn whistled low. "Classy, man. Very classy."

The rest of the day passed in a blur of drills and short skirmishes until it was time for free-swim before the kids were picked up.

"You've got five minutes to get changed and out onto the pool deck, or we're coming in to check on you," Glenn told the kids. "Or sending a lifeguard in for you," he added to the girls. "Three, two, one, go!"

The foyer between the two change rooms was empty in seconds.

"Let's get our trunks on," Glenn said, heading for the staff room. "Then you can see your girlfriend."

"Stop it," Tony said half-heartedly. He honestly couldn't wait to see Amanda again.

The second he stepped onto the pool deck, he scanned over the faces of the lifeguards. James was on duty near the hot tub, but Amanda wasn't on deck, meaning she was on her break in the pool break room. They'd explained the rotation system to him years ago when they'd first become lifeguards; fifteen minutes in each position so that their minds were fresh, and fifteen minutes every hour and a half to rest in the break room.

Tony counted heads for his kids. "Great, you're all here. Buddy up, don't drown, listen to the lifeguards, and have fun."

"Yes, coach!"

He caught several of the new kids eyeing his body and tattoos admiringly, but gave them the courtesy of ignoring them. He headed over to the tiny break room, beaming when he saw Amanda sitting at the desk with her head resting on her arms. "Shouldn't you be working, darlin'?" he asked her.

Her head flew up. "Tony! I missed you today."

"We can't spend every waking moment together," he said. "How did your day go?"

"No emergencies." She smiled at him. "Pretty slow."

"That's great." He glanced over at Glenn, who was being splashed by their kids. "I should go rescue him. See you for the walk home."

Amanda blew him a little kiss, making him feel all warm and fuzzy. Sure-footed, he ran the two steps to the edge of the pool and yelled "Cannonball!" as he leapt next to Glenn.

A short whistle blast met his ears when he surfaced, and he saw James looking down at him with barely contained amusement. "Just because you know how to run on a pool deck doesn't mean the kids do. No running, please."

"Right. Sorry, Jamie." Tony could feel his cheeks flushing with color. He turned to his kids. "I'm not perfect. Don't run on the pool deck. It's too easy to slip and bang your head when you fall."

"He's hot," Amber said dreamily.

"He's my best friend," Tony replied. "And he'll tell me off even worse when we walk home for wasting his time."

Amanda left the break room and made her way over to James. He said something to her, his mouth close to her ear, and her eyes found his, a teasing smile on her face. Then James moved on, rotating to his next guard position.

"Are they dating?" Dan asked, who was watching them.

"Amanda's my other best friend," Tony said absentmindedly, still watching her as she made the circuit of the hot tub next to the part of the pool they were standing in.

"She's hot," Joe added.

"Don't be rude," Tony admonished. "Hey, do y'all want to play water polo?"

When their time in the pool was over, he and Glenn sent the kids off to get changed and then collapsed against the wall near the change room doors.

"And to think, it's only Monday," Tony said with a little groan, closing his eyes against the bright lighting.

"I like hearing that sound come out of your mouth." A small hand with sharp fingernails snaked its way onto his torso.

Tony's eyes snapped open and he wrenched himself away from Carolina. "What the actual fuck?" he hissed at her. "Not only did I not consent to you touching me, but there are kids around!"

"I was just touching your abs," Carolina whined, her eyes fixed on Tony's body. "They're so beautiful."

Tony made a face. "Carolina, you will *never* have my permission to touch my body," he said clearly. "Leave me alone."

"Nothing to see here. Please get ready for your parents to pick you up," Amanda said, ushering the last stragglers past them to the change rooms. Once they were in, she locked the doors and joined the trio. "Is something wrong?" she asked.

Tony could see the tension in her shoulders. She knew something was up.

"I was just letting Tony know that he can always come to me for comfort when he gets tired of being a third wheel," Carolina sneered, crossing her arms.

While every instinct in his gut was screaming at him that Carolina was way off base, a small part of him couldn't help but wonder... Would Amanda and James have gotten together if it had been just the two of them? Was he intruding and they were just putting up with him?

"Third wheel?" Amanda said, raising her eyebrows. "A tricycle would fall over if it didn't have all three wheels."

"Human beings aren't tricycles," Carolina scoffed. "They need more balance than that."

"While I'm liking the metaphors, I'm not sure I fully understand," Glenn said, looking from one person to another.

"She's fucking both of them, the little slut," Carolina snapped.

Tony's blood boiled at the insult, but Amanda stared at her impassionately. "Why would you think that?"

"I feel like I should have popcorn," Glenn muttered to himself. "This is better than a soap opera."

"It's obvious! You were practically eye-fucking each other the instant you—" she pointed at Tony "—walked onto the pool deck."

"Excuse you, but I was working," Amanda said with a frown. "As was he. And if we exchanged glances, that's not exactly news. We're best friends, in case you missed the memo. This doesn't sound like proof to me."

Carolina flushed. "You're disgusting," she spat.

"Hmm, no," Amanda said thoughtfully. She looked Tony in the eye and winked. "You know what I think?" She lowered her voice, "You *wish* you were me."

Carolina's jaw dropped.

"Oh, and since you groped Tony in front of some kids, we can finally write you up for harassment," Amanda said cheerfully, her hands on her hips. "I don't care if your daddy owns the place. He won't be able to keep you here once the parents hear about your behavior."

"*My* behavior?" Carolina shrieked. "What about *your* behavior?"

Glenn raised his hand. "I haven't seen her do anything wrong."

"She—" Carolina pointed at Tony and James, who was approaching them.

"She's been nothing but professional," Glenn pointed out. "She hasn't touched either one of them. And I haven't seen any proof, as much as I'd love to." He grinned at Amanda, who chuckled. "However, you left your kids this morning to come bother Tony while we were working, you've been sexually harassing him since camp started, and you groped him in front of some kids without his consent," he counted on his fingers. "You're in big trouble, and there's nothing we can do to protect you, even if we wanted to."

"I'll...I'll tell my father that Tony was asking for it!" Carolina said, her face turning white.

"Tony's been working here for years," James said quietly. "He has a proven record."

"Not to mention our kids will stand up for him," Glenn put in.

"My father will believe me," Carolina said weakly.

"Will he, though?" Amanda said mildly. "Over multiple eye-witnesses, many of which are the kids of parents who pay to entrust them to our care?"

Carolina gulped.

Amanda waved to her. "Goodbye."

Without another word, Carolina turned on her heel and stalked away.

"So, after all that, I still don't get it," Glenn said. "Are you really taking them both for tricycle rides?"

Amanda laughed. "Maybe you should have another party. We're at work right now, and trying to be professional."

"Shit, we'd better go get changed," Tony said, catching a glimpse of the large clock on the wall. "The kids'll be waiting for us in the foyer."

Glenn sighed and pushed off the wall. "No shower until I get home, I guess. Shall I plan another party for the long weekend?"

"We always have fun at your parties, man," Tony said. "But if Carolina shows up, we're leaving."

"Fair."

On the walk home, he and James flanked Amanda, fingers linked loosely together, his thoughts were in turmoil.

"You're awfully quiet," Amanda said, tugging on his hand. "Did Carolina rattle you that much?"

"I try not to let anything she says get to me," Tony began. He took a deep breath, "But I can't help wondering if I'm a bonus."

"What do you mean?" James asked, his dark eyes troubled.

"I came in later to our little group. If my parents had decided to stay in Texas or go anywhere else, I wouldn't be here. Would you two have gotten together and been happy without me?"

Amanda frowned. "That's like asking if I love peaches more than pears when I'd never even heard of them."

"You balance us out," James interrupted. "You're not a bonus, not by a long shot."

"I love you," Amanda said. "I want you and James *both* in my life as my partners. I know it's not conventional, but I don't give a shit. We work together, as the three of us. You know me." She stopped walking, pulling him to a halt beside her, and took his chin between her fingertips. "I have never lied to you. You have half of my heart. Never doubt that."

Tony let her words wash over him, soothing him and healing his bruised heart. "I hear you," he whispered.

"Good." She pressed a light kiss to his lips before taking his hand again. "Whenever those intrusive thoughts take hold, come see me. I'll banish them."

"Have I made you feel like you don't belong with us?" James asked. "I'm not looking for reassurance here. I'm asking you to really think about it. If there's anything I can do to make things easier for you, I'll do it."

Tony didn't answer right away. "No. You've always been there for me. I'm sorry I'm insecure."

"We'll work on that." Amanda squeezed his hand. "Thanks for talking about it with us."

"It helped."

"You know what else will help?" James winked at him.

"Making our girl scream our names multiple times?" Tony replied with a grin. "I can't think of anything better."

Chapter Twenty-Two

Flashback: Wendy

Tony walked into his early morning class on Friday, anxiously looking around the room for Wendy's dark hair. She was sitting near the front next to the aisle. Taking a breath for fortification, Tony walked up to her.

"May I sit with you?" he asked.

She looked up, startled. "Tony! Of course." She shifted her chair closer to the table so that he could slide behind her. "What's up?"

Tony sat down. "Straight to the point," he said dryly. "Does something have to be up for me to sit with you?"

"Well, you usually sit by yourself during classes," Wendy pointed out. "I'm assuming to avoid distractions."

He smirked. "Do you know what all your classmates are thinking?" he asked her.

"I want to become a profiler," laughed Wendy. "It's good practice."

"Then why do you suppose I asked to sit beside you today?" asked Tony, rocking his chair back on two legs. He was enjoying himself immensely.

Wendy studied his face. "You want to talk to me about something, and it's fairly important. It can't wait until after class because you know I have to run to my next one immediately after this. You don't look upset, so it's nothing serious. There aren't any big projects assigned yet, so maybe you want to get a head start on asking for a partner?"

Tony grinned. "Close. But not really. I wanted to ask you out for dinner tonight."

Wendy blinked at him, surprised. "Oh," she said, surprised. "That's a little unexpected."

"I'd like to get to know you better and want to see if we're compatible," Tony said.

"I'd like that," said Wendy shyly.

"Is fish and chips okay?" asked Tony as they walked up to a fresh fish stand. "I considered suggesting something fancier, but this is more who I am, you know?"

"This is perfect! I love this place," Wendy said happily.

They found a booth that faced the ocean, and enjoyed the sunset while they gorged themselves on the fresh food.

Tony felt like he did most of the talking during dinner. He kept trying to draw Wendy into the conversation, talking about his childhood, their classes, and various genres of media. She listened avidly, but didn't volunteer much information about herself.

"You should have let me pay my half," protested Wendy afterwards.

Tony smiled. "How about you buy me an ice cream, and we'll call it even."

Wendy gaped at him. "You can still eat after that meal?"

"You can't call ice cream eating," laughed Tony. "I think of it as filling in the spaces." He patted his muscled stomach.

After buying their ice creams, they walked silently along the boardwalk beside the beach.

"You're awfully quiet," said Tony finally. "Have I upset you in any way?"

"Well, you certainly surprised me," replied Wendy with a small smile. "No, I'm just trying to find the courage to tell you…" She stopped and sat on a nearby bench.

Tony sat down beside her without a word. He watched Wendy wrestle internally before she turned to look at him.

"I've never been in a relationship before," she admitted.

Tony's mouth dropped open. "No one has asked you out? I find that incredibly hard to believe!"

Wendy smiled. "I've been on dates. There's just never been a reason to continue seeing the guy before." She took a breath. "And so I've never told anyone this before."

Tony nodded encouragingly.

"I'm trans." Wendy closed her eyes. When he didn't say anything, she opened them again.

"Thank you for trusting me," said Tony softly, looking into her eyes. "That doesn't change anything."

"Really?" asked Wendy incredulously.

He shrugged. "Doesn't bother me."

Wendy gave a choked laugh. "Where were you when I was transitioning? I could have used someone like you by my side."

"How old were you when you knew?" asked Tony curiously.

"I knew I was a girl when I was five, but I started transitioning the summer before my last year of high school." Wendy sighed. "The other kids were awful. But I dealt with it the best I could, and I moved across the country as soon as possible. My parents were incredibly supportive when I came out to them. They paid for everything, the facial electrolysis, the therapy, the hormones, everything. Fortunately for me, my features passed easily." She smiled. "By the time I started the training camp the summer before our freshman year, I was accepted as a girl. It was such a relief!"

"That must have been so difficult," said Tony sympathetically. "I can't imagine what high school must have been like for you."

She grinned. "You have no idea how great it feels to talk about this!"

"If you want to talk to more people who will accept you for who you are, you should talk to my best friends, Amanda and James," said Tony, chuckling. "They would love to meet you."

Wendy chewed her lower lip. "Maybe later? We'll see how this goes first."

"Whenever you want," Tony reassured her. His eyes focused on her abused lip. He licked his own before tearing his gaze away.

"Aren't you going to ask me if I've had surgery?" she asked neutrally.

"No," replied Tony. "It's none of my business."

"So you want to be surprised?" she teased.

"Oh?" He smirked, one eyebrow ticking up.

She blushed. "I'm not saying that anything will happen, but if it does..."

Tony grinned. "It doesn't matter either way. And nice to know you're considering the idea."

"Will you walk me home?" she asked shyly.

"Of course," he responded promptly. "We can talk about what we want to do for our second date."

Wendy smiled shyly at him as he stood up. He held out a hand for her, and she placed her own in it.

"I like that you have such big hands," she confided. "It makes mine feel delicate and feminine."

"They are feminine, because they're attached to you." Tony winked at her.

She blushed. "Stop being so charming. I can't resist you when you say things like that."

"Who says you have to resist me?" Tony asked with a cheeky grin, spinning her into an impromptu waltz. "I think we should go dancing next time, what do you think?"

"Oh!" gasped Wendy, her hand firmly grasped in his, the other pressed against his chest where she had caught herself. She followed his lead as he spun her along the boardwalk, her skirt billowing softly around her. "Yes, please," she laughed. "Where did you learn to dance like this?"

"Our families were always big on group activities, and when we were in eleventh grade, we all took ballroom classes together, parents included." He dipped her gently, and then set her back upright. "It was fun learning to do something together. James's dad is amazing at swing dancing. I wish I was that good."

"I am envious of how close you guys are to each other," admitted Wendy. "That's something I never really had growing up."

"Neither did I, until I moved to Northampton," said Tony quietly. "I had a very unhappy childhood—a very lonely one, until then. I am grateful every day for the chance that my parents, and Amanda and James, gave me."

"I'm glad I got to know you," said Wendy shyly, as they stopped in front of her apartment building. "I had fun tonight."

"So did I." Tony looked down at their interlaced fingers. "I don't want to pressure you..." he hesitated.

"No, you can't come upstairs," teased Wendy.

Tony laughed, and then sobered. "Can I kiss you good night?"

Wendy bit her lip. "I would like that," she replied.

Hardly daring to breathe, Tony stepped forwards until she had to tilt her head back to look up at him. He cradled her face in one hand, his thumb along her cheekbone, his fingers speared through her hair at the base of her neck. Slowly he lowered his head until his lips just brushed hers. She gasped and clenched his shirt in her hands. He groaned and pressed his lips more firmly against hers, letting his tongue trace along the seam of her lips.

Tentatively, she opened to him, and he slipped in. She tasted like the chocolate from her ice cream cone. Head spinning, he wrapped his free arm around her shoulders as he continued to explore her mouth with his. Her tongue brushed his lightly, and they both moaned.

He pulled back slowly. "Wow," he said, dazed.

"Apt description," panted Wendy.

He cleared his throat. "If you can still talk intelligently, I'm not doing my job right," he teased. He bent his head to hers again, hungrily kissing her until she was only standing upright because he was holding onto her.

"Better?" he asked, smirking.

"Mmhmm," moaned Wendy, her eyes still closed.

"God, you're gorgeous." He brushed his lips over her eyelids, and they fluttered open.

"You're just saying that to get into my skirt," she accused him playfully.

"Is it working?" He waggled his eyebrows at her.

"Maybe, if you keep saying it every time you see me," she laughed.

"I promise I will, if only to ensure you believe me," said Tony seriously, dipping his head to kiss along her jaw to her ear.

"I really should go, or else I'll invite you upstairs," Wendy moaned.

Tony took a deep breath. "I won't do anything you might regret. I'll see you in class on Monday." He pressed one last quick kiss to her lips before slowly backing away. "Good night!" He waved as she opened the door to the apartment building.

"Good night," she called back.

Tony walked back to his dorm, a huge grin on his face. His lips were still tingling from the kisses they'd shared.

"Are you cold?" Tony asked Wendy. "Do you want my jacket?"

"No, thank you," she replied. "It's just a bit windy, and it's hard to eat when my hair keeps blowing in my mouth." She laughed when she tried to take a bite of her sandwich, and another strand of hair blew in front of her face.

Tony reached into his backpack and pulled out a binder clip. "Do you have anything better than this?" he chuckled.

Wendy shook her head and smiled. "That will do the job!"

With careful hands, Tony pulled the front pieces of her hair back from her face and pinned them with the clip, before tucking the rest of her long hair down the back of her jacket. "There! That should help."

"Thanks, Tony, you're the best." She took a big bite of her sandwich.

He copied her, and ignored the buzz of his phone, signaling an email.

"Aren't you going to see what that is?" she asked, swallowing.

"It can wait until I'm not spending time with you."

"You're sweet. Go ahead and check who it's from, at least." She took another bite.

Tony flipped his phone over. "It's from Boston U's Masters Program!" he exclaimed. He turned it back over and swallowed hard. "I'm terrified to read it!"

"Tony Carlson, scared of an email?" Wendy teased. "Wait until I tell the guys."

"They'll understand," he retorted. "We all have dreams. Did you get yours yet?"

With perfect timing, her phone buzzed the receipt of an email. She wiped her fingers on her jeans and pulled out her phone. "Just now!" Her eyes danced with amusement. "Shall we open them together?"

Tony swallowed hard. "Okay, yes. I can do this." He grabbed his phone again and quickly opened the email. Then he let out a whoop of joy. "I'm in!" He grabbed her shoulders. "They said that I was their number one choice!" He laughed happily. "I've got to text James and Amanda!"

"And your parents?" murmured Wendy.

"Yes of course, them too!" He tapped out a second text quickly, and then glanced up. "Wait, what about you? Did you get accepted?"

"I did," she said quietly.

"Why aren't you more excited? This is awesome!" He hugged her again.

"Tony, I think we need to talk," she continued softly.

His grin dropped from his face. "What's wrong?"

"I've been thinking about us since Christmas," she hesitated, and then continued, "and I don't think we're on the same page."

"What do you mean?" Tony gaped at her. "And you've been thinking about this for two months? Why haven't you talked to me about this sooner? We could have worked through it!"

"That's the thing." Wendy shook her head sadly. "I don't think we can work through it. I truly believe you care about me, but seeing how you lit up at the airport when James came home, seeing the three of you together in your own little bubble, that showed me how much love you have for them. And not for me."

"What…" Tony started to speak, but she held up a hand.

"Even today, you got your acceptance, the first people you wanted to tell were James and Amanda. You forgot to tell your own parents! And you didn't think to ask me if I was accepted until after all that. I mean, I can't really blame you, they're pretty awesome. Did you even realize you were in love with them?"

Tony opened and closed his mouth a couple times. "In love?"

Wendy nodded. "In love," she said firmly.

"I'm sorry," whispered Tony. "I never wanted to hurt you."

"You fooled yourself, too. I guess having a whole country in between you guys made it a little less obvious," she added. "But get you back in the same zip code, and it was like I was hit over the head with a two by four. The past two months, I was lying to myself. You really are a perfect boyfriend, you know. Every time I thought 'There is no way I could ever be enough for him, he's in love with them, I should end it,' you would do something sweet, like bringing me chicken noodle soup when I was sick, or sending me flowers on Valentine's Day. I thought that maybe you were in love with me, and I was imagining what I had seen at the airport."

Wendy took a shuddering breath. She had tears running down her cheeks. "I can't even be mad at you. I just want what you have. I want that all-consuming love. And it's time for me to stop looking for it with you."

Tony passed her a tissue. "I'm sorry I got you involved in this mess," he said sadly. "I didn't realize how much I loved them. Or how obvious it was. I do care about you, though, and that won't change. Is there anything I can do for you?"

"Keep being you." Wendy smiled. "Don't run away from love. Talk to them and tell them how you feel." She wiped her cheeks with the tissue. "And don't forget about me."

"I couldn't forget you if I tried." Tony looked down at his phone. There were four texts waiting for him to read. "What are you going to do when you graduate? Are you going to come to Boston?"

Wendy shook her head. "I applied to San Fran's program when I got back from the holidays. They accepted me yesterday. I think I'll stay here."

"Yesterday," echoed Tony. "I am a really sucky boyfriend. Not only did I not know that you had applied elsewhere, but I didn't ask you about it. You deserve someone who will focus all their attention on you. I hope you find them."

"Me too," she whispered. "I've thought of one more thing you can do for me."

"Name it," he answered promptly.

"Be my friend?" she asked.

"Does being your friend include being allowed to give you hugs?" he asked.

"I could use one right now."

"Me too."

Part Three:

A Golden
Wedding

Chapter Twenty-Three

James

The sun streaming through the vines on the porch woke James, as it had almost every morning for the past month that he slept with his best friends. A delicate hand traced up his body, rubbing through his chest hair, and then a mouth was on his, gently sucking on his lower lip.

His eyes slowly opened. "Now that's the best way to wake up," he groaned, before nibbling at her mouth. Amanda opened to him and his tongue darted in to flick against hers, pulling out slowly so that she chased after him.

"More," she gasped into his mouth.

James gave her what she asked for, but she seemed distracted. Her head tipped back and he mouthed along her jaw.

"Faster, oh God, *Tony!*" she ended in a squeak.

Ah, that makes more sense. James pushed a hand under her shirt to tease at a nipple, lightly pinching and rolling the tip between his fingers.

Amanda started to shake and James captured her mouth with his, swallowing her cries as he and Tony made her body sing with pleasure.

"Oh wow," breathed Amanda after a minute. "Just...wow."

Tony drew his hand slowly from her shorts, and she whimpered at the loss of contact. She rolled over to face him, and gave him a slow, deep kiss. James brushed her hair out of the way and bit her lightly on the neck, making her gasp.

"We should probably get out of bed before my parents discover us naked," whimpered Amanda, as Tony started kissing her ear.

"But we're not naked," murmured James against her shoulder.

Tony bit her earlobe lightly.

"We will be soon," Amanda gasped and writhed, grinding her ass roughly into James.

He groaned at the contact. "I take your point."

"Besides, we have to get ready to go to the airport. Our flight's at noon." Amanda wiggled out from between them to the edge of the mattress. "Or had you forgotten that it's Adam's wedding in San Francisco this weekend?"

"How could I forget?" Tony replied. "I'd be getting ready for work right now otherwise."

"It's all my parents have been talking about for ages," James said.

"Mine, too." Amanda stretched, checked the kitchen windows for her parents and turned to face them. "A quick dip in the pool before we shower?"

"I don't have my...suit..." Tony trailed off as Amanda stripped out of her pyjamas, leaving her bare. "That never gets old," he said admiringly.

"Come on, I don't have sunscreen on." She ran down the grass to the pool, disappearing behind the privacy screen in seconds.

"How is she so awake at..." Tony dug his phone out of his pants at the edge of the mattress. "Ugh! Five-thirty in the morning?"

"You're the one who gave her an orgasm," James pointed out, shucking his boxers.

"She was thrusting against me! I thought I was dreaming," Tony protested, getting naked and following James down the lawn.

"When did you notice you weren't?" James chuckled.

"When my fingers got wet." Tony rolled his eyes.

"Mmm." James eyed his friend's hand, hungry for a taste of their girlfriend. *Would it be weird to lick his fingers? Probably.*

"There you are," Amanda said. She was sitting on the far side of the pool, moving her feet lazily through the water. "First one in gets the first kiss."

The men chuckled. James pushed Tony backwards and sprinted to the pool, launching himself into a shallow dive that brought him right to her feet.

"Cheater." James heard Tony grumble behind him and he laughed, shaking his head, his hair flinging droplets around him.

He'd had his braids released the day before and he was enjoying the freedom of having his hair loose again.

James pulled Amanda to the very edge of the pool by her knees and then pushed them apart, exposing her sex to his greedy eyes. "You didn't say *where* we could kiss you," he said, eyebrows rising in question.

"Oh, if you must," Amanda said with a smile, leaning back on her hands.

"I must." James bent forwards and gave her the filthiest kiss he could manage, tongue delving deep inside her. He felt her thighs tense under his hands and redoubled his efforts.

"James!" Amanda gasped, her fingers gripping his hair.

I missed the tug on my roots, James thought, almost dizzy with desire. *Feels damn good.* He hummed happily against her clit and her body spasmed, a flood of juices weeping from her that he eagerly lapped up.

"Oh fuck, yes," Amanda said dreamily, slipping into the water while clinging to his shoulders. She wrapped her legs around his waist, pressing herself against him, and brushed her lips over his jawline.

James's hands grasped her by her waist, lightly traced patterns over her rib cage, and then floated down over her ass. Her mouth reached his and she bit his lower lip lightly, drawing a groan from him. His hands tightened convulsively on her ass, pulling her tighter against him. She rubbed herself along his length and he twitched against her. She moaned into his mouth, and he took control of the kiss, his tongue darting into her mouth to dance with hers. God, he wanted to take her right then and there.

Finally, she pulled away from the kiss. James's heart raced as he panted.

Giving him a mischievous smile, Amanda swam away from him to Tony.

She twined her pale body around Tony's tan one, rubbing herself against him until he grabbed her roughly by her hips and hauled her upright.

Tony slid one hand up her body into her hair and pressed her mouth to his. He alternated between light kisses and deep, bone shattering ones. He pulled away from her mouth and started nipping along her collarbone.

James came up behind her and kissed across her shoulder blades.

Amanda gasped, grinding her hips between them. "I want you," she moaned.

"Fuck," Tony groaned.

"It's not safe to have sex in water, you know that," James reminded her.

"On the grass then?" Amanda begged. "Come on, please?" She wrapped her arms around Tony's neck. "You know you want to fuck into me, feel my heat against your cock, come deep inside me." She pulled on Tony's lower lip with her teeth.

"If you don't stop talking like that, I'm going to come in the pool," Tony growled.

"I can't help it." Amanda tightened her legs around Tony's waist. "Do you think there's time to have sex before my parents wake up?"

"Breakfast time, kids!" Mrs. Beyer called from the porch.

"No."

Amanda giggled. "I guess I'll do the walk of shame to get your clothes?"

"Wouldn't want to scar your mom?" Tony teased.

"Just for that, you're coming with me." Amanda stuck her nose in the air.

Mrs. Beyer must have counted clothing items and done the math because she was nowhere to be found when they returned to the porch and put their pyjamas back on.

They inhaled their food, having worked up an appetite the night before and separated to go home and shower after numerous kisses.

James crossed the street to his house and ran up the stairs to his room. His mother came out of her room and called to him.

"We've got an hour before we have to leave for the airport. Are you packed?"

"Toothbrush and deodorant after my shower and then I'm good to go," he replied after a moment's thought. "Everything fit in my carry-on without a problem."

"It's too bad you're losing two days of work because of the flights getting in so late," she said, frowning.

James shrugged. "It doesn't really affect Amanda and I that much because we took extra shifts, but Tony is only working weekdays like an adult." He smirked at his mom. "Are you and dad okay with taking the time off?"

"It'll be nice to have a mini vacation," she responded, smiling. "Our work can wait until next week."

"Must be nice to be settled in your field," James said.

"You'll get there. Now go shower, or we'll be late."

They were not late. All three families moved through the Hartford airport security to their gate with no trouble.

"Do you three have any plans during the day tomorrow?" Mr. Lavallee asked them once they were settled.

"Check out the Pier, go to the Golden Gate Bridge, typical touristy stuff," Amanda said. "Oh and there's this little tattoo shop that we want to go to."

"You're getting tattoos? All of you?" Mrs. Carlson asked, eyebrows rising in surprise. "What is it? Where is it going to be?"

"A little heart made out of three puzzle pieces in our prom colors," Tony said.

"Right over our hearts," Amanda added.

"We've been in contact with the artist by email. He's going to see us first thing in the morning," James finished.

"Good thing we don't get in too late tonight," Mrs. Beyer said. "Although traveling west always makes me wake up earlier."

"We'll probably take a nap in the afternoon. The bachelor parties are tomorrow night and we'll be up until sunrise with those, I'm sure!" Amanda said with a laugh.

"Any idea what you'll be doing?" Mrs. Beyer asked.

"I was told to wear something I can dance in," Amanda said. "So I've got a low-cut halter and a short skirt."

"We were told to dress for a club," Tony said. "I've got dress pants and a shirt. I'll roll the sleeves and keep the collar open."

"I brought the same as Tony," James said to the expectant faces. "What are you guys going to do while we're at the bachelor parties?"

"Oh, I don't know, maybe we'll go to a swinger's club," Mr. Carlson teased.

"Dad! Do you even know what that means?" Tony asked, horrified.

"My son, one of the men in a polycule, is asking me if I did some research into the types of things we can do in San Francisco," Mr. Carlson said to the other parents, who chuckled. "Does the thought of your parents having sex gross you out?"

Tony's face flamed. "I really don't think about it. Ever."

"You three have been so open with your sexuality, we thought it might be nice to try to...spice things up a bit!" Mrs. Beyer said, smirking at the three young people.

"If you can't explore your sexuality with your friends, who *can* you explore with?" Mrs. Lavallee added, mischief in her eyes.

"Please tell me you're joking," Amanda said, blushing. "You're just teasing us because we're a little unabashed?"

"Would that make you feel better?" Mrs. Carlson asked. "We could pretend that we're going swing dancing instead."

James groaned. "Now I don't know whether you're joking about *that*! Just...if you're swinging, be safe, communicate, be honest with each other, and have fun. If you're swing *dancing*, have fun."

"Oh, that's not fair, pulling the mature card on us!" pouted Mrs. Beyer.

Mr. Lavallee laughed. "Son, you've got an excellent head on your shoulders. Thank you for the advice."

"We couldn't resist the little joke when we were searching for dancing clubs and came across the *other* type of swing clubs," Mr. Beyer said, eyes twinkling.

"Granted, we *did* have to Google what it meant," Mrs. Lavallee said sheepishly.

"How do *you* know what it means?" Mr. Lavallee asked.

"Porn," James said with a shrug. Tony nodded.

"They told me." Amanda pointed at her boyfriends. "It came up in a rumor in high school."

Mrs. Beyer winced. "The rumor mill in our town is rabid. Do you know, I am constantly being asked if one of you is cheating?"

Amanda snorted. "Why would anyone think that?"

"I get asked that, too," Mrs. Lavallee put in.

"Me too," Mrs. Carlson said. "I was in the pharmacy the other day buying bandaids and one of the cashiers informed me that all three of you had been in to buy...ummm...lubricant—"

"You can just say lube," Amanda interrupted.

Mrs. Carlson blushed. "Lube, then, separately that week. Obviously you just hadn't communicated with each other and you all bought bottles by accident."

"Oh! Yeah, no...we wanted to make sure we had enough," Amanda said, blushing.

"But...three bottles?" Mrs. Lavallee said, gasping.

"That *is* more than we'd need normally, but we wanted a travel size bottle. And they've got different sensations." Amanda shrugged. "It's not like they expire any time soon."

"Damn, I wish I had that stamina," Mr. Lavallee muttered under his breath.

James huffed a laugh.

Mrs. Beyer looked alarmed. "You're sure you're alright, sweetheart?" she asked Amanda.

"Mom, if I even so much as wince, one of them notices, and they react like I'm made of china. I'm great. Better than great. I've got endorphins producing overtime." Amanda grinned. "Don't worry. They're taking excellent care of me."

"I'll say," murmured Mrs. Carlson, making Amanda giggle.

James followed the GPS on his phone, leading the way along San Francisco's windy streets until they reached their destination: Moth and Dagger Tattoo Studio. Eagerly, Amanda and Tony followed him into the brightly lit studio.

"Are you ready for this?" asked Tony, grinning. "You don't look excited."

Amanda stuck her tongue out at him.

The artist shook everyone's hands. "Welcome! Nice to meet all of you in person."

"Great to meet you, Joe," said Tony, introducing himself, James and Amanda following suit.

"Pleasure. Who would like to go first?" said Joe, shaking their hands.

"Me, please," said Amanda.

"Thanks for seeing us so early in the morning," James said. "We really appreciate it."

"Not a problem at all! We rarely get walk-ins at seven." The man chuckled, showing them to the chairs. "Something this small won't take more than an hour, even with filling it in. Get comfortable. Are you still good with the location we discussed?"

Amanda settled on the comfortable leather chair while he collected the materials he would need. "Yes."

Tony and James pulled folding chairs up beside her.

"You won't be able to wear a bra while it heals," Joe reminded her. "Shirt up and bra off whenever you're ready." He pulled a screen around the chair, enclosing the four of them in the small space.

"How high..." She flushed and stopped talking.

He twinkled at her. "You can still keep covered. If it helps, I'm going to be focused on the skin under my needle, nothing else. Did you want them to leave?" he asked, indicating Tony and James.

"Nothing they haven't seen before," she said, chuckling. She lifted her shirt, arranging it so that she still covered her breasts, but the space over her heart was visible. "I didn't wear a bra today, because I knew it would interfere," she told him.

"And you wore a soft cotton shirt that isn't too tight," he approved. He applied the transfer paper with the design and held up a mirror for her to see. "Okay?"

"That looks great."

James and Tony nodded agreement.

Joe dipped his needle into the black ink needed for the outline. "Ready?"

She took a deep breath and stretched her hand out to James. He took it, squeezing gently. "Yes, I'm ready," Amanda said firmly.

The buzzing of the needle started.

"You're doing great," murmured Joe as he changed the ink. "I'm going to fill it in now. This will take a bit longer."

"It feels like a cat is scratching at me," she whispered. "Over and over again in the same place."

"Don't think about it," suggested Tony.

James rubbed her knuckles with his thumb. "Look at us, love. Talk about people at work this summer."

Amanda told them about her students, some of the things that the patrons of the pool got up to and some of the wild incidents that the other guards had managed to fall into while Joe brushed her skin with ink. At last, it was over.

Joe placed a loose bandage over the fresh ink and handed her a list of care instructions. "No swimming for two to four weeks until it heals completely. Chlorine will eat at the color, and you might get an infection. Keep it dry and clean. No rubbing or scratching, no matter how itchy it gets. Do you have someone back home you can go to if you have trouble?"

"Yes," replied Tony. "I know a guy." He helped Amanda off the leather chair, and she sat in James' vacant seat before cuddling up to Tony.

Joe changed his needles and inks while James got settled on the chair. He slipped his shirt over his head and handed it to Amanda.

"Lighter colored inks show up differently on dark skin," advised Joe. "There won't be a problem with the pink or gray, but we'll have to see how the white turns out."

"Could we make the gray a darker gray, and the white a paler gray?" asked James. "Would that make a difference?"

"Possibly," Joe said thoughtfully. "I'll try the white first, and then you can decide."

The first touch of the needle to his skin was almost a disappointment. Then prickles followed the path of the needle as Joe traced the outline of the heart. The needle's path went over a bone, sending vibrations through his chest. He focused on the feeling of Amanda's hand holding his own and took shallow breaths while Joe finished the outline.

The white didn't show up, so he got the two shades of gray. The light one was better than the white.

Finally, it was Tony's turn.

After everyone was done, they thanked Joe and paid before walking along the streets of San Francisco.

"We're not too far from the Golden Gate Bridge," Tony mused. "We should be able to see it soon."

"I'm excited!" exclaimed Amanda.

They turned a corner, and the harbor stretched before them, the bridge arching across it.

"I don't care how many movies I've seen with this bridge in them, seeing it in person is something else," marveled James. "Seeing it with you two makes it even more special."

"Aww, aren't you sappy," teased Tony.

"What's next on the list?" asked Amanda. "I'd like to see the Pier."

"That is number one on my list," Tony declared. "And then I remember you mentioning something about a nap?"

"A nap after some fun?" James suggested, a half smile curving his lips. "It was nice to wake up this morning and not panic about being found naked."

"It was, wasn't it?" Amanda squeezed his hand. "We'll get to do that every night in Boston. Only one more week!"

"Can't wait!" said Tony fervently.

Chapter Twenty-Four

Amanda

Amanda waited patiently at the front entrance of the hotel, chatting happily with the other girls. The groom's limo had picked up James and Tony and the other guys a couple minutes before, and Adam had assured her that the bride's limo wasn't too far behind.

Sophia, the bride-to-be, greeted her with an enthusiastic hug. "We're practically sisters!" she exclaimed happily. "I've always wanted a sister!"

"Hey!" another girl said with a laugh. "What am I, chopped liver?"

Amanda chuckled and greeted the older sister of the bride with a wave. "Hello, Violet."

"I meant a younger sister," Sophia corrected herself.

"Sophia's a little tipsy," another girl told Amanda. "I'm Lucy, one of the bridesmaids."

That prompted all the other girls to introduce themselves as well. Amanda tried to remember everyone's name, but there were ten more and she forgot half by the time they were done.

The girls laughed off her apologies. "We'll remind you until you get used to us," they reassured her.

Finally, a limo pulled up and the doorman helped her into the back with the other girls.

"Where are we headed?" Amanda asked, curious.

She resisted the urge to scratch at her brand new tattoo and was grateful for the protective covering the artist had placed over it. Her shirt wasn't the most practical garment to wear over a new tattoo; it was heavily beaded and the inside was full of tiny ticklish threads. *I'll get used to the feeling soon, I hope. Or else be so distracted that I don't notice.*

"Ooooh we need to put the paint on her!" squealed one of the girls. "She didn't come to the pre-drinking."

"Paint?" Amanda asked, eyes wide. None of the other girls had paint on and she wondered if she was being pranked.

"It's blacklight paint," Sophia reassured her. "Goes on clear, shows up at the club."

Amanda submitted to the painting from the older girls, letting them contour her body and face.

"This is such a perfect shirt for the club!" exclaimed one girl, getting ready to paint her back. "Flower or heart?"

"Both?" Amanda said cautiously.

"Both is good!" shouted the others in the limo.

"We're big fans of *The Road to El Dorado*," Lucy explained. "We watched it all the time at Lambda Nu."

"Is that how you all know each other?" Amanda asked.

There were enthusiastic nods from everyone but Violet and another girl.

"I'm a cousin. Paula," she added.

Amanda smiled gratefully at her for including her name again.

"Don't lean back until the paint is dry. Shouldn't be long," said the girl from behind her as she slid her long legs away.

"So we're going to a blacklight club?" Amanda asked.

"We've reserved a private suite, but we can dance with the rest of the club goers if we want."

"We've got a bunch of games to play, so the suite will help keep the noise level down."

"After that club, we're going to a different club–a private one, and we're going to learn how to pole dance from an exotic dancer!" Violet said.

"Really?" Amanda bounced excitedly. "That sounds like so much fun!"

The other girls grinned at her.

"I knew you'd fit in," Sophia exclaimed.

"And then we'll perform our routine for the guys!" Lucy finished. "We'll all go up on stage together; they have plenty of poles for all of us, so it won't be massively intimidating to perform by ourselves."

"There's an uneven number, though," Violet said, checking her phone as a text came through. "Ben says that Adam's brother's friend means that there's an extra guy."

"Were you not expecting James?" Amanda asked anxiously. "We all got personalized invites."

"No, of course we were expecting him." Violet scrunched up her forehead in a frown. "We just thought that we had matched up everyone's significant other so nobody's left out."

"Oh!" Amanda glanced sideways at Sophia, who smirked. "You didn't tell them?"

"It's not up to me to out you," Sophia said playfully.

"What does she mean?" Paula asked.

Every eye was on her and Amanda flushed. "Ummm, both is good?"

"You're dating both of them at the same time?" Lucy squeaked.

"They must be gorgeous!"

"How do you manage? I'm exhausted from just one!"

"Are their dicks impressive?" That last was from the girl with the long legs.

"Raya!" several of the girls half-screamed.

Raya shrugged. "What? Like you all weren't thinking it."

"Does Adam's brother look like him?" Paula asked.

"Ah, no, Tony's adopted." Amanda fished her phone out of her purse and opened the photo app, pulling up a picture of the three of them at their layover the day before in Minneapolis. "Here we are."

"Oh my God, girl!" squealed Raya, grabbing the phone on its way past. "They are gorgeous!"

"How did you end up with both of them?"

"Do they ever get in fights over you?"

"How do you manage your time with them?"

"How does sex work?"

"Raya!"

"What? Like you weren't thinking it!" Raya repeated with a smirk.

"We've been friends forever, James since birth and Tony since we were twelve," Amanda said. "We finally acted on the attraction between us last month. No, they don't get in fights—at least, not that I know of. We spend all our time together when we're not working and we're moving in together next week. We're going to Boston for post-grad degrees."

"And the sex?" Raya prompted eagerly.

There was no shushing her this time, as everyone waited eagerly for Amanda's answer.

"Ummm... it's really good?" Amanda blushed.

"Like, do you take one away and then the other? If you spend all your time together..." Raya's eyes widened dramatically.

Amanda smirked. "I think you just answered your own question."

The girls all shrieked in delight.

"Oh, you're going to have fun during 'Never have I ever!'" Violet said with a chuckle. "We might have to restrict you to sips instead of full drinks or else you'll be sent to the hospital!"

"I don't mind switching to water every other drink."

"What's your drink of choice? Sex on the beach?" Raya asked with a wink.

"The act or the drink?"

The girls burst into laughter.

"Both is good!"

Amanda giggled. "We haven't done anything in the sand, but does beside a pool count? The drink is one of my favorites."

"Ooooh, I like you." Raya wrapped her arm around Amanda's shoulders. "Sophia, your little sister is awesome."

Sophia beamed.

"We're here, ladies," the driver informed them. "I'll park around the corner. When you're ready to go to the next location, send me a text and I'll come pick you up."

"Perfect," said Violet. "I've got your number right here. Thank you."

Everyone piled out and were escorted to the club. Once the bouncers caught a glimpse of the bride sash Sophia was wearing and Violet slipped them a bill, they let them jump the line.

Their suite was on the second floor of the club, with a window looking down over the dance floor. Once they closed the door, the thumping bass was reduced to a low throb and they could hear each other speak.

Violet sent their drink orders down. It was filled quickly and everyone found seats on the low couches as they started to play.

Amanda had a lot of fun and felt herself relaxing the longer she was in their presence. Raya had taken her under her wing, giving tiny anecdotes about each girl and reminding her of their names when she forgot them. Raya also took a picture of Amanda's back so she could see the colorful paint splashed across it in a heart and flower pattern. She sent the picture to her boyfriends along with a quick text saying she was having fun.

They were halfway through their drinks, and everyone seemed determined to see if they could think of something that they hadn't done that Amanda wouldn't drink to.

"Never have I ever had two cocks in me at once!"

"Hey, if a baby can come out, two cocks can go in," Amanda said after taking a sip.

"I meant mouth and vagina!" Paula squeaked. "It never even occurred to me to think...!"

"Oh! Do I have to drink again then?" Amanda said with a smirk at the shrieks from the girls.

"Never have I ever given head in public," Sophia said.

"At a party. There was a race to see who could make their boyfriend come first. I won." Amanda winked.

"With who?"

"Both."

"Both is good!" everyone shouted.

"I think it's my turn," Amanda said. "Never have I ever been engaged."

The girls all laughed and a quarter of them drank.

"Never have I ever gone skinny dipping," said Lucy.

Half the room drank to that one.

"Never have I ever participated in a bachelorette scavenger hunt," said Violet.

Nobody drank.

"Really? Well, get ready to do one now!" Violet said happily. "Everyone have your phones ready?" She read out the list of tasks. "Pictures or it didn't happen!"

"What are you going to start with?" Raya asked Amanda as they left the suite and headed for the stairs.

"I was thinking of getting the DJ to play a song. That way he's not annoyed by all the requests."

"Smart," Raya said approvingly. "Mind if I follow along and go after you?"

"Sure!" Amanda led the way directly to the DJ's booth and leaned on one of the tables, her arms framing her cleavage that had been outlined in paint. Once she got his attention, she shouted her song request at him. He gave her a thumbs up. She took a picture with him and winked at Raya. "Good luck!" she shouted and moved on to the next task on her list.

"Find and take a picture of yourself dancing with two guys," Amanda muttered to herself. "Shouldn't be too hard." She looked around the club until she spotted a group of guys standing by the bar. She grinned.

Her song started playing as she found her way over to the group of guys. "Hey!" she shouted. "I'm with a bachelorette party and we're doing a scavenger hunt. Can I get a couple of you to help me out?"

The guys laughed. "We're here for a bachelor party and we need some help too. What have you got?"

Amanda told them and they smiled.

"Easy peasy. We need the opposite."

"Oh, let me grab one of the other girls! I'm sure she'd be willing to help you out for a similar exchange." Amanda peered through the dark club, looking for Raya's paint work. "Hey!" she called, once she spotted the tall girl. Amanda waved her over and explained.

Raya grinned. "Yeah, I think we can manage that."

"Good luck!" they said to the men a little later, waving cheerfully as they moved on to the next part of their hunt.

"Might as well stick together," Amanda said to Raya, who nodded. "Only two left. Which do you want to do first?"

"I was thinking the bouncer's signature," Raya said.

"Shouldn't be too hard to get," Amanda agreed. They each grabbed a napkin from the bar and walked up to the bouncer nearest them, explaining what they wanted.

The man smiled and laughed. "Not the first time tonight I've been asked. Large group of you?"

"There are fourteen of us," Raya said, smiling. "Sorry to have bothered you."

"It's not a bother at all to have so many pretty girls ask for my autograph." The man winked as he signed their napkins.

"Last one. A selfie with the bride." Amanda turned to the stairs. "This was fun!"

They returned to the suite to find they were the first. They snapped selfies with Sophia and gave their phones to Violet for approval.

"Are you having fun?" Amanda asked Sophia. "I feel like your friends were focused a little too much on me rather than you for the 'never' game."

"Oh, that's alright." Sophia gave a little chuckle. "They already know everything about me. You're the new face. I'm glad, actually. It means I'm not super drunk and I'll be able to pay attention to the pole lesson."

"I'm glad I'm not stepping on your toes," Amanda said, relieved. She took a gulp of water. Her buzz wasn't too bad, thanks to only having taken sips of the alcoholic drink earlier.

"You're not," Sophia reassured her. She bit her lip, flushing. "Can I ask you something?"

"Of course!"

"Do you think Adam's parents like me?"

Amanda broke into a genuine smile. "They *adore* you! What on earth would make you think otherwise?"

"I haven't really spent much time with them," Sophia said shyly. "We're hoping to come visit this Christmas, since we spent last Christmas with my family. And, well, I'm just nervous."

Amanda hugged her. "You will love them once you get to know them. They are wonderful people who love their children. And I include James and I in that, because we have been welcomed into their home since day one. They already think of you as their daughter. They told us so yesterday."

"Really?" Tears threatened to spill over Sophia's cheeks.

"Really. You make Adam so happy, and that's all they wanted for him."

"Thank you!" Sophia hugged Amanda tightly.

"Not a problem!" Amanda gasped. She hugged back until more girls poured into the room.

Sophia pulled back. "Is my make-up alright?" she asked Amanda quietly, her back to the others.

Amanda wiped away a streak of black with a knuckle. "You look gorgeous."

Sophia smiled. "Thank you." She turned to take selfies with the other girls.

"Make sure you have everything," Violet said over the chatter. "We're heading for the pole club now!"

Full of high spirits, the girls cleared the room, checking for belongings in between cushions and under the couches, and then hurried down the stairs and out to the limo.

"So, Amanda, you still haven't told us," Georgia said.

"What could I possibly *not* have told you?" Amanda asked with a chuckle.

"How big their dicks are!" Lisa finished, smirking.

"Oh, right!" Amanda thought about it for a moment. "More than enough to satisfy me."

The girls all laughed.

"Do you gag when you go down on them?" Violet asked. "I can't get Ben fully in my mouth unless he's still soft."

Amid more laughter, Amanda managed to say, "Yeah, there's no way I could fit them all the way in my mouth, even soft." She furrowed her brow. "Not that I see them soft often."

"Show-ers, not grow-ers," Raya said, nodding wisely. "Arslan is like that, but the guy I was with before him? I thought something was wrong with him the first time he took his pants off!"

The limo filled with giggles.

"Is Adam like his brother?" Paula asked Sophia.

"Not at all," Sophia said. "I wouldn't say he's exceptionally long, but he thickens a lot when he's aroused. My jaw aches if I go down on him for too long."

"Ugh, I know what you mean!" groaned Amanda along with several others.

"But it feels great inside me," Sophia finished, blushing.

The ones who had groaned before now nodded their agreement.

"Hang on... Amanda, both your guys are hung like horses, and you stuffed both of them inside you? That can't have been comfortable for anyone!" Lucy said with a gasp.

"Well, we've only done it once so far," Amanda said. "But it felt incredible, and the guys seemed to really enjoy it. I was stretched beforehand and we'd already had sex three... maybe four?... times each that afternoon, not counting the oral, so I was super relaxed."

"Six times in one day!" Raya repeated, amazed.

"I guess that's what happens when you've got two men seeing to your needs!" Violet said with a chuckle and a wink.

"How are you surviving the sexual appetites of two men?" Georgia said.

"They've got to survive mine!" Amanda laughed. "I crave them all the time."

"You go girl!" Raya said cheerfully.

"I can't wait to see you with them after the pole class," Sophia said. "From what Adam's told me, you were always close, but now?" She grinned. "Sounds like you know each other better than ever."

"We really do."

"We have arrived, ladies," announced the driver. "Have fun."

"Oh, we will!"

They walked into an empty club, the lights brightly lighting every stage.

A stately woman walked forwards from the bar to greet them. "Welcome! My name is Jewel, stage name Bijou. Where is the bride?"

Sophia was pushed forwards and was greeted with a hug and a kiss on each cheek.

"Now, you ladies won't be removing your clothing, so I'll just teach you some seductive moves and some simple spins on the pole. If you do well, I might be able to teach you some more complex moves. Finally, you'll learn a simple dance, which you'll perform together for your men when they come in from next door."

"They're already here?" Amanda asked eagerly.

Jewel smiled. "Yes, they're doing karaoke in the other half of the club."

"They're *singing*?" Raya practically had to hold Amanda back from running into the next room. "Can't we just peek at them? For a minute?"

Jewel laughed. "It's a full club on the other side, not just your men. It could be ages before their turn, or they could have already gone."

Amanda sighed, but focused on the instructor for the lesson. The group of them put their purses in a locker and kicked off their shoes to learn the steps.

It turned out she wasn't the only one who had a dance or gymnastic background, as everyone picked up the seductive moves quickly. Jewel taught them the simple spins on the pole, increasing the complexity once everyone showed their competence.

"I'm really impressed with all of you," Jewel told them during a water break. "I don't think I've ever had an entire group learn this fast. Are you having fun?"

A chorus of yesses answered her.

"Alright!" Jewel grinned. "We're going to learn the routine now. You'll have a bit of freestyle time in the middle. I can help you come up with something if you want."

The routine was a combination of sultry and sexy moves on a chair, the floor, and around the pole with a couple spins to break things up. The song was Beyonce's *Dance for You*, which Amanda was feeling in her soul.

"Let's try it from the top!" Jewel said, clapping her hands together. "You can pick your poles now. Sophia, you get the center stage, of course. Everyone else spread out around the room. Bring your chairs with you. Ready? Five, six, seven, eight!"

Amanda worked herself hard throughout the routine, keeping an eye on the other girls to make sure she was sticking to the steps properly.

"And freestyle!" Jewel said. "You've got until the chorus starts again. Slow and seductive, ladies!"

Amanda froze. *I'm not sure what to do!* her mind was screaming at her.

Jewel came over and leaned on the stage in front of her. "You're the younger sister, right?"

Amanda nodded, embarrassed. "Sorry, I'm not great at improv. I'd like to do something on the pole, but..."

"Not to worry. I can teach you something fun. You're very strong and flexible. How do you feel about being upside down?" Jewel asked.

"I think my boys would love that."

"Okay. I'll help you after the run-through." Jewel raised her voice. "Chorus is starting in five, six, seven, eight!"

Right on cue, the chorus started. Amanda was impressed that Jewel could carry on a conversation and keep track of the music at the same time. The girls completed the routine and cheered for each other.

"Anyone who would like some help with their freestyle portion, come see me now," Jewel said.

Raya, Sophia, and Violet joined Amanda on stage with Jewel.

"I've got three options for you: chair, floor, or pole. You don't have to stick to what I show you exactly, just remember to keep your movements slow."

Jewel taught all four of them the floor and chair routines before turning to Amanda. "Anyone else want to watch the pole routine?"

A couple more girls raised their hands.

Jewel took hold of the pole and swung herself up, legs splaying out in the splits upside down. "I'm holding the pole here and here," she said, indicating the two spots. "If you feel yourself slipping, don't delay in grabbing with your other hand as well and return to an upright position. Then you can transition to the floor or chair, your preference."

Jewel performed the move once more, slowly, so that Amanda could follow, and then said, "Give it a shot."

Amanda nodded, her brow furrowed in concentration, and gripped the pole where Jewel indicated. She carefully lifted herself upside down, legs in a full split.

The other girls cheered and Amanda carefully lowered herself off the pole.

"Oh wow, that was awesome!" Sophia said, clapping her hands.

"Try again, smoother and quicker," Jewel suggested.

Amanda did the move again, starting with a slow spin that Jewel had taught them all earlier before transitioning to the split.

"Very nice," Jewel said approvingly. "I think you've got it. Alright, we're going to run through the routine again, but we're going to start with your entrances. Sophia, because you're in the center of the room, you'll come in on the floor, and someone will help you up onto the stage. Everyone ready?"

Chapter Twenty-Five

Tony

Tony and James hadn't liked leaving Amanda outside the hotel when their ride had arrived first, even though the rest of the girls had been with her.

Adam picked up on their anxiety during the limo ride. "What's up?"

Tony winced. "Amanda doesn't have a great track record with other girls. I think she intimidates them."

"These girls aren't like the ones in your class back home," Adam said reassuringly. "Almost all of them are Sophia's sorority sisters, and the other two are her older sister and her cousin. I know every single one of them and not only do they not get intimidated easily, but they will love her. Chill, baby bro. Your girl is in good hands."

Ben was doing a headcount. "We've got fifteen guys here." He tapped something out on his phone. "Weren't there fourteen girls? I thought we had an even number," he asked Adam.

"Why would you need an even number?" Tony asked, curious.

"There's something at the end that involves the girlfriends. And fiancée. And my wife," Ben said. "Who's the guy without one?"

"Ah," said Tony. He glanced at James. "I think I understand the problem."

Adam smirked at them. "It was bound to come out sooner or later."

"Yeah, I know," Tony said sheepishly, running a hand through his hair. "We're not keeping it a secret. James and I are both seeing the same girl," he explained to Ben.

"Oh, okay, that's a relief then," Ben said, relaxing in the seat. "I was worried the extra guy would feel left out."

James chuckled. "Definitely not something to worry about with us."

"How is it that every guy here is dating a girl from the same sorority?" Tony asked. "Is that a coincidence?"

Adam laughed. "The Delta Phi fraternity is super close with the Lambda Nu sorority. It is a coincidence, I guess, that we all ended up dating from the same house, but not unusual."

"We have similar interests and goals," a man named Arslan interjected. "We think a lot alike. Much like you and your girl, correct?"

Tony and James glanced at each other again. "Definitely similar interests. Our career paths are very different, though," James finally said.

"Career paths are not the same as goals." Arslan shook his head. "Work ethic, values, ethics, family importance, that sort of thing. The things that really matter in the long run. Those goals."

"Oh. Yeah, I think we're on the same wavelength for the goals, too," Tony said tentatively.

"You don't have to have all the answers right away, little brother," Adam said. "You're only twenty-two. The biggest changes in your life will happen over the next five years."

"Who you are as a person will mature. The people you surround yourself with will help shape you into the men you'll become," Ben added.

"This is getting rather philosophical for a bachelor party," said a man named Phillip.

"When else would you suggest we discuss philosophy?" said another man, but Tony hadn't caught his name. "Over dessert?"

The other men groaned. "Not again!" shouted several others.

"Sounds like there's a story here," Tony said.

"Matt just likes to have intense conversations." Adam laughed. "So what's first on the agenda, Ben?"

"Karaoke," Ben said cheerfully. "And then we're going to an exotic dancing club, so get ready to have your socks knocked off!"

"Ben..." Adam hissed in warning.

"Hey, just trust me, alright," Ben said with a smile. "Don't worry. Violet approved and you know she wouldn't do anything to jeopardize her sister's happiness."

"Hey Adam, maybe it's a male club and you can finally learn how to look cool while taking off your clothes," Tony teased.

"It's not how you take off your clothes, but what you do afterwards," Adam rebutted, sniffing disdainfully.

"It's all part of the same package," Tony said with a grin.

"Ouch, low blow, brother." Adam pretended to be shot in the heart. "At least this package can satisfy by itself!"

The other men in the limo "ooh'd" simultaneously.

"I think he thinks that's an insult," Tony said to James with a smirk.

"He does, doesn't he." James returned the grin. "And how many times can your package satisfy in one evening? Refractory periods in men can take a while to recover. Women can go all night long."

"Well, ours can, because she doesn't need to wait in between packages," Tony finished with a flourish.

Arslan whistled. "I hadn't thought of it like that. Damn, that's a good setup you've got going."

Adam pouted. "Are you saying that one man isn't enough for a woman?"

Tony relented with a sigh. "No, brother. We're just teasing. I'm sure you more than satisfy Sophia all by yourself."

"Just for the record, how many times *have* you gone in one night?" whispered Phillip.

"Each?" James asked. "Three, but to be honest, that was pushing it. I lost track of how many times Amanda was satisfied. I was exhausted the next day."

"Mmm, yeah, but we all came earlier that day, too, so wouldn't that count as four?" Tony said thoughtfully.

They glanced around at the shocked faces in the limo.

"Sorry, is that a lot?" James asked. "That was our first time together, so we had a lot of pent up sexual tension to work through."

Adam burst into laughter. "Did you ever! Godammit, I was not expecting my little brother to be so sexually proficient. You're all grown up!" He pretended to wipe a tear from his cheek.

"Gentlemen, we have arrived," the driver announced, putting the car in park. "Enjoy your evening."

The men filed out of the limo into the karaoke bar. There was a large table reserved for them near the middle of the room.

"Round of shots!" Arslan shouted. "Who's up for a Screaming Orgasm?"

There were whoops and cheers from the other guys.

Drinks received, Ben held his out to toast Adam. "May you always satisfy your wife with one of these!"

Everyone cheered and slammed their shot back.

As the liquid slid down his throat, Tony felt himself relax. His brother's friends were a good sort. A tablet was being passed around the table and Tony leaned over to see what it was. The song list for the bar was extensive and Tony started thinking about what song he should sing.

"Any suggestions?" he asked James.

James shrugged. "Something you know well enough that you won't mess up?"

Tony chuckled. "Yeah, that doesn't really help."

The tablet was passed to him and Tony flicked through the categories, hoping something would jump out at him.

"Oh, hey, I want this one," James said over his shoulder, clicking on Ed Sheeran's *Shape of You*. "I know it pretty well."

"Nice," Tony said absentmindedly. "I was hoping for a different vibe for my song... Oh my God this is perfect!" He showed James his choice, making the other man nearly choke on his laughter.

"Adam's going to bust a gut," James wheezed. "That's perfect. Go for it, dude."

Tony made his selection and passed the tablet on to the next guy.

Their phones announced the arrival of a text from Amanda and they eagerly grabbed them to see a picture of Amanda's painted back.

"She looks like she's having fun," James said, smiling.

Adam overheard. "I told you the girls would take good care of her," he said with a smile.

The first guy from their group was called up to the microphone not long after and the group applauded boisterously when he was done. A few more people sang from their group before James was called up. He did a great job, from Tony's point of view, his deeper voice suiting the song quite well. He was welcomed back to the table with cheers and back slaps.

Tony was getting excited for his turn. He knew the song so well he wouldn't need the prompter and he planned on making use of the mobility of the microphone to really play up to the audience. He rolled up his sleeves, exposing the tattoo on his forearm with James's name hidden amongst the black ink Monstera leaves and flowers. *God, I wish I could tell him how I feel about him. That he has the other half of my heart.*

Finally he was called up, Adam's jaw dropping when he heard the name of the song he had chosen.

"Tony will be singing *Pretty Fly For A White Guy* by The Offspring!" said the announcer.

The guys at their table whooped and hollered as he bounded up to the stage, taking the microphone out of the stand.

"I dedicate this song to my brother, the whitest guy I know, who is getting *married* tomorrow to an amazing woman. I really do wish you all the happiness in the world, bro," Tony said before the music started, making the room cheer. He spun to put his back to the room and nodded at the DJ.

The music started and Tony pitched his voice high for the beginning of the chorus, rocking his hips back and forth.

He spun around, pointing at his brother as he sang the end of the chorus with a smirk. Tony strutted across the stage, working the crowd and cheesing it up. He got to the chorus again and held out the microphone for the audience to sing along with him.

Jumping off the stage closest to their table, he sang as he pointed at them, making them cheer wildly. He worked his hips in front of his brother's chair, pretending to give him a lap dance for a few seconds before heading back onto the stage.

At the line about a tattoo, Tony lifted his shirt to show off his new ink, drawing loud cheers from the crowd as he showed off his body. He winked at his table and finished the song with a flourish, ending in the same pose he had started.

The entire bar exploded with applause. Tony walked back to the table grinning from ear to ear. "Hope you enjoyed that, brother!" he said to Adam, giving his cheek a wet smooch.

"*You* are a menace and not allowed to sing any more tonight," Adam retorted.

"Of course I won't," Tony scoffed. "It would make everyone else look bad."

The entire table burst into laughter.

"Come on, Superstar," James called over to him. "You can sit by me. I'm not intimidated by you."

"Oooh!" the men at the table said excitedly.

"Pfff! You think I'm intimidated?" Adam scoffed. "Where's that tablet? I have a last minute addition to make."

Tony smirked at his brother, enjoying their banter. When Adam's name was finally called, Tony whooped to hear that Adam's song choice was *Ice Ice Baby* by Vanilla Ice, the rapper mentioned in *his* song.

Adam went all-in, making ridiculous over-the-top movements to make the audience laugh. "And *that's* how a white boy throws down!" Adam said at the end, chest heaving from the exertion.

Nobody clapped louder than Tony, who jumped to his feet to cheer his brother on. He swept his brother up in a hug when he got back to the table. "You're a great sport, man. Love you," Tony murmured in Adam's ear.

"I love you, too, you rascal," Adam whispered back.

Ben clapped his hands for attention. "Now that everyone's had their turn on stage, we're going to go and watch some lovely ladies on stages of their own. Everyone follow me!"

Tony and James exchanged glances as they followed behind the other men to a door at the back of the club. "You think Amanda will be okay with this?" James asked Tony.

"I think she'll be disappointed she missed out," Tony replied.

The door led to a small room. They waited there for less than a minute before the other door opened, admitting a beautiful regal woman with a clipboard.

"Good evening, gentlemen. My name is Jewel. Did you enjoy yourselves at karaoke?" She smiled at their enthusiasm. "We are ready for you. If you'll follow me, please." She led them into a room lit with blue lights, soft music playing in the background. There were several stages, each with multiple poles on it. They were the only people present.

"Adam, you are at the center stage, please have a seat." Jewel proceeded to direct each man to sit in front of a different pole. At last, just James and Tony were left. "You two are over here." Raising her voice, she addressed the entire room. "Enjoy yourselves!"

She walked to the other end of the room and pressed a button on the sound system. The soft music changed to an upbeat tempo and spotlights appeared on each pole.

"Hang on a second..." James said slowly. "We're together..."

At that moment, the curtains behind each pole opened, revealing the girls, who stepped forwards into the light and posed.

Tony's world faded to the girl on the stage in front of him.

It was Amanda, and though she was wearing the same outfit she'd been wearing earlier that night, there was something about the way she was holding herself that made it even sexier.

"No fucking way," James murmured beside him.

Tony spared a glance at his friend and saw beyond him that Sophia was walking to the center pole. Adam stood up to help her onto the stage, holding her hand as she walked up the steps at the back of the platform. The moment she was placed and Adam had retaken his seat, the music changed again.

The sultry music and vocals of Beyoncé filtered through the speakers, but Tony barely noticed other than to realize that Amanda was hitting every beat with her hips. She moved around the pole seductively, spreading her legs in a low squat facing away from them and running her hands over her body as she walked. A chair near the pole became a prop, Amanda dropping into it and grinding her hips down against the seat. She dropped to the floor and crawled towards them, spinning around at the last second and spreading her knees. Her hands roamed her body again and Tony gripped the edge of his chair convulsively.

"Fuck me," whispered James, his voice sounding wrecked.

Amanda grasped the pole in front of her and used it to climb back to her feet. The beat of the song changed, getting even slower. Amanda gripped the pole and spun around it, flipping upside down into the splits.

Tony found himself on his feet without knowing how he got there.

Amanda hung there for a few more beats, winking at them, before she returned upright, touching down lightly. She dropped to the floor in a slow split that was giving Tony ideas not fit for the very public space they were in.

He sat down again, breathing hard.

Not two beats later, Amanda flipped herself over the edge of the stage and landed on her feet in front of them. She rocked her hips in a figure eight, fingers drawing up the edge of her skirt hypnotically.

Tony wet his lips, eyes fixed on the skin that was being revealed. He was rewarded by a lapful of his girlfriend, Amanda's arms around his neck, gripping the back of his chair. She pressed down against him, swiveling her hips against his groin. Her forehead connected with his, their breath mingling in the tiny space between them. He could feel himself hardening underneath her and drew in a sharp breath.

Amanda smirked at him and got up, spinning as she moved from one chair to the other, and treating James to the same grinding dance.

Tony watched his friends, fascinated by the tension in James's jaw and neck as Amanda rubbed over his lap.

The song slowed and Amanda got up, swinging herself back up on stage and going to the pole for one last seductive spin.

The music stopped and there was silence for a moment before every single man got to his feet and started clapping.

Tony startled at the extra noise, having forgotten that there were others in the room with them.

James helped Amanda back down from the stage and they hugged her between them. "That was amazing!"

"You were incredible, darlin'," Tony said.

"All of us worked really hard," Amanda said, beaming at them. "We were perfectly in sync."

"If you say so," James said with a laugh. "The moment you stepped out, I only had eyes for you."

"I watched Adam greet Sophia," Tony admitted, "but as soon as the music started, I couldn't take my eyes off you."

"Aww, aren't you two sweet," Amanda said, batting her eyelashes at them. "Now please kiss me, because I got all riled up from that dance and I need—"

James bent and cut off her next words, pressing her against Tony as his mouth claimed hers. He pulled back after a minute, spinning her around for Tony to kiss.

Tony slid his tongue in to dance with hers, feeling the resistance as her head connected with James's shoulder.

"They're calling on everyone to leave now," James murmured to them. "I think all the others are as eager to get back to the hotel as we are."

"Yeah, I want to take off all my clothes and scream your names," Amanda said breathlessly, pulling back from Tony. "Let's go."

"I now pronounce you husband and wife. You may kiss the bride."

Tony watched, hand-in-hand with his girlfriend, as his brother gently cupped his new wife's face and brought their lips together. He chuckled when Sophia wrapped her arms around Adam's neck, bringing him in for a much deeper kiss than Adam had intended.

The men from the bachelor party the night before cheered loudly, echoed by their girlfriends.

"I like Sophia," Amanda said happily. "She's a great sister."

"Sister?" Tony asked, surprised.

"Oh, well..." Amanda blushed. "She said I'm practically family, all things considered."

Tony glanced up at James, who looked thoughtful. "I think all three of our families consider us their children, biological or not."

"Does that make you my brothers?" Amanda wrinkled her nose.

Tony laughed quietly. "Not in any way that matters." He glanced down at the hot pink dress she was wearing today; it was the same dress she had worn to the prom with them a little over four years ago, and it looked even better on her today than it had then. "I certainly wouldn't want to pull my sister's dress off with my teeth."

Amanda shivered and smiled up at him. "Maybe in the future we could be family in a different way."

"I rather like the sound of that," James said.

Tony grinned. "Where there's a will, there's a way. It might not be considered strictly legal, but who the fuck cares when it's true love?"

"Mawwage bwings us togevver today," Amanda said, mimicking the priest from *The Princess Bride*.

"God, I love you," Tony whispered to her. He glanced up at James as he made the same vow in his head. *Maybe someday I'll get the courage to tell him as well. Maybe someday we'll all be together. I can only hope!*

Author's Afterward

I hope you enjoyed reading this as much as I enjoyed writing it. Honestly, it's such a dream come true for me. To be able to hold this book, pinkpiggy's gorgeous art on the cover—it's all thanks to the amazing Amber at River City Siren Press. Stay tuned on my socials for Book 2, coming December 2025. I'd better get writing, hmm?

Much love!

Desiree DuBois